NOT QUITE ENEMIES

AMY LARK

berry lark

CHAPTER 1

AFTER A LONG DAY in the office, the last person Morgan Taylor wanted to hang out at a bar with was Drew King. Not that they were alone by any stretch of the imagination, but somehow even with ten coworkers, he'd ended up right beside her at the table.

In all the large northeast coast cities, he had to be in the same one as her.

"Who has the next round?" Phoebe yelled right in Morgan's ear. They had a tab open and would split the cost later, but with no server, they had to get the drinks from the bar to the table.

"Morgan and I will," Drew announced.

Morgan tried holding her breath for a count of three before turning to look at Drew, forcing a smile to her lips. *What the fuck was wrong with him?* They weren't friends. Any other person would have been happy to go with him, and she would happily go with anyone else to the bar. He purposely singled her out because she wouldn't want to go with him. But if she said no, she'd be the bad guy. "Sure."

Resigned to helping him bring back the drinks for this

round, she slid off her stool and followed him. Towering over her by almost a foot, he completely blocked her view. So when he suddenly stopped for no apparent reason, she crashed into his rock-hard back.

"Sorry," he said over his shoulder and continued forward.

She rubbed her nose. He was *sorry*? The trigger reaction word was almost an insult coming from him. The guy was never truly sorry. He was too busy teasing or kissing up to be sorry. This morning at the weekly meeting with their boss, when the presentations were all but over and everyone needed to get back to work, Drew decided to tell a joke to their boss. Not just a short one either, but a long, complicated one that kept them all sitting there to listen to the punchline ten minutes after the meeting was supposed to end. Like no one had anything else to do but listen to Drew King speak. Even though everyone chuckled, personally, she hadn't found it funny at all. Fucking kiss-up.

He reached the bar and ordered another pitcher of beer and margaritas before turning to face her with an expectant smile.

Oh God, did he actually want to talk? Morgan pulled her phone out of her pocket as if it had just notified her of something really important (even a notification that Beth liked Robert's picture on Facebook would be better than talking with Drew). She stared at the screen, hoping it would deter Mr. I'm Everyone's Best Buddy from starting a conversation.

"Did you get the memo from corporate?"

"Of course."

"Wonder if people were hooking up in the office."

She really tried not to roll her eyes, but he made it so hard. Why were they even having this conversation at all? The memo basically said no dating fellow employees or face the consequences. No issue here.

She kept her eyes on her phone. "Probably too many complaints of people being harassed by coworkers."

No dating where she worked was one of her rules. Her friends who had dipped their pens in the company ink had always ended up regretting it. When she broke up with a guy, she didn't want to show up at work the next day and have to deal with him. Working with an ex was the worst, and the only way to get away from him was to change jobs. Not good. No thank you.

Not that she was in any danger with present company.

Drew shifted his weight and one of his hands went through that curly mop of dark brown hair that would look ridiculous on a Muppet, but she supposed it gave him a boyish look everyone else in the office gobbled up like candy. She glanced at him while his attention focused somewhere past her shoulder. Okay, so even she could admit he was hot; if he didn't open his mouth and ruin the moment with his stupid words. He was physically fit and tall. Based on his social media pictures from high school (that Phoebe had shown her), he'd been amongst the popular crowd. At least popular enough to win prom king. King Drew King, like it was prophesied.

The only possible reason the memo upset Drew would be because his groupies at the office could never be graced with his presence outside of work. At least not in his bed. The horror.

"Hey." The word was soft in that low rumbling voice of his, but even with the noise at the bar, she heard it. It resonated in her bones.

Resigning herself, she lifted her gaze to meet his. Those eyes of his were part of the problem, though. Blue eyes, the ridiculous color of sapphires. Way too pretty, with dark lashes settled into a pretty boy face, which still managed to be masculine even when his dimple made an appearance. Blech.

That dimple winked into existence as his eyes softened. "How do you get your pita bread to stay toasty like that?"

Oh, he wanted to bring *that* up, did he? She narrowed her eyes. "I use arsenic."

"Mmm." His lips curved into a satisfied smile. "Just like mom used to make."

"If you don't like it, stop stealing my lunch."

"If I didn't steal your lunch, I'd be forced to eat my own." He leaned down toward her, sucking all the available air away from her, and gave her a conspiratorial look. "Between you and me, I really suck at making lunches."

She tightened her lips, refusing to back away as he invaded her space. The heat between them had everything to do with her rising temper. What kind of asshole stole someone else's lunch at work and then bragged about it? "Then go out to eat."

The bartender set the pitchers on the bar, breaking the tension between them. Straightening, Drew handed her the margarita pitcher and, for one second, she imagined the look on his pretty face if she lifted the pitcher and poured the icy cold margarita all over him. His gasping shock from the cold would be worth it. When he turned with the beer, he lifted an eyebrow as if he knew what she'd been contemplating and dared her to do it.

Her small smile vanished. She tightened her lips and spun on her heel to head to the table. Somehow, he made her feel like they were in middle school. Everything he did made her want to respond with juvenile actions. But she did her best not to sink to his level. His low chuckle behind her skittered down her spine. *Asshole.*

She managed to make it to the table without incident and poured herself a margarita before passing the pitcher. Drew's shirt sleeve brushed her arm as he took his seat next to her. Of course, no one had decided to move while they were gone, so she wouldn't get stuck next to him again.

Ignoring him, she turned to talk to Phoebe and Robin. While they discussed the most recent viral video and how to incorporate viral marketing into their new campaign, Morgan was acutely aware of Drew's body heat. The man had to run at over a hundred degrees. Just another thing she hated about him.

"Mr. Baker," Drew shouted their boss's name directly in her ear.

Thomas Baker went straight to Drew and shook his hand. "How's it going, gang?"

Morgan put on her work smile as everyone turned their attention to the boss.

"Good," Drew said. "Just having a drink to celebrate a stellar week. Do you want to join us?"

"No, thank you. I'm afraid I'm going to have to pass." Mr. Baker met everyone's eyes before returning his attention to Drew, who had apparently elected himself leader of their small group of the single people from the office. "I'm meeting someone for dinner. Are we still on for golf tomorrow, Drew?"

"Definitely. I've got a new driver to break in."

Golf? The guy had only been part of their company for a month and was already golfing with the boss? Morgan had been with Hart Association for the past five years and only golfed with the boss on the company's annual golf outing. Of course, she wasn't a member of whatever fraternity both Drew and Thomas had belonged to, which had instantly bonded them over their shared college experience of being frat boys.

"I'll see you then." Mr. Baker put a fifty on the table. "Next round is on me, guys. Good job this week."

Everyone thanked him as he left. Morgan glared at the back of Drew King's curly head. He had it so easy. The man had no filter and still ended up on top. If Morgan did or said half the things Drew did and said, she'd probably get written up. During her presentations, he constantly interrupted her with inane facts or to make some smart-ass comment just for a laugh.

Everything was a joke to him. He flirted with anyone with two legs, and his lips had to be sore from all the kissing up he did.

Drew turned so quickly she didn't have time to look away, so she didn't even bother changing her expression.

"What?" His dimple flashed in his cheek.

She shook her head disapprovingly and lifted her phone to check to see if she had any messages.

"You want to go golfing with me and the boss tomorrow afternoon?" He lifted his drink to his mouth and winked. "I could hook you up."

"I'm good." Inside, she was seething though. She worked hard to get recognition for doing her actual job and didn't need to kiss up to the boss like Drew obviously felt the need to do.

His hand snaked out and took her phone from her before she could react.

"Hey!"

He clicked a few times, and then his own phone lit up. "In case you change your mind, you have my number and I have yours."

"Gee, thanks." She rolled her eyes as she snatched her phone back and turned away from him again. The last thing she wanted was to owe Drew King a favor.

~

WHEN THE WORK group broke up, Morgan and Phoebe moved to a smaller booth to catch up. They'd started together at the agency just out of college and both worked in the luxury division under Allison Cross, who was currently on maternity leave.

"Do you think I should go golfing with Drew and Thomas?" Morgan fiddled with the straw in her water.

"I don't know. It could be good to get face time with the boss, but it doesn't sound like much fun." Phoebe leaned back and squinted at the bar door. She was definitely on the prowl tonight. "Do you really want to sink to the same level as Drew King? Or even spend an afternoon with him while he's in full suck-up mode?"

"Probably not." She shrugged. "He's just so irritating."

"The other women in the office don't seem to think so. Of course, he turns on the charm with them. It's like he's on a mission to antagonize you. You'd think he'd avoid you, but no, he just keeps picking you out. Just be glad we're not in the same division as him."

"Right? It's like he needs my attention and will do anything to get it. Him and his attitude kick my competitive nature into overdrive."

A group of guys entered the bar, all wearing scrubs and laughing. They were good-looking guys. A blond one with pretty brown eyes and a gentle smile caught her looking at him. She returned his smile before returning her gaze to Phoebe.

"He's cute." Phoebe leaned her chin on her hands and assessed the group that had walked in. "So is his friend, and that friend, and that friend. Oh my. Maybe we should invite them over."

"How would you ever choose?" Morgan glanced up at the guys as they ordered from the bar. The blond looked over and gave her an easy smile that touched his eyes. Heat went straight to her cheeks. Of course, Morgan knew who she'd choose. "I don't know how good of company I can be. You made me sit next to Drew King for an hour. I think I got his cooties."

Phoebe laughed. Before either of them could gesture, two guys broke off and made their way through the bar to their table.

"Hi," the blond said.

"Hi." Morgan tried not to stare, but he really was handsome. He had that boy next door look down.

"Mind if we join you? I'm Alex," the other guy said.

"Phoebe." She slid over to let Alex sit next to her in the booth. "And this is Morgan."

Morgan slid over, giving a speculative look to Phoebe.

"Drew," the blond said as he sat.

As if he'd thrown cold water at her, Morgan squeaked out, "Excuse me?"

"Andrew Walker." He held out his hand, and she took it. His hand was warm and soft.

What an unfortunate name. "Morgan."

"So what do you do, Morgan?"

She would think of him as Andrew, because every time she thought of Drew, she saw that jackass's smiling face. "I'm the Assistant Creative Director at an ad agency."

"Any ads I might have seen?" Andrew had one of those chin dimples. He was far more pleasing to look at than Drew King and his ridiculous Muppet hair.

"Did you see the one for Valentine's Day with the jewelry and the butterflies for Avalon Jewelry?"

He smiled and shook his head. "I don't always get to watch a lot of TV. The hospital has them on in some rooms, so I see stuff occasionally, but I didn't catch that one."

"You work at the hospital?"

"St. Peter's. I'm a surgeon." He gestured to his light blue

scrubs. "I usually dress better for going out, but we just finished a training day and weren't on call for the night, so we figured we'd make do."

"I don't mind scrubs." Especially on him.

He smiled again. He had really nice white teeth. They ordered another drink. The two doctors told them outrageous stories about things they'd found on x-rays. Everyone seemed to have a good time. Even Morgan relaxed and tried to forget about the other Drew. After about an hour, Phoebe motioned to Morgan they should go.

"It was nice meeting you, Andrew." And she meant every word. He was nice, easygoing, and good-looking.

"You can call me Drew. Here, let me give you my number. Maybe we can meet up on purpose next time."

She handed him her phone. "I'd like that."

Within minutes, Phoebe and Morgan were in a cab, heading back to their apartment building.

"You know the best thing about doctors?" Phoebe sighed, leaning against the back of the seat. She smiled up at the ceiling of the cab.

"Earning potential?" Morgan teased.

Phoebe ignored her. "Timing."

"Not what I expected, but I'm listening."

"Well, they have limited time, so you have to work all the fun stuff around their schedule. Sometimes that means nooners or late-night hookups. The best thing is they don't get bent out of shape about having me home for dinner at a certain time." Phoebe started texting.

"Are you texting the doctor?" Morgan tried to read over Phoebe's shoulder, but she tilted the screen away. Morgan glanced at her own black screen. No new notifications.

"Maybe." Phoebe smiled as her phone dinged a response. "You should too. When's the last time you hooked up with anyone? I bet Dr. Walker could help you release your stress from the work week. In a purely professional way, of course."

It had been a while. Not that she usually indulged in hookups, but boyfriends hadn't been a consideration given her schedule. Besides, Andrew was pretty hot.

Phoebe grabbed her phone.

"Hey!"

"You need a reward for your grueling week." Phoebe pressed a bunch of things on the screen while holding Morgan off with her other hand. "Consider him your gold star for a job well done."

Morgan's face flushed, but it wasn't that bad of an idea. She'd hit kind of a dry spell with guys, and work had been so busy lately she hadn't even attempted to find someone. And she definitely didn't want a relationship with all the strings attached. But the thought of apps like Tinder made her shudder and not in a good way. She wanted to meet first to see if they had a spark before committing an evening to a guy. It all took time, but Dr. Walker had said he wasn't on call tonight, and he was good looking. Maybe a hint of a spark there.

Her phone dinged. Morgan wrenched the phone from Phoebe. And read the texts that had been sent and apparently received.

Hey, I'm not tired and thought maybe you'd like to come over and help keep me awake tonight.

Morgan glared at Phoebe. "That's the best opening line you could think of?"

Phoebe shrugged. "It worked."

Morgan looked down at the response.

Morgan?

"That's working?" Morgan shook her head.

"At least he knows who you are." Phoebe started texting on her own phone. "Cut to the chase."

"Fine. But I don't think just because I ask him to my apartment, he's going to hop to it."

"He's a man, isn't he?"

"He seems like a nice guy."

"Even nice guys like to get laid."

Morgan scoffed. "What should I type?"

"Hmm." Phoebe looked out the window of the taxi as they pulled up to the apartment building. "Well, it depends. . . do you want a relationship or just a night?"

"I guess I should be open to a relationship, but I don't really have time for one right now. Work is pretty busy with Allison gone." Morgan paid the taxi, and they got out. "Screw it."

Obviously we clicked tonight. I thought we could skip the bullshit and just do what both of us want.

"Damn, girl." Phoebe laughed. "And I thought you were a good girl."

Morgan shrugged. "Why play games?"

"Because games can be fun."

"Games just end up with someone getting hurt."

They let themselves into the building and headed up the elevator.

Morgan's phone dinged as they reached her door. Phoebe's apartment was down the hallway a little farther. She glanced at the phone and then held it up to Phoebe.

I'm in.

CHAPTER 2

To say he'd been shocked to receive Morgan's text would be an understatement for Drew King. The ice princess of Hart Association rarely acknowledged his presence except to let him know he was beneath her. Who knew that was exactly where she wanted him to be?

As the Uber car pulled up to the apartment building, he still couldn't believe this wasn't some sort of elaborate trap where their teammates would wait inside to laugh their asses off at his eagerness to thaw those frozen eyes of hers.

But if it weren't a joke. . . . She quickly buzzed him in.

Fuck, he was nervous. This felt like an audition he hadn't prepared for. An interview when he hadn't even realized a position was open.

Most of their problems happened when they tried to talk to each other. He'd tried to make her relax at the bar by teasing her, but as always, it had backfired. And those eyes. The palest blue eyes so huge in her small face as to make her appear like an elf or some cartoon Disney princess. Every time she looked at him, his brain turned into a bowl of Spaghetti-O's.

Unfortunately, her body made his mind slip into the gutter and into fantasies far naughtier than Disney. She had the curves of a pinup model, and her pencil skirts and high heels made him feel like the cartoon big bad wolf with his tongue dragging on the ground and his eyes bulging out of his head.

Every now and then, he'd glimpse a chunk of her golden hair dyed a deep blue. It usually hid tucked up in whatever hairstyle she put her hair in for the day, but it was there, flitting in and out of existence. It teased him with thoughts that the ice princess might be more than she seemed. That a wild streak lay just beyond the facade.

He stepped off the elevator and ran his hand over his head. What was he doing? They worked together. That memo he'd mentioned earlier had been really clear: corporate didn't want people within the company dating each other. But she hadn't asked him to *date* her.

Taking a deep breath, he knocked on the door.

"Just a sec." The door muffled her voice, but he didn't hear sounds of the entire office snickering accompanying it, so he took that as a good sign.

He released the breath he'd been holding and glanced down the endless hallway. It wasn't a joke. Right? Even if it was, he could laugh it off. If the pranks his frat brothers had pulled in college hadn't gotten under his skin, this wouldn't. If it was a prank.

Fuck it.

The door opened and a quick glance showed only a barely clothed Morgan Taylor standing there in an empty apartment living room. Her forehead scrunched up and her mouth opened. Maybe she already regretted asking him over.

Fuck it.

He stepped into the doorway and pulled her flush against him, capturing her mouth before she could utter a sound.

A million puzzle pieces fell into place as her mouth softened against his. He backed them up a step and kicked the door closed behind him. Mint with a hint of the lime from the margaritas she'd drank earlier filled his senses. The jolt of desire between them coursed through his body and his thoughts scattered.

Her hands burned into his shoulders. His slid home to her small waist. She was so tiny, but so strong. While her eyes might be cold, her kiss scorched through him like a blaze.

All those contradictions about her drove him insane. But there was a rightness about her lips against his. Her soft body pressed to his. Any hesitation had disappeared the minute their lips met.

She pulled back slightly. Reluctantly, he opened his eyes. Afraid to break the spell.

"Um." Her expression seemed puzzled, which didn't do a thing for his ego.

Had he misread the text? Fuck, did he just royally screw this up? Had she not felt the same jolt when they'd kissed? Was he in for a write up on Monday morning and an impromptu meeting with HR about sexual harassment?

Evaluate the situation. She hadn't slapped him. She hadn't pulled any farther away, and he didn't think he could release his grip on her hips if he wanted to. He would if she asked, but he was thankful she didn't seem to be completely immune to him. She seemed to be considering him and he didn't want to do anything that would put her off, like speaking.

"Would you. . . ." She cleared her throat and her usually icy eyes thawed. "Would you do that again?"

He leaned down and kissed her. This time more slowly, exploring. She put her hand on his chest and pressed. He stopped and lifted his head.

He wanted to reclaim her lips, but maybe she needed to lay some ground rules. She needed control of everything at work. Or maybe she liked to be out of control when it came to sex. He couldn't wait to make her so out of her mind she couldn't even think straight.

Her tongue darted out to lick her lips. She searched his eyes and seemed to come to a decision. "Only tonight."

Relief swept through him. At this point, if she'd said only five minutes, he'd work with it and make the most of it. He lowered his head until his mouth touched her earlobe and whispered, "Tonight."

Her body shuddered against his. "No one else can know."

He ran his teeth against her earlobe. Her breath caught, and she pressed into him. This was happening. It was his to mess up now. And no way he'd mess this up.

Drew King blew her mind. His lips against her ear shattered any semblance of sanity she could conjure. She hated this man, but the minute his lips had touched hers (after the initial shock of seeing him at her door), everything inside her had gone into full meltdown mode.

She'd had to take a moment to process what the fuck was happening, but she knew she wouldn't let him leave without exploring this further. Not if that kiss had been any indicator of what could happen between them. Fully expecting a different Andrew to be on the other side of the door, she'd changed into a pair of sleep shorts and a tank top before he'd arrived.

"One more thing." She waited until she could look into his eyes.

"What?" The rumble of his voice went through her like liquid heat. That was definitely new. He wore a pair of jeans and a black T-shirt. Not his normal office wear. In the office, she'd never noticed how muscular his arms were. Her fingertips ached as she fought the urge to touch those muscles to see if they were as hard as they looked.

She met his eyes. This was important. "We aren't going to break this down later and talk about what happens. Whatever happens stays to tonight. I'm not going to suddenly be in love with you because we have sex. Even if it's good sex."

"It'll be good sex."

She rolled her eyes. "Honestly, you need to just stay quiet or this isn't—"

His lips captured her last words, and she gave up. They say love and hate are two sides of the same coin. Passion seemed to be required of both. Maybe hate explained the sudden attraction. But she wouldn't overthink this.

She'd wanted to get laid tonight and had expected the cute doctor, but somehow Drew showing up at her door had been. . . inevitable? Better? Hell, she'd never know. And didn't care.

This could complicate things at work, but right now, her mind lined up with her body. It was lust, pure and simple. After all, she hated this guy. The sex might be amazing or it could fall flat, but it wouldn't make her like him. However, he had a nice body and the chemistry between them was explosive.

Her hands smoothed up his shoulders, feeling the muscles ripple beneath the surface. Her fingers hesitated when she felt the brush of the surprisingly soft curls of his hair against the backs. Somehow, she'd always thought that they would be crispy with gel. His hands slid over her hips and cradled her butt, pulling her in tight against his arousal.

At the same time, his tongue slipped past her lips, tentatively at first. Desire flowed starkly through her. Her fingers grabbed into his stupid hair and pulled him closer. Needing him closer.

She pulled away from him and searched his eyes. Those fucking impossible eyes that seemed to glow with the intensity of a million faceted gemstones even in the dimly lit room. "The bedroom is down the hallway."

He lifted her so quickly; she squeaked and wrapped her legs around his waist and her arms around his neck.

"That's an interesting noise." His dimple flashed in his cheek. "What other undignified noises can I get you to make?"

"Again with the talking." Morgan shook her head.

"You have to admit you like a little talking." He jostled her, and she wrapped herself tighter around him.

"Asshole."

"Bitch." He lifted his eyebrow.

"Can you just fucking kiss me again?" she said in the most exasperated voice she could manage.

"Which way to this mythical bed?"

She lifted her arm and pointed.

He rewarded her with a fervent kiss against her mouth before carrying her down the hallway. "So, how controlling are you going to be? Will I need to ask permission before removing your clothes? Would you like me to do a striptease?"

That caught her off guard, and she laughed.

He dropped her on the bed and stared at her with shock on his face.

"What?" She leaned up on her elbows.

"I didn't think you could laugh." His tone held a sort of mock wonder in it.

She fell back against the bed and stared up at the ceiling. "Maybe this is too much work for one night."

He grabbed her legs and pulled her to the edge of the bed,

causing another squeak to come out. "I'm up two squeaks and a laugh. I'm definitely going to get another laugh tonight. Surely there will be a ticklish spot somewhere on that compact body of yours, but I think there are a lot more noises I'd like to explore first."

"Talk, talk, talk." She held up her hand to puppet him talking. "All words, no action."

He leaned over her, pressing her down onto the bed. His body wedged between her thighs, breath warm against her lips. "Talking is part of it."

His hand stroked up over her hip, along her waist. Her breath caught and held as she stared into his eyes and waited for his hand to touch her breast. His fingers slipped beneath the fabric of her tank, grazing her bare skin.

His eyes darkened, and his head dipped to brush his lips lightly against hers. She arched up into his touch, needing more than he was giving her. His fingers skimmed along her side, trailing around the back to find the clasp to her bra.

She grabbed the bottom of his T-shirt and pulled it up, catching it on his head.

"Damn, girl." Drew lifted off her and finished taking off his shirt.

She leaned up on her elbows and took in his fit body that usually hid beneath button-down shirts. "Damn yourself."

Drew's physical body had never been her problem with him. He was a good-looking, fit man and even though he drove her freaking batty, she could appreciate a nice piece of man candy. But his office wear didn't show just how fucking rock-hard he was.

Muppet hair, notwithstanding.

She took off her tank and bra and tossed them over near his T-shirt.

His eyes went wide and greedy as they took in her body. "We're actually doing this."

"You don't have to sound so surprised." But then again, maybe he should; this was all a little shocking to her. It felt good to be needed and wanted, even if it was Drew King doing the wanting.

He lifted an eyebrow.

"Shut up," she said.

He grabbed her hands and pulled her to stand against him. The slide of his heated skin against hers made her sigh in surrender. It really had been way too long. Especially if Drew was the one making her feel this way.

"I like that sound." His voice was low and reverent, no teasing this time.

She ran her fingertips between them. Following the muscles in his abs, up his sides. Grazing his nipples. He inhaled sharply but didn't stop her. His skin was tight and hot as she explored his shoulders, down to those beautifully sculpted biceps.

"You're a beautiful man." The words came out with no forethought.

He leaned down and took her lips with his, tenderly, slowly. Exploring as if they had forever to linger on just this kiss. Lips, teeth, tongue. Figuring out what the other liked.

Her heart raced in anticipation. One small rational part of her mind kept blinking in protest like a gigantic neon sign. This was Drew King. The guy who routinely stole her lunch. Who had a habit of trying to make her flustered in meetings. Who she loathed and complained about to her best friend. Who she made comments about overcompensating for something.

His hands swept beneath her shorts and cupped her ass, drawing her tighter against his erection, and that little voice popped like a bubble. He definitely wasn't overcompensating for a lack below the belt. She reached between them to undo his jeans.

He lifted his mouth from hers and pressed his forehead against hers as she reached into his open jeans, stroking him through his boxer briefs. He was warm and firm against her palm.

His fingers tightened into the flesh of her bottom. Her own body tingled in anticipation, waiting for him. Hot and needy. Ready for him to claim whatever he needed.

Drew stepped back, away from her touch. "Slowly."

His hands pushed her shorts and underwear down and he kneeled before her to help her out of them. He looked up at her from his knees. A world of passion shone in his eyes. The fact he liked what he saw was clear. It lifted her and made her feel powerful with this man kneeling before her naked body.

His head swept forward and his lips touched the top of her mound. A chaste kiss that barely registered as a touch, but longing flooded her.

"Beautiful," he whispered against her stomach, filling her with butterflies of sensations. His hand stroked up her leg from her ankle. "Lay back." He pressed her backward, his eyes locked on hers, until she sat on the bed.

She did as he asked and squeaked once more when he pulled her legs over his shoulders. Her fingers curled into the bedspread, hanging onto the edge of the bed for dear life, as his mouth descended on her. Her thoughts scattered into fireworks at the touch of his tongue.

White hot heat spread from his tongue to every inch of her. Filling her and leaving her empty at the same time. He held her with reverence. Her breath caught. Existence ceased for a moment as his tongue and lips made her a mass of sensations. Her breathing chaotic.

Climbing higher and higher until her body shattered into a million pieces, she arched into him. He didn't let up, pushing her further than she could take. The heat engulfed her and a noise she didn't even know she could make emanated from her lungs as her body hit another orgasm.

She collapsed against the bed and pulled air into her starved lungs as she came back to herself. "Oh, wow."

He pressed a kiss to her thigh, and an aftershock racked her body.

"Fuck," she hissed.

He stood and pulled off his jeans and underwear. Somewhere she registered his nudity and acknowledged he was truly gorgeous, but her brain had vacated the premises, leaving a tangle of nerves ready to respond to his every expert touch.

He lifted her limp body and repositioned her more fully on the bed. Laying down beside her, he trailed his hand over her body, sparking like lightning across her skin.

She lifted her hand and gestured. "Condoms are in the drawer—"

He cut her off with a kiss. "Patience."

Meeting his eyes, she'd never been self-conscious about her body. Not anymore than most people, but she couldn't even bring any of that forward or the fact this was Drew. It didn't matter right now. All that mattered was this connection forged out of need and desire. Her breath caught at the depth of his eyes. His hand made its leisurely way over her body, tracing her curves, making the fire burn brighter and brighter. She brushed her hand over his cock.

He sucked in a breath, but it didn't hurry him along. She pushed up on her elbow, turning her body in to his and wrapped her hand around his cock, stroking gently. She needed him to feel as out of control as she'd been. Needed him to want her so badly there would be no "slowly" or "patience."

She wanted him as shredded as she felt. She pressed her open mouth to his. Exploring him with a recklessness born of lust. Her hand kept up the steady pressure on his cock, feeling every ridge, every vein. Softly cupping his balls.

She heard the catch in his throat before a soft rumble emanated from his chest. His mouth took control of the kiss and he rolled her onto her back, caging her in his arms.

He lifted his head. "You don't play fair."

She smiled as he reached over for a condom and made quick work of it.

"No one said we had to fight fair." She stretched her body along his, loving the feel of his heat against her. The knowledge that she cut into his patience made her reckless. "You take too long."

His eyes snapped to hers and the smile he gave her should have warned her. He spread over her, trapping her beneath him. "Who's in charge, Morgan?"

She trailed her hand down his back and wrapped her legs around his waist. He didn't let her take him in, though. "Obviously I have seniority."

"I'm older." He leaned down, and his mouth closed on her neck.

Her mind went blank as he nuzzled and suckled a spot that fried her brain. "Age. . . has. . . nothing to do with it."

"Experience, then." He thrust, but his cock rubbed between her folds, not inside where she needed him. Her core pulsed with desire. It helped fuel the fire, but she needed more.

"You definitely talk a good game." She tried to rub against him again, wanting that connection, but he held himself away. "But you leave a lot to be desired in actual action."

He answered with a dark chuckle. "You won't give in, will you?"

"Never." She smiled.

He lifted her hips and entered her in a swift motion.

She moaned.

Drew held himself there for a moment, his mouth next to her ear. "That's the sound I want."

When he moved within her, everything scaled down to their joined flesh. The brush of his chest against hers. His unsteady breathing in her ear. Her own unhindered moans called up from somewhere within her.

"That's my girl." His voice in her ear was her undoing. The world pivoted into a spiral of feelings. Her body stiffened as she found her release. He moved a few more times and then joined her before collapsing on her overwrought body.

The sound of their breathing was the only sound in the room as their hearts slowed down. The weight of him over her body felt way too good, as though she could stay like this forever.

"Is the bathroom. . .?"

She lifted her arm and gestured toward the door. He pressed a kiss to her lips before slipping away.

She drew in a deep breath. What had she just done? She couldn't even move to cover herself. Every nerve ending twittered happily about finding release. She'd just had sex with Drew King. Fuck.

The scary thing was. . . she wasn't sorry. At least not right now. Tomorrow, in the light of day, she'd probably be mortified. But tonight, in her bedroom, she couldn't care about tomorrow. All the tension she'd been piling up seemed to have eased out of her.

She heard the water, and then the door opened and closed. Drew returned to the bed and sprawled beside her. She was surprised he hadn't just gone for his clothes, but she couldn't protest too much, not in her current state.

"Give me a minute," he said to the ceiling.

She chuckled. "For what?"

"Round two." He rested his hand on her hip.

Her body leapt to attention for a second before relaxing back into the bed. "You're kidding, right?"

He turned his face toward her and waited until she met his eyes. His ridiculous mop of curls hung in a riot around his face. "There will be a round two. You said tonight only. It's only. . . ." He lifted his head and looked around the room for a clock. "Early."

She shook her head. "You really are impossible."

"You're gorgeous." His words were soft. "And intelligent. And so damn aggravating."

"You have Muppet hair."

"What?" He rolled onto his side and looked down at her.

"You have Muppet hair." She shrugged, and his eyes were drawn to the motion of her breasts.

"Muppet?" His fingers followed his gaze, lightly tracing her nipples into stark peaks.

Her breathing hitched from his touch. "You know, like Kermit the Frog."

"Kermit doesn't have hair." He took her nipple into his mouth while working the other between his thumb and finger.

She struggled to keep from moaning. "Like Animal then."

"I do not have Muppet hair." He blew softly over her nipple, sending an electric pulse to her core, and looked up at her face.

She reached out and put both her hands in his hair. The silky strands rubbed between her fingers. "Totally Muppet hair."

He rolled his body, bracing himself over her so their faces aligned. "At least I don't have Disney princess eyes."

She laughed. "What's that supposed to mean?"

"Your eyes are enormous." He pressed a kiss to her lips. "Like you are some lost soul in need of rescue."

"Hah." She ran her hands down his sides. "They are

normal sized eyes, and at least they aren't some weird shade of blue that looks fake."

"Are you saying I have fake eyes?" He batted his lashes a few times.

"Do you wear contacts?" She searched his eyes as if she could see the lenses in the dim room.

"Sorry. Perfect eyesight." He rested his body on hers and kept most of his weight on his arms. "Most women love my curls."

She shrugged and settled her body more in line with his growing arousal. "Your hair is stupid."

"Stupid?" He laughed. "That's the best adjective you can find with that amazing advertising brain of yours? Stupid?"

"I call 'em like I see 'em." Her fingers trailed over his tight ass. "And your Muppet hair is stupid."

"Hmm." He leaned down and kissed her neck, his soft hair brushing against her cheek. Her breath caught as her focus went to where his mouth lingered. Vaguely, she registered him moving and putting on a condom, but the sensations inching over her skin from his teeth and lips were over-powering.

He slid into her, and she gasped. His movements were slow and methodical. Driving her closer and closer to the edge again. All the while he kept up his attack on her neck and that stupid soft hair of his kept sliding softly against her skin, adding a whole extra dimension of sensation.

His lips moved up to hers and he explored her mouth in time with his hips. He lifted his face from hers.

"Open those beautiful eyes," he whispered.

She did. The stark desire on his face made her come undone. She watched his eyes widen, and the satisfied smile made his dimple flicker in his cheek as he felt her response to him. It unhinged her further. For a moment, a thought drifted through her. How on earth would she face him in the office on Monday? But it skittered away as he lost his steadiness.

She threaded her fingers into his hair and pulled his mouth to hers. If he was going to make her lose control, he'd better prepare for her counterattack. She met him thrust for thrust and pushed them faster, driving into his mouth with her tongue the way he drove into her.

His cadence stumbled until they were both just moving together in a chaotic rhythm.

"Fuck." He slammed into her and clutched her to him. Her body shuddered against his, finding its way to another release even as he found his.

He collapsed over her. The bed melted around them, cradling their spent bodies. Thoughts drifted away as her heart slowed. She barely registered when he pulled away for what seemed like a few seconds before the heat of him engulfed her and drew her down into sleep.

CHAPTER 3

HER FINGERS WERE TANGLED in something soft, and her bed was unusually hot. Morgan stretched and the body half on hers moved with her. Her eyes popped open, and she turned to stare into Drew King's sleeping face.

Well, that happened. Maybe she could blame the margaritas.

Her hand clutched his hair and his leg lay across hers. They were both still very nude. Even in the pale light of morning, he was a really fascinating specimen of a man. His features were too pretty, but his body was cut.

This wouldn't change anything.

They didn't really like each other still. Though their body parts definitely got along just fine and that mouth of his. . . . When he used it for things other than talking. . . . Her body warmed just thinking of how wicked that mouth could be.

She hadn't really expected him to sleep over. Not that she hooked up all that much. But after that last round, she'd just fallen right to sleep, and he'd been so warm. . . . This was bad. She sighed.

"Mmm, that didn't sound like a happy sigh." He stretched

and pulled her tighter against his body without opening his eyes.

"It's morning." She didn't resist when he pressed her head down on his shoulder.

"Impossible. I specifically ordered more tonight." He took in a deep breath.

She rolled her eyes.

"I felt that." He stroked his hand down her back.

"You couldn't possibly have felt that." She glanced up at his face.

He smiled but didn't open his eyes. "Shh. I'm sleeping."

His hand stroked over her back again.

"I don't even know what time it is." She shifted to get up, but he pulled her back down.

"It's Saturday. Who cares?"

Saturday. His day to suck up to the boss. Her body stiffened. "Don't you have golf?"

"This afternoon." Another pass of his hand over her back, like he was trying to soothe her or pet her. "I'm not worried."

Of course not. He could probably be a no show and still earn the boss's favor. Especially if it was because he got laid. Frat boy mentality.

"We should get up." She pressed against him a little harder and managed to sit up.

His eyes opened, and his gaze swept over her. She might have felt a little self-conscious if they hadn't been all over each other last night. The time to be shy had definitely passed. His hand reached up and threaded into her hair. "There it is."

"What?"

"I knew it existed." He pulled her blue streak out from under her hair.

"You are weird." She tugged the strand from his fingers and pulled her hair back away from her face.

His eyes warmed. "I think it's still Friday."

"Friday is definitely over." She attempted to scoot to the edge of the bed.

His fingers closed over her hands and dragged her back toward him. "Nope. I'm pretty sure it's Friday."

He pulled her down until their lips met. She would have liked to think she would only kiss him one more time and then usher him out of her life before getting ready for the day, but the minute his lips touched hers, her brain threw in the towel.

Things heated quickly. Maybe there was an edge of desperation. But his hands were in her hair, down her back, over her breasts, between her legs. His mouth followed closely behind wherever his hands led until she was a writhing mess beneath him.

She gave as good as she got. Squeezing the hardness of his muscles. Tasting the salt of his skin. Making him groan made her smile.

When he sank into her, they both released a breath, like coming home for the last time. They moved slowly together, building the fire higher and higher. Until they finally combusted.

They didn't move after. Lying there with Drew's head on her breasts, her fingers played with his soft curls. His hand played with the fingers of her other hand. She was scared to say anything. What could she say?

If that hadn't been goodbye, she didn't know what would be.

But neither of them moved. Reality would close in soon enough.

~

"So. . . ." Phoebe stood in Morgan's doorway Sunday morning, dressed for their weekly run. "Was it just what the doctor ordered?"

Morgan's face grew hot as she looked behind her toward her bedroom. She'd spent Saturday afternoon doing laundry to wash away Drew's scent from her bed: a clean masculine scent with a hint of sandalwood. Every time she got near it, her insides went soft, and she thought about texting him for another night. That would be insanity, though. She could chalk up Friday night to having a few too many margaritas and getting caught up in the moment, but sober...

Much easier to wash the sheets.

"It was good." She grabbed her shoes and busied herself with putting them on to hide her expression. It was fucking fantastic, but Monday would be horrifying. What would she say to him? How could she look at him in meetings across the board table when he knew exactly what she sounded like during sex? At least what she sounded like when she had sex with him...

Her dreams last night had starred him on repeat. She'd woken in a tangle of sheets and in desperate need of a cold shower.

Phoebe stretched. "Alex was okay, but not sure if I'll make a habit of him. Are you going to see Drew again?"

"What?" Morgan couldn't hide the guilty look. For a moment, she'd forgotten about the other Drew. She coughed to cover up. "No. I don't think I'll be seeing him again."

"That sucks. Guess we both struck out. He seemed like a nice guy. Actually had some potential to be a good match." Phoebe shrugged. "You never know with doctors. Ready?"

"Yes. So only okay?"

They took the stairs down to the lobby and headed out to the park as Phoebe told her all about how things with Doctor Alex didn't exactly blow her mind. As always, she overshared about Alex's crooked penis and how that had been the only good thing about the night. About a half dozen times, Morgan thought about telling Phoebe about Drew King. She'd told him she hadn't wanted to analyze it afterwards and just let it be what it was. One night of sex.

But her mind kept spinning around to it and him. She wanted to know what Phoebe thought, but how mortifying would it be to admit to her friend she'd slept with Drew. On purpose. That he'd broken her down so thoroughly she'd had some pretty amazing orgasms.

And that she hadn't stopped thinking about him since he'd left.

It was stupid. He was stupid.

They were walking to cool down when Morgan finally asked, "Do you think hate sex is a thing?"

"Hate sex?"

Morgan shrugged and took a gulp of water. "Sex with someone you don't like."

"Is this hypothetical or are you talking about someone in specific?"

"Hypothetically."

Phoebe stopped and stretched on the bench. "I guess it could be okay. I mean, they say that love and hate are kind of the same thing. Heightened emotions or some such thing. I don't know that I've ever had hate sex, though. Why, are you planning on having some? Or just fantasizing about it?"

"Neither," Morgan said quickly. "I mean, I just read something about it on the internet this morning and it got me thinking. . . ."

"Since the only person you've actively hated is Drew King, I'm assuming this doesn't mean you are going to put the theory to the test."

Heat sliced through her. Three fucking times. Her body was still pleasantly tender in spots. "God, no."

"Good, because that would be a disaster. Though I suspect he has a killer body beneath his work clothes."

"How do you mean?"

"He rolled up his sleeves one time—"

"Not about the body." Which she could attest was damn fine and didn't need the reminder. "The disaster part."

"Could you imagine how much that man would gloat if he'd had you naked? You'd never hear the end of it. I mean, he's already obnoxious and thinks he's God's gift."

Morgan made a non-committal sound even as her throat tightened. What had she done? Phoebe was right. She'd given him so much ammunition he could bring her down in flames.

"Fortunately, that ain't happening." Phoebe stood up. "Drew King. Could you imagine? You ready?"

"Yeah." Morgan was in deep shit, and it would hit the fan come Monday morning.

CHAPTER 4

Drew stood at the coffee maker waiting for it to finish brewing. He'd barely slept all weekend. He hadn't been able to keep Morgan out of his thoughts, pulling up her messages at least twelve times a night to text her when he should have been sleeping. Surely she couldn't have meant it when she claimed it was one-night-only, never to be talked about again.

She was a woman. Women liked to talk over these things. And talking could lead to all sorts of interesting possibilities. The chemistry between them had been epic. Maybe she always had sex that good, but. . . .

He shook his head and filled his coffee mug to the brim before heading out of the breakroom. His eyes scanned for her like they had since he'd arrived this morning.

"Hey, Drew," Thomas Baker called to him from his office door. "Can you come here for a moment? I need to talk to you."

Drew glanced toward the elevator as the doors opened. Morgan stepped out, looking cool as a cucumber. Her cold eyes swept over him just like every other morning, and she just kept walking toward her office.

He let out a breath. Maybe he'd hit his head this weekend and had imagined it all. Maybe someone had spiked his beer at the bar. Even so, while he had a good imagination, he didn't think it was that good. Not when it came to Morgan under him.

He dropped his coffee off on his desk and went into Thomas's office.

"Hold on a second." Thomas pressed a button on his phone and his assistant answered. "Ask Ms. Taylor to join us please."

Fuck. Thomas knew and this would be his "sorry, but corporate doesn't like employees sleeping together so you're fired" speech. Drew hadn't spilled the beans. Maybe Morgan had. But she had initiated with the text. Had that been her game all along? To get him fired?

Worth it.

Thomas gestured to a chair. "Good game on Saturday."

"You definitely had the advantage over me." Mostly because Drew had barely slept the night before. He tried to relax into the chair, but this wasn't how he wanted to see Morgan after Friday. He didn't know how he'd thought it would happen, but being called into the boss's office didn't bode well. He didn't actually want to lose his job.

"You wanted to see me?" Morgan's voice sliced through him.

He forced himself not to turn to look at her. Fuck, she was in his head. He just had to pretend he hadn't taken her under him and forget those sounds she'd made and the sound of her voice, soft and rough after orgasm. He shifted in his seat.

"Join us and close the door please." Thomas leaned back in his chair and waited for Morgan to sit.

Her scent, a soft gentle thing, swept over him as she settled next to him. He kept his eyes front, sure that if this wasn't about their extracurricular activities Friday night, he'd give it away by looking at her.

"Allison Cross, our Creative Director for the luxury goods division, has decided to extend her maternity leave indefinitely."

Morgan crossed her legs, helplessly drawing his gaze to them. Her black pencil skirt moved up her thigh slightly.

Drew refused to loosen his tightening collar or shift in his chair.

"Corporate and I have two candidates in mind as her replacement."

Drew sensed Morgan glance at him. Ice cold eyes that he'd seen melted in passion swept over him as if measuring him and finding him wanting.

"Morgan has been a loyal employee since college and has moved up organically within our corporation. She's Allison's assistant and the logical choice for the promotion. However, she's a few years shy of the experience we generally require for this position."

Neither of them said anything.

"Drew is new to our organization but has the experience required as the Assistant Creative Director in beverages. Unfortunately, it's not in the luxury goods line. So, while he's a good fit on paper, we worry about how his experience will translate."

All thoughts of intimate relations put aside, Drew dared a look at Morgan then. Her jaw was tight, but not a single hair dared to be out of place. Her smile was the same as always, frozen.

"Where does that leave us?" Morgan asked.

"We want Drew and you to work together for the next two weeks. You'll catch him up to speed on the current campaigns, and we'll see what each of you has to bring to this position. We'll decide who will advance at the end of two weeks. We want you to become a team so the other person will take over the position of Assistant Creative Director in the luxury goods division."

"Sounds fair," Drew said.

"Great." Thomas stood and shook both their hands. "I know you two will fit well together and won't let me down."

Drew clenched his fist at his side. They had fit well together, but how the hell were they supposed to work together now? And for the foreseeable future. Being near her in front of their boss had him already slightly aroused. And he was damned if he would let her get more into his head and make him mess up this opportunity. The opportunities for advancement were the reason he'd made the strategic leap to Hart Association.

He had a feeling neither of them were going to be happy about this arrangement.

~

Morgan couldn't leave Mr. Baker's office fast enough. Drew's heat followed her as she made her way to her office, and he was hot on her heels as she entered. The door closed behind him.

She took a deep breath. "Did you really have to follow me?"

"We need to talk."

She rounded her desk and settled in her chair before lifting her gaze to his, trying to maintain a cool and collected exterior. "Fine. Have a seat."

Drew sat in one of her office chairs. It should have made her feel superior to have the advantage of her office, but he took up all the breathing space. It felt way too intimate, but she wouldn't be the one making a fuss to open the door.

She pressed her lips together. She'd geared herself up all Sunday to face him today, but then Thomas blindsided her with this. "This is my job."

"Apparently it's either of our jobs." Drew leaned back arrogantly and crossed his ankle over his knee.

"What makes you think you can waltz in here and take what is rightfully mine?" Even as the words left her mouth, she wanted to kick herself. This would have been a lot less complicated if she hadn't slept with him this weekend. It still would have sucked but definitely not as complicated.

Why hadn't she turned him away when he'd shown up at her apartment? Told him it had been a mistake. Laughed it off. That she'd wanted some other guy, not him. That she wouldn't want him if he were the last man alive. That had all been the case… before he kissed her.

"It's not yours, yet." Drew uncrossed his leg and leaned forward. "We can make the most of these two weeks. You can show me—"

Her face flushed hot. "I'm not showing you anything else."

"Jesus, Morgan." He ran a hand over his Muppet hair she knew now was soft and silky to the touch. "I'm talking about work."

She tightened her lips.

He stood and closed in on her desk. "Look—"

"If this is going to be a lecture about work ethics—"

"Would you just let me talk?" He lifted his eyebrow and waited until she gave him a slight nod of acknowledgment. "This is both of our careers. With my experience and your knowledge of the line, we have the opportunity to make a great team, no matter which one of us gets the promotion. But neither of us can get there without the other one."

She rose slowly and leaned her hands on her desk. "Actually, I could probably make it on my own, but I have to hold your hand and show you the ropes, just so you can use it against me."

"Getting me up to speed isn't holding my hand. I have just as much right to this promotion as you do. I've put in the time and I'm just as qualified as you."

"I've worked my ass off for this company. You just waltz in with your frat boy attitude and they practically gave it to you."

A flash of heat lit his blue eyes and an answering flare lit deep inside her as he leaned in closer. The desk separating them might as well have been made of paper.

"I think we can fight fair for this position," he said.

"Since when do you fight fair?"

"Since when did you want me to?"

When had her office gotten so hot? And when had he gotten so close? An inch, maybe two, separated them. Everything in her wanted to lean in just a little more and press her lips against his. His gaze dropped to her lips, and she damn near ached.

Slowly, she backed away and stood up straight, as if a sudden move would trigger an attack. "If we don't work together, Mr. Baker won't be happy with either of us."

Drew didn't back off immediately. He seemed to be wrestling with something. Finally, he straightened, and she had to lift her chin to meet his eyes. "For now, we're in this together."

"I'm not going to be easy on you."

His eyes flashed hot. "I won't be easy on you either."

Images of him above her cascaded through her mind and she firmly knocked them away.

"I want this promotion," she said. A hell of a lot more than she wanted Drew King. Even if her body wasn't so sure.

He took a deep breath. "So do I."

"Meet me in the conference room in an hour, and we'll go through the current campaigns." She sat behind her desk and pulled her computer keyboard over, effectively dismissing him.

He opened his mouth as if to say something else and decided against it. "An hour."

CHAPTER 5

Tension wasn't quite the right word for what he felt. Drew sat in the conference room watching Morgan move around while she talked about the various ad campaigns and what stage they were in.

Her pencil skirt hugged her hips, and it had a slit that went a little higher than he thought was decent. Maybe because he kept fantasizing about what was under the skirt. Or more to the point, what might be lacking. Her legs were bare, silky skin. Her shirt was cream colored and made the flush on her chest stand out. Which made him just a bit more aroused to know that she wasn't immune to him.

"Avalon Jewelry is one of our key clients. They have an assortment of prices, ranging from low end to high end." She forwarded her PowerPoint presentation. "We're working on the Christmas campaign. They've designed a special heart pendant as well as a diamond and sapphire tennis bracelet they'd like to specifically endorse."

"What stage are we at in the campaign?"

Her eyes snapped to him as if remembering he was there.

He figured she'd been trying to ignore him while doing her presentation. This was nothing new. She'd always been like that with him, even before Friday night. It's why he teased her so much. She was just too uptight, too easy to screw with. Not that she'd been easy…

He fought off the urge to loosen his suddenly tight collar. Damn it. Focus on the task.

She pressed the button and a flow chart appeared. "Art is working on some initial sketches. Copywriting is working on the tagline. It's really in the beginning stages and we have time, so we were waiting for Allison to get back before rolling forward."

"Sounds like we have our first task then."

She glanced at the slide. "I guess so. I'm still amazed Allison is giving this all up."

"You don't ever think of starting a family?" The glare he received made him chuckle and hold up his hands. "What?"

"I'm focused on my career."

"What if the right man comes along?" He couldn't resist poking at her.

"I doubt that will happen." She turned to press a key on her keyboard and when she bent over, her skirt tightened over her perfect ass. His throat went dry. He clenched his fingers into the chair to keep from crossing the conference room and taking her in his arms. The wall of windows left them completely exposed to the rest of the office where everyone else busily worked. While he wasn't concerned about an audience—which he should have been, but when he was near her, he stopped thinking straight—Morgan would be concerned, especially given the hands-off notification from corporate. Fortunately, the room was soundproof.

The right man would be a fool not to grab her, but she didn't believe it would happen? "Why not?"

She turned and glared at him. "I'm not available for a relationship."

"Just sex then."

Her mouth dropped open and snapped shut. She gave a quick look out the conference room windows into the office. No one was paying attention to them. She gave him a glare that would have incinerated a lesser man.

He held up his hands in surrender. "Hey, I'm always game for sex."

"Sex is off the table."

"The floor will do."

She closed her eyes and pinched the bridge of her nose. "Oh my God. Seriously?"

"What?"

"We cannot have this conversation at work." Her eyes sparked with anger.

"Does that mean we can have it somewhere else?"

"No."

"But then what about the sex, can we have that?"

Her face flushed. "No."

"We aren't going to talk about it?" he said softly. He didn't move and neither did she, but the conference room felt smaller all of a sudden.

"No." Her voice lowered to an almost whisper. "You just need to stop."

"Why?" He let his gaze wander over her like a caress. "It was good. Better than good. It was awesome."

She turned her back on him and started messing with her computer.

"Can you honestly say you don't want to do it again?"

She shut her laptop and inhaled. "It was a mistake," she whispered.

That wasn't a no. "Best mistake I've ever made."

She packed up her laptop and turned to face him. Her

glacier eyes and strict mouth weren't as harsh as they used to be, before he knew what those lips felt like against his and how those eyes became a dark sea when she lost herself to passion.

"It was a mistake, and I don't repeat mistakes." She made her way to the door, but she had to pass by him to get there.

When she reached him, he stood in her way. He didn't touch her, but he was close. Close enough to see the warning flash in her eyes.

"There are two ways this can go, Morgan."

Her lips tightened and she narrowed her eyes.

"We can work together on these projects and prove to Thomas we are both qualified for the position. But we do it together." Drew flexed his fingers as he caught a glimpse of blue under her hair. God, he wanted her.

"I don't think we can work together." She didn't back down even though he invaded her personal space. He respected the hell out of her for that.

He stepped a little closer than what was appropriate at work, forcing her to either back up or crane her neck to meet his gaze. She held her ground but tilted her chin defiantly.

"The other way. . . ." His gaze dropped to her mouth. Her lips parted slightly. "Each of us is in this on our own, and don't expect me to be gentle."

"I never expected you to be gentle."

A brief memory of her pushing him over the edge made him clench his jaw. "Then let the games begin."

MORGAN SPENT the rest of the day putting out various fires and sending as much information as she could to Drew to keep him from coming to talk to her. It was bad enough when they had to be in the same office building, but this working together would be pure torture.

"Heading out for the day." Phoebe stuck her head in Morgan's office. "You need anything?"

"Someone to murder Drew King?" She leaned back in her chair and stared up at the ceiling. "At least make him disappear for a while?"

"You've got this, Morgan." Phoebe came through the door and sat on the arm of one of the chairs. "Allison has said for years this job was made to be yours."

"I wish she would have told that to Thomas." She stretched her arms up, feeling all her muscles protest at the movement.

"Personally, I think it would have been yours if they hadn't hired Drew." Phoebe glanced over her shoulder. "If you need me to do something to turn the odds in your favor, just let me know."

She leaned forward across her desk. "What did you have in mind?"

"Sabotage." Phoebe wiggled her eyebrows like a silent movie villain.

Morgan rolled her eyes. "I don't need to get us fired."

"I'm not talking anything really bad, but. . . ." She came closer. "What about putting a laxative in your lunch?"

Her nose scrunched up. "I don't know how that's supposed to help me."

"Doesn't he always steal your lunch?"

Morgan grinned. "That's wicked."

"When you get home tonight, we'll brainstorm over a bottle of Pinot." Phoebe gave her a conspiratorial wink and stood. "But not here. He could be listening."

"I'm holding you to this." Morgan laughed at Phoebe's secretive look before she vanished out the door.

After another hour, Morgan stood and stretched. The sky

had darkened rapidly outside her windows and most of the lights were off in the office. Her screen had begun to dance and blur from staring at it way too long. She needed to walk around and maybe get a cup of coffee. Most nights a handful of people worked late. But Mondays it always seemed to be a few steadfast souls.

Tonight wasn't much different, but instead of a few, it looked like it was down to her and Drew. His door was closed but she could see the light on. Made sense. He had a whole product line and production team to learn about. He was dedicated to his job if nothing else.

She wasn't proud of how she'd acted in the conference room. She wasn't sure if she would have acted much better if they hadn't slept together. Drew brought out her inner twelve-year-old emotionally. Rationally, it made sense to work together. After all, if he got the promotion, she'd be his assistant. She stopped dead in her tracks and stared at his door. Holy crap! Why hadn't she put that together before?

She'd have to quit or transfer. There was no way she could work for Drew King. Not after Friday. Hell, not even before Friday.

She hurried into the breakroom and shut the door behind her. She had to bring her A game to this. That meant absolutely no screwing around and definitely not giving too much advantage to her opponent.

As she waited for the Keurig to finish brewing her cup of caffeine, the door opened. Drew stepped in with his shirt collar undone and his sleeves rolled up. She glanced away from those strong arms as they sparked memories of laying in them.

Drew stepped up to the counter next to her and reached up for a cup from the shelf. His heat engulfed her like it always had. And even though it had always been unsettling, now it was unsettling in a different way. A familiarity she hadn't had before.

Drew spoke, shattering the silence. "Do you think the ads for the Rosenthal line are the right color?"

She exhaled the breath she hadn't realized she'd been holding. Work. She could manage to talk to him about work. "Art really wanted to push the status quo, so the ads would stand out in print."

"I saw one of the earlier mock-ups. The darker colors definitely lent it sophistication." Drew leaned against the counter and crossed his ankles. She refused to look at him; ignoring him was the only way to maintain her sanity.

She made a non-committal sound and took a sip.

"Also it was a bit sexier."

She choked a little on her coffee. Slippery slope and all that. She needed to extract herself quickly from this situation. "We can have a meeting with the art department tomorrow, if you want to go over things."

No one else was in the office. No one to witness anything. That was dangerous enough with Drew, but if they started talking about sexy stuff…. Well, she wasn't willing to risk it. She might not be strong enough. In fact, she knew she wasn't. His scent already filled her head with naughty thoughts. Her naughty bits were already aching for his naughty bits. And her brain was obviously stuck on naughty which was really bad.

"I need to get back to work." She edged toward the door.

"I didn't plan this." The sincerity in his voice gave her pause.

"What do you mean?"

"I didn't know about the promotion until this morning. I know you think I'm a kiss ass, but I left my previous employer because I wouldn't be able to move up there for years. The opportunities to advance at Hart Association were too good to pass up."

"Okay." She didn't think he had been specifically out for her job.

"I know you work hard, and you deserve this just as much as I do." He lifted his gaze to meet hers.

God, those eyes were her undoing. She'd known it the first time she'd met him. The unreal color caught her deep inside and tugged at something carnal within her and sparked her flight or fight instinct. Dangerous.

"I know you don't want anything more from me, but I still want you."

Her heart hammered.

He turned and set his cup of coffee in the machine, leaving her staring at his ridiculous hair. Her fingers itched with the need to feel that stupid hair. She should leave the room. He'd had his say.

She had no choice but to take him down career-wise. She couldn't work for him, and she didn't want to leave Hart Association.

It's not like Phoebe and she would actually actively sabotage him, just mess with him. The same way he'd been messing with her since he'd arrived at Hart Association. He'd brought this on himself. In for a penny, in for a pound.

If Phoebe hadn't accidentally texted him on Friday, nothing would hold Morgan back. If she'd turned him away at the door of her apartment and hadn't let him in. . . . But she had. If she were being honest with herself—even though she didn't like the idea—she wanted him too. Something had passed between them that night. He'd crawled under her skin and made her feel tight and needy every time he was close, but she had to hold firm to her resolve.

He grabbed his cup and seemed surprised to still see her there. "Morgan?"

She shook her head to wake herself the fuck up. What the hell was she doing?

He closed the distance between them, slowly, stalking her like she was a cornered wild animal that might turn and run. Her instincts were heightened, and part of her wanted to run. The other part was locked in place by the look in those eyes. He took her mug, setting it on the table next to his own. She pressed against the door behind her, suddenly trapped and not hating the feeling. Too caught in his eyes to mistake his intentions.

"It wasn't a mistake." He reached out a hand and brushed a stray piece of hair behind her ear.

She shuddered at his touch.

"It might have complicated things, but it was never a mistake."

Her eyes focused on his lips moving. Remembering how they felt against her skin. She licked her lips.

He gave her every opportunity to stop him, but she couldn't. His head lowered and she lifted her mouth to meet his. Her world focused down to him. Her whole body lit like a fucking Christmas tree when he pulled her into his arms. All day she'd been going through the motions, but the moment he touched her, she awakened.

His hands grabbed her ass and pressed her firmly into his arousal. Their mouths did battle. Fast and hard at first, but then he gentled. And spread tender kisses along her jaw.

"What the fuck are we doing?" she said. Her rational brain was still semi-aware that they were in the breakroom.

"I don't know." He took her mouth with his and the thoughts of work and appropriateness went out of her head. Especially when his wicked fingers started edging up her skirt. The assault on her senses was complete and devastating. She was lost.

His fingers worked their way into her panties and between her legs. He caught her gasp with his mouth.

She grabbed at his belt and made short work of undoing it and his pants. Reaching inside, she palmed his erection. A rush of desire, hot and heavy, poured through her.

"Fuck." He leaned against her. He opened his eyes and met hers. "We should stop."

"Don't you dare." She wasn't sure she could be rational where he was concerned.

Both of them had their hands on each other and it was too much. She could feel an orgasm closing in on her and she was helpless to stop.

He pulled his hand away and stripped down her underwear. He reached in his pocket and pulled out a condom. At this moment, she didn't care he had one in his pocket. That he thought this might happen. At this moment, he was the most brilliant man in the world.

She helped him put it on and yanked him down into a kiss when he lifted her onto him using the wall to support them. She had been so close before, that within a few moments, she came hard, pulling him quickly with her. It had been fast and reckless and just what her body wanted.

Her head rested back on the door, while his dropped to her shoulder. Their breathing was erratic. His warmth surrounding her felt way too good.

She opened her eyes to the office lights above them and the smell of coffee in her nose like a shock to her system. *What the fuck did I just do?*

"I. . . ." He started and then shook his head, still against her shoulder. He turned and pressed a kiss to her pulse. Her body responded with a slight aftershock.

Her face started to burn. This was where she worked. This is why that memo went out. "Can you put me down?"

He set her down and fixed himself. If someone saw that condom in the trash. . . .

"Do not throw that away in here." Her face still burned as she stepped back into her panties.

"I won't."

She had to get out of there. She straightened her skirt. What had she done? Again. With Drew. At work. She was so stupid.

"Morgan?" He reached out.

She stepped away from his touch. "Don't. I can't."

"I didn't mean to—"

"I said I can't." She left the breakroom and hurried into her office to close up. She had to get out of there. It was all too much. Drew and the promotion and everything. Her tears choked her. Tears? She didn't fucking cry.

Drew came to her door and watched her. "I'll walk you out."

She slammed her drawer shut. Mad at herself. Mad at him. Mad at her fucking weakness. Mad at the fucking tears. "I don't need you to try to make it all better."

Drew stood there, confusion on his face. He seemed so lost with his pretty boy looks. He had none of his usual bravado, which would have made it so much easier to be furious with him.

"Don't worry," she said. "I'm not going to report you or anything. It was totally consensual. I'm just mad at myself."

She grabbed her purse and laptop bag and headed for the door. He was in her way.

"I don't know what came over me." He shook his head. "I just. . ." He ran his hand through his hair. "You drive me crazy."

"We need to stop." She made sure to keep plenty of space between them. Keeping temptation out of reach. "We have to work together and that" —flinching, she gestured toward the breakroom— "can't happen again."

He nodded and moved to let her out of her office. She rushed to the elevator and felt him follow her. When the elevator arrived and it looked like he would join her, she shook her head. She couldn't trust herself to be alone with him. "I'll be fine."

His face was blank, but he nodded and said, "Good night, Morgan."

CHAPTER 6

"I BROUGHT WINE," Phoebe said as Morgan opened the door just before ten o'clock.

Even a shower and a fresh pair of pajamas hadn't washed Drew away. Her body was slightly sore and even though she was still angry at herself, the sex had felt amazing. She didn't even like him. But she hadn't been able to resist him.

He was definitely bad for her mental health.

"I need to get drunk." Morgan let Phoebe into her apartment and took the bottle to her kitchen. After uncorking it, she filled two glasses.

"What happened after I left?" Phoebe sat in the armchair with her feet curled up under her. "Drew didn't do something stupid, did he?"

Only if *she* was stupid. Morgan handed Phoebe a glass while deciding what to actually tell her. As long as the sex stayed between Drew and her, corporate wouldn't find out and fire them both. Not that Phoebe would blabber about it, but it just seemed better to keep it to herself. "Just typical infuriating Drew stuff."

She settled on the couch and drank half of her glass. *You know, Drew stuff. . . like orgasms. In the breakroom.*

"Okay." Phoebe looked less than convinced. "I've been doing some plotting of my own."

"I'm game for anything." At this point, she needed to be doused with a fucking water hose whenever she got near the man or she'd end up straddling him.

"Lunches for starters. It doesn't have to be laxatives, but we can figure out what he doesn't like, maybe if he has a slight food allergy—"

"Whoa, I was kidding about having him killed."

"Not that kind of allergy. You know the kind where they just get a little itchy." Phoebe shrugged.

"I think we should steer clear of allergies." She grabbed the bottle and topped off her glass. "We need something that will keep him on edge." And far away from her.

"What if we set up a Tinder profile for him?"

"I'm listening."

Phoebe smiled. "He's such a pretty boy. We could totally hook him up with all sorts of guys or just some really needy females."

"Interesting, but how does setting him up on dates sabotage his efforts to become Creative Director?" Not that she really wanted to hook him up with anyone else. Whoa. Not sure where that thought came from.

"What if we plan the dates when he has business lunches?"

"Oh, that's just evil." Morgan smiled, feeling a lot more relaxed and warm from the wine. She finished her glass. Coffee was the only thing she'd had today. She hadn't been able to stomach the thought of lunch after being slapped with the promotion news. So the wine hit her empty stomach and loosened her tongue. "I bet he'd like that. Some woman fawning over him while he tried to close a deal. And I bet she'd love his stupid hair and how soft it is."

"Soft?" Phoebe took the bottle from Morgan before she could add more to her glass. "Did you have dinner?"

"No."

"You always were a lightweight." Phoebe shook her head.

Morgan leaned her head on the couch to keep it from spinning. "He has such stupid eyes. Stupid Muppet hair. But his arms are really nice. Like, really nice. I didn't think I was an arm person, but damn, the boy must shred."

"Yeah, I'm cutting you off. When Drew starts to look good, you are too toasted to go on." Phoebe stood and went into the kitchen. "Do you have some bread to soak up that alcohol and turn off your beer goggles?"

"Maybe," Morgan yelled and slouched on the couch. More to herself, she added, "I bet he didn't have any issues eating tonight."

"Found some."

Still mumbling, she added, "He probably ate something really great and didn't even feel bad at all."

"What are you going on about? Eat this." Phoebe held out a piece of bread and cheese.

She took the bread and ate a bite. "He's going after my job, Phoebe."

"I know." Phoebe sat back down. "He's such a doody head."

"But he's not." Morgan shook her head. He could be annoying, but sometimes he was really nice. "He's not a doody head."

"Are you sure you aren't coming down with something?" Phoebe put the back of her hand against Morgan's forehead and looked concerned.

Morgan shook her head and ate the cheese. "Drew King is going to be the death of me. How on earth am I going to work under him?" She snickered. She'd had no problem working under him Friday. "Maybe I need to work *over* him."

It definitely had potential. So many positions they hadn't even tried and now they wouldn't because she couldn't trust herself around him.

"Seriously, what is wrong with you?" Phoebe took a drink. "If I didn't know better, I'd think you might actually like the guy."

"I don't like him." She shook her head furiously and regretted it as her brain felt like it sloshed around in her skull. She *lusted* after him. Huge difference. "I don't like him at all."

She liked his body and how it felt moving against hers. And the orgasms. . . yes please. She definitely didn't have anything against his mouth, except when it was talking.

"Good, let's keep it that way. I think I'll take the rest of this home."

"Aw." Morgan pouted. "You're no fun."

"I'm tempted to put your phone on lockdown. Wouldn't want you drunk texting." Phoebe stood and headed for the door. "But it's barely ten o'clock and I'm going to pretend you are a responsible adult. Maybe you could text Dr. Drew for round two. Give the guy another shot. Now that you are all relaxed."

Phoebe opened the door and stepped into the hallway. "Do it, Morgan. Do Dr. Drew." She blew a kiss and closed the door.

Morgan collapsed against the couch. "I already did Drew though."

She rolled her head. The phone was right there. She'd told Drew they couldn't do it at work, but she wasn't at work now. What the hell was she thinking? Too much wine, not enough food.

She stood and made her way into the kitchen. As she

made a Lean Cuisine, her phone dinged. She waited for the microwave to finish before heading into the living room with her dinner and a glass of water.

Picking up her phone, she unlocked it. One message from Drew.

You okay?

Fuck no, she wasn't. She couldn't get him out of her head. She'd freaked out after the impromptu office sex because she didn't do that. She didn't mix business with pleasure. She'd never so much as kissed a coworker.

At least not until Drew had shown up at her apartment.

She stared at the text while she ate her meal. When did he get to be so nice? It was easier when he was being a jerk. He was probably just afraid she'd turn him in to HR.

She sighed and picked up her phone. *I'm good.*

She pushed her phone aside before she did something stupid. Namely Drew King. Her phone pinged again.

Sighing, she picked it up.

We should talk.

Nothing to talk about. She hit the send button. She took her dishes into the kitchen before picking up her phone to take to the bedroom. She hooked it up to her charger and made sure the alarm was on before heading into the bathroom to get ready for bed.

Somehow she would have to work with Drew and manage to make a good impression on the boss so he would overlook the fact she lacked a few years of experience for the promotion. She also needed to figure out a way to keep her mind off dirty thoughts when she was close to Drew and to make sure he didn't get under her skin again.

Her phone pinged.

What about what happened at the office?

She sat cross-legged on her bed and held the phone in her hands. *No.*

She closed her eyes and took a deep breath. She would have this thing under control by tomorrow. Her job would keep her busy. She'd be as nice as she was before Friday and keep all talk to a minimum. It was a little tempting to block his number from her phone, but she wasn't that strong yet and they had to work together.

Tomorrow, she'd be stronger. Tomorrow, she'd figure out how to ruin Drew King's chances of being her boss. Tomorrow, she'd prove she was the right person for the job. Tomorrow. . . she'd have to work with Drew and not think about the breakroom incident.

CHAPTER 7

"It's not that hard," Morgan said, shaking her head.

"Maybe for you, but this is excruciating to look at." Drew pushed the sheet of proofs away. "I've always wondered why perfume ads were so surreal."

Morgan pulled the proofs across the conference table and queued up the proof in question on her computer to show on the screen. After a few awkward moments this morning, they had settled into the conference room to go over the proofs from the photoshoot for the new perfume, *Joli*.

This conference room was slightly smaller but still had a narrow window next to the door overlooking the office.

"It's supposed to evoke the Mad Hatter's tea party." Morgan crossed her legs and leaned back in her chair, staring up at the image. "In this photo, the woman playing Alice is more of a steampunk style with a short skirt and a barely there top. It's supposed to be art, not erotica. When people think scent, they think of being close and sex. What's sexier than skin?"

Drew cleared his throat, but she ignored him. The old

Drew would have thrown out a comment, but apparently, he was trying to be on his best behavior.

"This is work" was the mantra that played over and over in her head. Unfortunately, they weren't working on a dog food campaign where sex wouldn't be a primary component. Most luxury goods used sex or sex appeal as a selling tool, but perfume and cologne were the kings of sex in advertising.

"What's the Mad Hatter doing though?" Drew used a red laser pointer to indicate the Hatter's hand, which clearly disappeared under Alice's skirt.

Morgan recrossed her legs and cleared her throat. "Do I need to explain to you what a man and woman do?"

"I think we both know I know," Drew said softly. His voice was almost as devastating to her lack of willpower as his eyes. "This is a print campaign. Won't it trigger censors?"

"Perfume is about desire." Morgan kept her focus intentionally on the image on the screen. Her breath had shortened. It was bad enough being stuck in a small place with Drew, but when the primary focus of the campaign was sex. . . . Ugh. "It's beauty. Longing and want. It's about capturing what you can't have."

"What about the next one?" His voice went slightly deeper.

She clicked forward. The same couple, except the Mad Hatter only had a hat on. His side was to the camera, but he was all lean taut muscles. Alice had an expression that Morgan could only describe as orgasmic.

"Well?" Drew asked.

"Well what?" Morgan had to look away from the image. The male model had a very similar build to Drew, and her mind had started creeping to dragging her fingers down Drew's abs. . . . She met Drew's gaze accidentally and saw the heat there. She shoved her laptop away and straightened the proofs.

"Her O face? That's classy." His tone was deadpan.

"Don't tell me you are a prude, Drew King?" Morgan lifted her gaze to see him pressing his lips together.

"Hey, I like sex just as much as the next guy, but isn't this over the top?" He gestured helplessly to the image still on the screen.

Morgan studied him. He'd been okay to her all day. Not bringing up sex or making jokes about anything. It was almost as if he were taking the job seriously for once. Or maybe just taking her seriously for once. It was a little off-putting at first to be honest. She'd prepared for frat boy Drew, but working with nice Drew was a pleasant change. Although frat boy Drew would have been easier to ignore and be irritated at.

"Perfume is one of the hot holiday sellers. We need to stand out among the ads with scantily clad, household name celebrities. If it takes oiling up a couple of really pretty people and making them look like they are about to have sex or in the middle of having sex, then I'll oil them up myself. This is part of the job. Sex is one of our tools. We can't be shy about using it."

Drew locked his blue eyes on her and for a moment, it felt like he was physically touching her. "I get that. I've done my fair share of sexy ads, but this campaign takes a children's book and turns it into a porn shoot. You don't have a problem with that?"

"I know what it takes to make the client happy." Morgan stood and stacked her things together. "If they want me to have fully nude models, I will find a way to make it tasteful and appropriate for the advertising space they have available. Luxury goods is new to you, but it thrives on excess and pushing the envelope. You won't find Hip Hopping Hamsters or belching frogs."

"I know that." He rose from his chair and came around the table to grab the proofs again. That put him directly beside her and the smell of him. . . longing and desire mixed with sandalwood. If she could bottle him, she'd make a fortune.

"What about this though." He leaned in close to her and pointed at one of the images. "Can you pull this one up?"

She found the photo, projecting it to the smartboard. He didn't move away, and while he wasn't doing anything inappropriate, he was closer than she thought was necessary. At least closer than was good for her mental health.

The image was Alice and the Hatter from the waist up. The Hatter had his back to the camera, and he was completely naked with the exception of the hat. He had Alice pressed up against the wall with her leg hooked over his waist. His face turned in profile with his lips close to Alice's neck. Alice faced the camera with her head slightly tipped back, lips slightly parted, and her eyes closed. Her feathery, fake lashes dusted her cheeks.

Morgan swallowed. It was very reminiscent of last night. Had he brought this one up intentionally? She snuck a glance at him, but his thoughtful gaze stayed on the image.

"Okay, bear with me here while I work through this." Drew's voice was deep and quiet in the conference room.

Morgan glanced out into the rest of the office, but there didn't seem to be anyone else around. Not even Phoebe to save her.

She cleared her throat. He was being professional. She could be professional. "Okay."

"You said perfume ads were supposed to evoke desire and passion, right?" The heat of Drew made her sway a little toward him before she caught herself.

"Yes."

"Here's the problem I'm having with these photos." Drew stepped closer and reached around her to tap on her laptop. His hair brushed her arm, sending a jolt through her. Her breath caught. "Sometimes the things we want most are the things that we can't quite have. In this image, you are giving us the man, and he's got the woman. Where's the longing in this?"

"But does he really have her? Or is this just a moment and in the next she'll be gone?" Morgan's voice sounded breathy even to her ears. "Down the rabbit hole once more."

"That's just it." Drew's breath tickled her ear, but she didn't dare turn to face him. The heat his body radiated engulfed her. "If he wants her, he can have her. It's right there in the picture. In all these pictures. But what if he couldn't have her?"

"Like she is just out of reach?"

"Yeah." He scrolled through some of the photos and stopped on one. "Like here. The Hatter has finally found some pants. But look at Alice's face."

The air in the room had vanished during his speech. He took up too much space and he crowded into her. Every nerve ending in her body stood at attention, waiting, wanting, needing his touch.

She looked at Alice's face. She had a hint of flirtation about her mouth and eyes. Not sultry, but more come-hither. "It's softer."

"She wants him." His words were soft and hypnotic. "She's letting him know that she wants him, but she's not going to give it up easily. No. He's going to have to work for it. But when he does earn it, man is it going to be explosive. Look at his mouth. See the slightest hint of a smile. He knows she's his for the taking."

Holy fucking shit. That was the picture's story, but was he talking about the picture or about them?

"Maybe that's part of the appeal of the other photos." She had to extract herself carefully from this. "They had their fun and now that it's over, they can both move on."

"I don't think it's over." His body grazed hers as he changed the images again. Back to the one against the wall. "That. . . ." He pointed at the picture, more specifically at the woman's face. "That right there doesn't happen to just everyone. If you want longing, you go with the subtle photo. The flirtation. If you want desire, it's right in front of you. Ready for the taking."

She snapped her eyes to his, unable to take any more of his baiting. His sapphire eyes sparkled with intention and an underlying desire that probably reflected in her own. Her lips parted, but her brain lost track of what she was going to say. His gaze dropped to her lips and her body throbbed in response.

"Right." She clapped her hands to dispel the lingering desire hanging around them and walked away. Needing space and time. "So you think we should go with the flirty photo and not the porny photo."

His eyebrow shot up, his lips tilted, and his dimple appeared. "Porny?"

"That photo." She pointed and felt the heat rising in her cheeks.

"Is that a professional term? Porny? Should I use that when writing up my report?" Drew was having way too much fun with this.

"Yes." She smiled her plastic smile. "That's the term all senior management uses. In fact, you should use it when we pitch this at the next staff meeting."

"Well now, someone is feeling a little evil today." Drew

straightened and glanced out the window into the office. "Willing to throw me under a bus?"

"Gladly." The bickering took the edge of sensuality out of the room quite effectively.

"I'm hurt." He clasped his heart. "That you would so willingly let a colleague use inappropriate terminology at a meeting, just to make yourself look better. I'm shocked. And frankly, a little impressed."

"I'm not trying to impress you." Morgan picked up her stuff, making ready to beat a hasty retreat.

"Trust me, Morgan. You've impressed me." His words were soft and caressing again.

Damn it. Where was a water hose when you needed one? "Why don't we break for lunch, and then we can make a final decision about whether or not the Hatter gets pants?"

"Are you asking me out to lunch?" Drew moved forward so quickly she didn't have a chance to sidestep him. Suddenly he was there in her space, all warm body and sandalwood.

"No." She backed up a step.

"Why not? We could continue this discussion at the bar downstairs or maybe in a locked room somewhere." His eyes suggested the wicked things he had in mind.

"I think that's a horrible idea." She retreated a step.

He filled in the space. "But think of all the things we could get done."

"I'm not that hungry." She held her ground, mostly because her next step backward would put her up against the wall. Her heart raced. Her body was on board, but that would only lead to disaster.

His eyes caressed her face. "We don't have to eat. We could continue to discuss the intricacies of perfume ads and desire."

Fuck, he tempted her. If the whole office didn't have a view into this conference room, she didn't know if she would be strong enough to not jump his bones. And from the look on his face, he knew it.

She took a deep breath and slid away from him toward the door. "I need a break. See you in an hour."

His chuckle followed her as she escaped out the door.

An hour later, Drew sat in the conference room again with the proofs, waiting for Morgan, after eating his own lunch for a change. He'd tried his damnedest to keep things professional this morning, but those images and Morgan's shortness of breath . . .

He adjusted himself while the room was still empty. Morgan didn't want to talk about yesterday or Friday night. Clearly, she didn't want to think or talk about what happened between them today. She needed space, he understood that, but when she was close, his brain took a leave of absence.

The conference room door opened and in walked Morgan and Phoebe.

"I hope you don't mind. I thought Phoebe might be able to help us this afternoon." Morgan's eyes dared him to say no.

"Sure, the more the merrier." Drew leaned back in his chair as the women took seats across from him. "I spent lunch going over some of our other ad campaigns for perfume and cologne."

"That must have been exciting." Phoebe opened her laptop and hooked it up to the smartboard. "We've had some really successful campaigns."

Morgan met his eyes.

"Very evocative." Drew didn't drop his gaze from hers. "I could see what you meant about the tone of the campaigns.

Lots of skin, faces caught in passionate stares, even some oiled nudes, which I know are your favorite."

He ended with a wink which finally made Morgan drop her gaze.

"Yes." Morgan moved her stack of papers around. "This client had very specific ideas in mind when they contracted us. They wanted the Mad Hatter and Alice, grown up versions of course. And they wanted sex that smacked you when you looked at it."

"Art definitely delivered." Drew turned to Phoebe. "Could you put both fifteen and twenty-two on the screen please? Side by side."

"Sure." Phoebe dragged the images onto the smartboard.

"I think it's down to these two." Drew leaned back in his chair and studied Morgan. Her face was a mask of concentration and focus. "The flirty photo and the porny photo."

Her eyes snapped to him with a flash of anger.

He held his hands up and flashed her a smile. "Your words, not mine."

She went back to studying the photos. "Okay. Why these two?"

Drew stood and went to the smart board. "Both of these are sexy, but in different ways. The first Alice is flirty, while the Hatter is definitely interested. The undercurrent fascinates me about this one. Her body language is saying oh hell yeah, but her eyes are a little more mysterious. Like she might say no at any moment. He's obviously into her, but she holds all the power in this moment."

"You got that from the photo?" Phoebe shook her head. "I think I'm out of my depth here."

"Sure, she looks like she has the power in that first one." Morgan stood and walked to the other side of the smartboard toward the image of an orgasmic Alice pressed against the wall by a naked Mad Hatter. "But in this one, she has him.

There are no questions of will they or won't they. Just pure unadulterated sex. Even though she's his for the moment, she may not be his in the next. And him . . . well, he's giving it all he has so she'll come back to him. Longing is in the curve of his spine and the lift of her chin. They want each other, and they have each other."

"These two aren't just a flash in the pan." He moved in closer. "They have chemistry and something intangible. Sure the sex will be amazing, but isn't the chase the fun part?"

"If she wanted a chase, she would have asked for one. Obviously, she just wants the Mad Hatter to get the job done."

"Maybe the Mad Hatter is more than just a walking—"

"Whoa," Phoebe said from her chair. "I hope you aren't about to use the word I think you are going to use, because I don't want to have to sit in another HR seminar on appropriate workplace talk."

Morgan and Drew had drawn closer as they'd argued until they were close enough that he could feel her breath on his face. She inhaled deeply and fell back. He retreated to his spot at the table.

"Look, I may not be the one up for the Creative Director position, but even I know you guys are reading far too much into this." Phoebe leaned back in her chair and held her hands up to present the pictures. "Try looking at them together instead of picking your favorite."

Drew grunted but looked at the two photos side by side.

"It actually tells a pretty compelling story." Morgan sat in her chair. "Maybe as a dual ad where the flirty one is on one side and when you turn the page, the por—"

Phoebe made a buzzer noise. "HR?"

Morgan cleared her throat. "Okay, the *sexy* one on the next."

Drew nodded. "Kind of a before and after."

"Exactly." Morgan smiled. "Phoebe, sometimes you are a genius."

"Oh, I'm always a genius. I just don't like to flaunt it. Otherwise they might actually make me work more." Phoebe gave a horrified shudder.

Morgan's cell phone rang. She glanced down at the screen and blushed. Interesting.

"I need to take this." She showed the screen to Phoebe who snickered. And then Morgan left the conference room.

"What was that about?" Drew asked as he opened up their file documents to see which campaign they should work on next.

"Just this guy we met Friday at the bar. She almost didn't take a chance on him because of his name." Phoebe shrugged as she put together an email for art. "I thought she was over him after Friday though. I know my guy wasn't all that, but hey, maybe if she wanted to double, I might take another chance on the doctor."

Drew stared out the window at Morgan as she smiled while talking to whoever was on the other end of the phone. Friday night? His name? A sick feeling started in his gut. "What's the guy's name?"

"Well, he is a doctor. . . ." Phoebe slouched back in her chair as if trying to remember, then she sat up straight. "Walker or something like that."

"What's his *first* name?"

Phoebe laughed and shook her head. "You'll never believe me."

Morgan turned and met his eyes. Her smile vanished.

A tick started in his jaw. "Try me."

"His name is Andrew, but he goes by Drew too. Isn't that funny?"

"Hilarious."

CHAPTER 8

THE REST of the day went by in a blur for Morgan. They went through a couple more campaigns before returning to their respective corners. She made sure not to be one of the last ones at the office and headed home at a somewhat reasonable time, grabbing some Chinese on her way.

Drew had been surprisingly subdued after they made the decision on the perfume ad. She'd been shocked when Dr. Andrew Walker called her to ask her out this Saturday. A little surreal, considering he'd been who she'd wanted to hook up with last Friday. He was nice and sweet and good looking, but something didn't feel right about it. She was really busy with work after all. So, she'd asked for a rain check.

As she finished her Chinese food, she refused to admit the real reason she didn't want to go out with him was because she'd had sex with Drew King on multiple occasions now. He had crawled under her skin, and until she worked him out of her system, she wouldn't be very good company.

She put her leftovers in the fridge and looked around her

empty apartment. She could go see what Phoebe was doing. It was still early.

Her buzzer went off. She wasn't expecting anyone, but sometimes delivery guys pressed all the buttons to get in. She didn't go check. They could press the proper apartment number button if they wanted in that bad. Or they could just press all of them. A guy a floor down pretty much let everyone in.

When someone knocked at her door a few minutes later, she didn't think anything of it. Phoebe came over a lot in the evenings. Hopefully she'd brought another bottle of wine. Maybe if Morgan confessed about Drew, Phoebe would be able to talk her down off this ledge.

The knock came again.

"Just a minute. God, you're impatient, Phoebe." She opened the door and Drew stood there.

Her mouth dropped open.

"We need to talk." Drew didn't wait for an invitation but swept past her into her apartment.

"By all means, come in. Make yourself comfortable," she murmured as she shut the door. She stood for a moment facing the door and took a deep breath to steady herself before facing him. She could do this. Alone. In her apartment. With a bed within sprinting distance. She took another breath. He wanted to talk. Fine.

She turned. He had her phone in his hand at the coffee table. "Hey!"

She charged over to take back her phone, but he held it higher.

"That's not fair."

"It isn't, is it," he said, still messing with her phone.

She wasn't about to jump up and down or climb on the couch to grab her phone. Even if he was provoking her to do just that. She still had some decorum. "May I ask what you are looking for?"

"Contacts."

"What, you don't have enough numbers and you want mine now?"

He must have found what he was looking for, because he nodded and set the phone back on the coffee table.

She backed up a step as he turned, suddenly aware of how close she'd gotten to him.

"I was surprised when you texted me on Friday." Drew paced to her front door and back to the couch. "I mean, really surprised."

She sat on the couch to get out of his way and tucked her feet under her. "Do you want to sit down?"

He ignored her.

"I thought maybe it was a prank. Morgan Taylor texted me to hook up. Who would have thought of such a thing? I thought you hated me. Or at least really didn't like me. So, why would you text me? But then I always felt this underlying attraction to you even if you were an ice princess, so maybe you felt the same way. Sex to get the tension out of the way."

Morgan's heart raced. He made her living room feel small. He made *her* feel small.

"I honestly expected your apartment to be filled with our coworkers ready to laugh at the new guy." He stopped pacing and ran a hand through his curls before lifting his eyes to her. "But then you opened the door. . . . You were in hardly anything and you looked surprised to see me."

He began to pace again and gesture. "See, that should have clued me in. That bit of surprise on your face. Had it been because you hadn't seen me in a T-shirt and jeans, and I look damned fine in a T-shirt and jeans?"

She couldn't answer. The phone was her major clue. She knew he knew.

"But I was like fuck it, and then I kissed you and you went soft and pliant in my arms. And that spark. . . ." He gave her a look that curled her toes. "Damn. I swore the heat would melt the floor."

He watched her for a moment before he started pacing again. "Who knew under that frigid exterior was a sex kitten waiting to be released? I'd hoped of course, but I'm sure glad I got to find out firsthand."

He stopped with his back to her, facing the door.

She didn't know what to say. They weren't really having a discussion. He obviously had stuff he needed to get off his chest. All she could do was listen and wait for the axe to fall.

"You texted *me*." He didn't turn around. Didn't continue to pace. "I gave you my number at the bar, and you texted me."

Her heart clattered, and her throat felt thick. Maybe this would finally end it all. They'd go back to just hating each other and no more sexual tension.

"But it wasn't me, was it?"

He turned then, and his face was emotionless. "Oh, you wanted a Drew, but not this Drew. How'd you end up texting the wrong guy, Morgan?"

She cleared her throat of the lump lodged there. "Phoebe started the texting. I only saw she texted Drew."

"Why didn't you say anything when I showed up at your door?" He moved closer to her, and her insides tingled.

"You kissed me before I could do anything," she accused.

"And any Drew will do?" His chuckle was dark.

"I didn't know you would be showing up at my door. I thought, what are the odds of having met another Drew?" She uncurled from the couch and padded across her floor until she stood toe to toe with him. "I was surprised when I opened the door. I was shocked when you kissed me. And then I was glad it was you and not him that showed up."

His eyes glittered like hard sapphires. His curls were more manic than usual. Unable to resist, she reached up and slid her fingers along one of his silky curls.

"I wanted *you*." Morgan traced her finger along his strong tense jawline. "I want you."

"But?" Drew's hands clenched at his sides, waiting for the other shoe to drop.

"We can't keep doing this." Her fingers sank into his hair, and she released a sigh. She didn't mean it. But she did. He was dangerous for her mental stability.

"What exactly are we doing, Morgan?" A muscle ticked in his jaw.

She shook her head. She didn't know. She didn't want to say. Tomorrow they'd be working toward the same position. One of them would lose. They weren't friends. They were barely coworkers, but when he touched her. . . hell, when he looked at her, she melted.

"Please," she whispered. Just one last time. Just one more hit. Then she'd be good.

"Fuck," he said. Whatever battle he'd been waging, he'd lost, or maybe he'd won, Morgan had no idea. But his hands were on her finally and his mouth descended onto hers, hard and a little brutal. She welcomed the punishment.

He pressed her backward while undoing her shirt and skirt, letting them drop as he moved her. His body, always warm, was like a furnace, heating hers into a frenzy. She worked on his buttons while he worked her bra. His mouth took control of hers until she didn't know where she ended and he began.

This was insane. It was dangerous. It was everything she wanted.

Her bare chest pressed against his. The back of her knees

hit the edge of her bed, and his momentum carried them down. He made quick work of her underwear and the rest of his clothes, and joined her on the bed.

He reclaimed her mouth as his hands skimmed over her body. She never wanted this to end but knew it had to. A desperation to not break the spell came over her. His mouth trailed over her chin and down her neck. When he closed over her nipple, she nearly came off the bed. His hand pressed her down into the mattress as he teased and tortured her breasts.

How could this be wrong when it felt so right? Together they were epic.

He trailed hot kisses over her stomach and down. Her fingers wove into his curls and held on as he pressed his mouth to the very center of her. His tongue and lips drove her insane as they pushed her closer and closer to the edge. He stopped right as she was about to come and grabbed a condom.

He moved over her, and she opened for him. He paused above her. She opened her eyes to his face hovering over hers. His eyes were dark and unreadable in the darkness.

"Who's in charge, Morgan?" The words, once a challenge, were more than that now.

Even as she bristled at the words, she knew this wasn't about work anymore. In his mind, she had wanted another man and had made do with him. He needed to know that he wasn't second to some other guy or to her whims. He wanted to know if she was his.

The problem was, as much as she wanted to deny it, she was. He tied her up in knots and broke her down into pieces. He was in control, and she wasn't. But he wouldn't take her until she admitted it to him.

"You are," she whispered. At least right now. He had taken control of her body and made it his own. She had no will when it came to him. She wanted him. She needed him. All of him.

He sank into her in one powerful thrust. Her body shuddered in welcome. She wrapped herself around him and followed his pace. He took her mouth, hard, as he thrust into her. When he increased the tempo, she couldn't hold back. She came in a silent scream. Her whole body tensed around him, dragging him into his own release.

For a moment they stayed like that, bound together, in the center of her bed. Reluctantly she released him so he could take care of the condom. The curve of his ass was a pleasant view as he made his way to the bathroom. She released a breath. Maybe this wasn't a bad thing. Maybe they could continue to have sex without it interfering with work.

When he came out of the bathroom, he didn't come back to the bed, but went to his pants and started getting dressed, his face a blank mask. He picked up all his stuff and had dressed within minutes.

She laid there, speechless, as she watched him. He was leaving her.

He didn't say a word, never even looked at her, and then he was gone.

DREW WAS DONE TRYING to talk out something that could never work. Instead, he decided to focus on what really mattered, which was getting the promotion. Wednesday and Thursday flew by in a haze of business meetings. He'd managed to avoid being alone with Morgan.

He didn't have to try hard as she seemed to be avoiding him too. Thursday afternoon, the staff meeting dragged on. Drew checked his phone for the time and saw that only five minutes had passed since he'd last checked.

The copy department droned on about sales for dog food and how the copy could be better. Morgan sat across the table from him, fiddling with her pen. She'd worn her hair up in a bun with a conservative blouse and one of her tight pencil skirts that went down to her knees. Her eyes were frozen ice when they met his.

He deserved it. He'd been an ass the other night, but it was exactly what she'd wanted from him. Sex and nothing else. A good lay. Granted, he hadn't been the one she'd originally wanted, but he'd been the one she got.

Thank God, the copy guy finished up and the meeting was officially over. Drew closed his notepad and stood.

"Drew, Morgan, I need to see you in my office," Thomas announced.

Drew glanced at Morgan, but she just shrugged.

They entered Thomas's office and he gestured for them to sit. He closed the door and took his seat. Whatever this was about, it couldn't be good by the look on Thomas's face.

"I was excited about your proposal for *Joli*. The client seemed to love the idea as well. The concept of the dual photos was brilliant."

So far so good. Maybe this was a pat on the back meeting.

"Unfortunately. . ."

Or not.

"Something has come up, and I need you two to come in this weekend to work on it."

"Not a problem," Morgan said, daring him to say he was busy.

"No problem here," Drew said, without glancing at her.

"That's the spirit." Thomas turned his monitor around. On it were three products, a cologne, a diamond engagement ring, and a high-end vodka. "We've been tasked with creating ad campaigns for these three products. Or rather a pitch for the ads. We don't have Bradbury Industries as a client yet, but they are very unhappy with their current advertising firm."

"That would be R&F Group?" Morgan waited for Thomas's nod before adding, "We were one of the original bidders for a previous campaign, but the client decided to go with R&F Group. I can pull up what we've previously pitched and our notes on their pitch."

"That would be great." Thomas leaned back in his chair. "If we could add this client to our roster, we'd be set to meet our financial goals for this year. I want you two to put your heads together to figure this one out. After all, no matter which one of you gets the Creative Director position, you'll be working together for the foreseeable future."

Morgan glanced over at Drew with her lips tight. She didn't like the idea of working for him. Tough cookies. He sure as hell wouldn't stay in a job where she had power over him.

But Thomas didn't need to know that. "Of course, sir. We'll get right on it."

"That's the spirit."

They both stood and left the room. Once the door shut and they were walking in the hallway, Morgan stopped him.

"Can we call a truce so we can get through this weekend?" She looked up at him with those Disney princess eyes.

"You've already conceded that I'm in charge." Drew leaned back against the wall and crossed his arms.

Her face flushed bright red. "You really are an asshole."

"Language, Ms. Taylor."

"Fuck off," she said quietly and started down the hallway again.

He reached out and grabbed her arm. She tugged away from his touch and looked at him like he was a cockroach. "Hey, I promise to be on my best behavior. After all, when this is my job, these will be my clients to look after."

She closed the distance between them and lifted her chin defiantly. "You mean when this is my job, and you are my lowly assistant."

"C'mon, Morgan, you know you mean lovely assistant because you aren't going anywhere but under me."

Her huge eyes lit with a fire he'd seen in them many times. The attraction between them still lingered there. Huge and omnipresent, but he wouldn't be her booty call again. She'd have to beg him. Which actually sounded like a damn good idea. Having her on her knees groveling.

She huffed out a breath and looked around as if remembering where they were. "I'll send you the old files, and we'll start tomorrow."

"My office."

"Fine."

He watched her spin on her heel and walk away with determination before he headed to his own office. He'd just settled in to work when a knock sounded on his doorframe. He looked up as Thomas entered his office.

"I wouldn't get too comfortable in here," Thomas said as he sat across from Drew. "You'll have more room once you have the director's office."

Drew mulled over the choice of wording. "Unless I end up in Morgan's office."

Thomas turned and looked out into the main office before leaning back in the chair. "HR insisted on having Allison's choice looked at too, but we both know you're the man for the job."

His words weren't lost on Drew, but they definitely made his insides turn. It wasn't the first time Thomas had said something bordering on sexist. Drew wanted the job because he was the most qualified applicant. Not the best male applicant. But in this case, he did have more experience. "I think it's a pretty fair fight. Morgan has a lot of potential."

"With a few more years under her belt, maybe." Thomas smiled. "Just make sure you don't lose her. She's a hard worker and knows these clients. They all like her, but I'm sure they'll like you too."

Drew nodded, his stomach churning. "I won't let you down, sir."

"That's the spirit." Thomas stood and went to the doorway. "I'll have my assistant bring the products down to your office."

As soon as Thomas left, Drew took a breath. Maybe he had read too much into Thomas's choice of words. But if he wasn't, apparently the job was his to lose.

CHAPTER 9

THE NEXT MORNING, Morgan was a bundle of nerves. She'd already spilled her coffee once and that was even before she'd had to interact with Drew.

Phoebe poked her head in Morgan's office. "Do you want me to referee?"

Morgan buried her face in her hands but shook her head. "No. I need to be a grown-up and do it myself."

"Have you thought about pranking anymore?" Phoebe slipped in and closed the door behind her, pulling out her cell phone. She came around the desk. "I might have taken a picture of Drew and set up a profile. . . ."

She handed Morgan the phone. The picture showed Drew in his suit sitting behind his desk. "Subtle." Morgan read the Tinder profile. "Only furries need swipe right?"

"Can you imagine a giant mouse showing up to a business meeting?" Phoebe snickered.

Morgan tightened her lips and shook her head. She handed back the phone. "I don't think I'm quite ready for furries."

"What about the lyrics to 'Baby Got Back'?" Phoebe

looked at the photo. "I could totally photoshop some gold chains around his neck."

"Not yet." Morgan's phone dinged with the reminder it was time to go to Drew's office. "But if I'm not here on Monday, you have my permission to go full medieval on his ass."

Phoebe mock-saluted Morgan. "I won't let you go down without avenging you."

Morgan headed to Drew's office with her laptop and some pictures from their previous attempt to win the client. She should have suggested they meet in Allison's office. It was bigger and a more neutral space. But he'd made her mad, so she'd agreed to his office just to finish the conversation. If she were being honest with herself, she'd wanted to drag him into a closet and check his pockets to see if he had any condoms in them. Which didn't bode well to working with him all weekend.

Steeling herself, she went through his open door. He was on his phone, but held up his hand to wave her in.

"Sorry I can't make golf this weekend." Drew's eyes flowed over her, taking in her red blouse and black pencil skirt. His eyes landed on her "Always Red" colored lips, and she felt the familiar tug of desire before she bashed it down. "Something's come up."

She took a seat at the small table and chairs in the corner of his office and started arranging her things.

"I think that'll work. Definitely." He hung up and typed into his computer before turning to her.

"Cancelling your golf outing with the boss?"

"Actually the boss's nephew. We were part of the foursome last weekend. Zack's new to town." Drew picked up his laptop and set it at the seat across from her before going and closing the door.

The click of the door sent a shudder through her. There

were no windows for someone in the office to see him and her together. No way someone would rescue her. They were alone.

"I wouldn't want to keep you from your kissing up." Morgan kept busy pulling up files on her laptop, avoiding his eyes as he sat.

"Don't worry, I'll have plenty of opportunities to kiss up." Drew nudged a box by his feet. "The client sent over the products to help inspire us."

She raised an eyebrow. "And they delivered them to you?"

"Thomas sent them over." He shrugged. But he had an advantage over her. Thomas clearly wanted him to win, which would leave her with the decision of whether to throw away six years at Hart Association or deal with Drew King as her boss. She basically had a week to find out if she could work with him.

He reached into the box and started setting smaller boxes on the table. She grabbed the biggest and pulled out a vodka bottle.

"For when we need inspiration?" She set the bottle in the middle of the table and opened the smallest box. A gorgeous square-cut diamond with triangle-cut sapphires on the sides sat in the burgundy box. "Pretty."

She placed it on the table and Drew pulled out the final item: a bottle of cologne. He turned the label toward her and smirked. "Censured?"

"Really?" She reached out and grabbed the bottle without thought, but the moment her fingers touched his, she snatched them back. Her gaze flew to his eyes. She forgot to breathe. This was ridiculous.

He cleared his throat and set the cologne down. "I reviewed the previous campaign and the notes. Did R&F Group really use completely nude models for the perfume ad?"

She breathed out and nodded. "Multiple couples. It was a huge orgy and the execs loved it."

"Do we know how that perfume sold?"

Work was safe. Even with the sexy ads, it was just part of the job. She did a quick search through the documents. "It looks like the product didn't do well."

"Which is why they are looking to switch things up? Makes sense." Drew loosened his tie.

"What do we want to work on first?" Morgan set the items side-by-side between them.

"What are your thoughts?" Drew looked contemplatively at the items.

"If we want art to get started with a concept, the cologne is going to be the toughest as far as our idea for it goes. If we get an idea to the art department today, they could have a concept drawing to us by the pitch. The cologne might be the thing that wins us the account, given the poor sales of the perfume."

"Sounds reasonable." Drew picked up the cologne and sprayed some in the air.

Sandalwood with cedar notes hit her nose. It was a little heavier than whatever Drew used, but her body barely noticed the distinction. To her body, the scent meant really great sex.

She crossed her legs. "It's nice."

"Do we need to figure out our demographics?"

The work discussion went on for hours as they researched whether to market to athletes or executives. Young men or older. They pulled up comparable ads. From the very sophisticated with a man in a very nice suit to bare chested men to scantily clad women to scantily clad women on men with suits. To the more provocative images with a whole lot more skin showing.

"Most of these are clothed. Any notes from the client on

what direction they want to go?" Morgan leaned back in the chair and stretched her arms over her head. They hadn't moved for hours.

When she opened her eyes, Drew stared at the gap in her shirt like a starved man.

"Notes?" she repeated.

He glanced at his computer. "No notes. Guess we're flying blind. Is it time for lunch?"

Morgan looked at her phone. It was already 1 p.m. "Past."

"You want to go down to the bar to get something to eat? We could see if they have Foxx Vodka." He held up the clear bottle.

They were about to spend the next two days together working and potentially eating together. She didn't really want to spend more time than necessary with him, especially after the way he'd left the other night. Not that she blamed him. It's what she'd asked for that first night. He was only giving her what she wanted.

It hadn't hurt any less though.

Maybe this was an olive branch or maybe this was a mistake.

"No drinking during business hours," Morgan chastised. "But I could go for a burger."

"WHAT IF WE have a business suit guy relaxing in a hotel room?" Drew threw out the idea as he shoved another fry in his mouth.

Morgan had just taken a bite of her burger like it was the last thing she would eat for the rest of her life. The expression on her face tugged at something primal in Drew, and he shifted on his bar stool. Her red lipstick hadn't even faded with the food which made him just want to mess it up even more.

"This is the best burger ever." She set the burger down and proceeded to lick the sauce that had dripped out off her fingers.

If he'd been uncomfortable before, he definitely wouldn't be moving anytime soon. At least not until he got himself under control. This was a dangerous game. He would be completely alone with Morgan for the weekend. The office would be empty with the exception of the two of them.

The last time that happened, he hadn't been able to control himself. But neither had she.

He'd dealt with the fact she hadn't been reaching out to ease some perceived tension between him and her. Maybe she hadn't felt the tension before that night. But he had. Something about her frozen eyes had made him want to see if he could thaw her. Instead of solving the problem though, one night hadn't been enough.

Before, he could only imagine; now he knew what her mouth tasted like, how she liked to be touched, how she could drive him out of his mind with wanting her.

He understood her desire to hook up with someone. Work took all of their time. She was early in and one of the last to leave. With the new job and trying to make a good impression, it had been a while for him too. Even if she had expected Dr. Drew, she'd let him in.

She had let him into her space and into her bed. But that's all she'd wanted. *Tonight.* Just something to take the edge off.

Unfortunately, it backfired. He couldn't be in the same room without wanting her. Without remembering the feel of her lips pressed against his. The slide of her palm against his cock. Those fucking erotic sounds she made.

"Hello, Drew?" She waved her hand in front of his face.

"Yeah." His voice dipped a little lower than normal, and

dwelling on them having sex hadn't exactly helped the situation downstairs.

"As I was saying, I like the idea of sophisticated elegance for the cologne. I think if we introduce a woman, she should have on a formal dress, long and slinky. Maybe a blonde with a gold dress, but no shoes." She popped a fry into her mouth.

"Why no shoes?"

"Mmm. She could be holding them as she crosses the room to him."

His brain focused back on work. "So like an end of the evening. . . . Wait what if his tie is hanging loose around his neck and a couple buttons are undone. His feet are up on an ottoman."

"Oh, and she comes up behind him and smooths her hands down his chest to his abs." Her eyes glowed.

"If he's in a low back armchair and she's leaning over him, that image could be gold." He grabbed a napkin and his pen and quickly sketched what he was thinking. He handed it to her before taking another fry.

"I'm impressed."

"You helped."

"Not the idea," she said. "Though it's good. You've got some talent with art."

He shrugged. "I took visual arts throughout high school, but I wasn't good enough for art school. Besides, 'how can you make a living as an artist, you should get a business degree.'"

She smiled and set down the napkin. "Dad or mom?"

"Both." He shook his head. "I ended up falling in love with marketing, so no loss."

"I can only draw stick figures, so you're damn near Van Gogh compared to me."

"Don't expect me to cut off my ear. I get ill at the sight of blood."

She laughed. The sound bounced off his heart in a joyous rhythm, softening it. She didn't laugh enough.

"Trust me, I am not into disfigurement for the sake of art or love." Her smile was still bright with laughter as she met his eyes.

When she looked at him like that, he wanted to forget their argument. All he wanted was to kiss her until he found all her sounds again. The ones she only made in the dark. The ones she made for him.

He cleared his throat to disrupt the spell that had slowly woven around them. "Sounds like we have a solid idea to go to art with when we get back."

She pushed her plate back and wiped her hands. "We should come up with a couple more concepts so we have some choices when their renderings come back. Maybe we can go through some of the stock photos from previous shoots to see if there's anything we like."

They paid and headed back upstairs, ending up shoulder to shoulder in the overcrowded elevator on the way up. The back of his fingers brushed hers and the contact made his blood boil. Her quick inhale of breath sounded loud in his ears.

Drew let her get off the elevator first and followed her back to his office. He closed the door behind them. She took her seat as if nothing had passed between them. She tried to stay cold to him like before, but now cracks formed in those glacier eyes of hers to reveal the heat of her.

As they settled into work, they found several images that might do the trick. Thankfully, cologne ads showed a lot less flesh than perfume ads. No talk about skin and nudity required. After an hour, they went to the art department together and composed a good idea board to present to the client.

Afterward, they went to copy to see if they could come up

with a tag line for the ad. The copy writers asked for a few hours to brainstorm.

"I have to take care of a few things in my office," Morgan said in the elevator back to their floor. They were the only ones going up at this time of the day. They stayed on opposite sides of the elevator.

"We're working tonight," Drew said. It wasn't a question. They both needed to put in full days if they were going to put this together for the presentation on Tuesday morning.

"Yeah." She leaned against the wall of the elevator. "Do you want to reconvene for delivery dinner and start on the vodka?"

She stifled a yawn as the elevator stopped at their floor. His instinct wanted him to wrap his arm around her to keep her upright. But that was against the rules.

"Asian or pizza?" He followed her to his office, where she grabbed her stuff.

"Pizza, whatever toppings you want."

"Sure, boss, I'll get right on that." He gave her a mock salute.

Her lips tried to curl into a smile, but she managed to restrain it. "Better get used to taking orders from me."

"I won't." But he winked to take the edge off.

She leaned on the door frame. "Can we work in Allison's office? She's got the right setup for group projects. Not that your office isn't nice."

He nodded. "Makes sense. See you in two hours."

CHAPTER 10

THE PAST FEW nights of tossing and turning caught up to Morgan as she entered Allison's corner office. It felt weird to be in here, knowing Allison wouldn't be returning and either she or Drew would be taking this office. The windows overlooked the lights of the darkened city surrounding them.

A couch and chairs were positioned in the window corner with a low coffee table to work on. Allison's desk sat opposite them. The office was a lot larger than either hers or Drew's. And it was neutral space. Although, Drew had done a good job of not being a total asshole working in his office today.

It would be a lot easier if there weren't the lingering feelings that popped up every time he got close. An energy that pulsed between them. She'd managed to shake it off during the day, but it was late, and she was tired. Most of the staff had already left, and more lights shut off which made the office feel a little more intimate. Intimacy was the last thing they needed.

"Pizza delivery."

She turned at Drew's voice. He set the pizza box on the

coffee table, along with a couple of Solo cups and a two liter of Mountain Dew.

"Why do I suddenly feel like we're in college?" Morgan walked over and opened the pizza box. "Huh."

"What?" Drew peered into the box.

"I figured you'd take full advantage and order something disgusting." She shrugged.

"Sorry, I'm a simple man with simple tastes. Pepperoni. Cheese. Period."

"Let me grab some napkins."

He held up a couple with a smirk.

"See, you'll make a wonderful assistant, Mr. King." She sat on the couch.

"Don't get used to it, Ms. Taylor." He poured them both a cup of soda and sat in one of the armchairs. "This office is nice."

"Don't get used to it." She raised her eyebrow in challenge.

"How long have you worked with Allison?" Drew started eating his pizza.

"Allison got the promotion two years ago and moved me up to her assistant immediately." She took a bite before continuing. "We've done a lot to rebuild the luxury goods division. Brought in some really amazing clients who seem happy with the work we provide."

"I can tell."

She mocked him with shocked eyes.

"What?" Drew chugged his soda. "I can see that you worked hard. I've gone through all the files you've given me. There's some truly brilliant work in there. I have no doubt in my mind that you are an integral part of the team."

A stiff breeze could have knocked her over. "I don't know what to do with compliments from you."

"Don't get used to it." He shrugged. "I'm not denying you wouldn't be good at the job. I just think I would be better."

"The world can start spinning again. Everything's back in order. Drew King's ego is still huge." She gave him a look that said, try to deny it.

He smiled. "Guilty as charged."

"Lock him up." She finished her pizza and took a drink of Mountain Dew. College had been the last time she'd drank it. It was really sweet. She must have made a face because Drew laughed.

That dark rich sound went straight to the core of her.

"Not your favorite?" He took another drink. His sapphire eyes danced in the light.

"Not for a while at least. But I need the caffeine." She took another drink and made another face. "Maybe I'll switch to coffee or tea."

"Wimp."

She shook her head. "We need to get our product samples."

"Still in my office, along with my laptop."

After a few minutes of putting away the leftover pizza, grabbing the products and his laptop, and getting settled into Allison's office, they were finally ready to work.

"I've been thinking about the cologne." Morgan picked it up and sprayed it in the air again. "What if we're looking at it wrong?"

"Explain." He'd taken off his tie and unbuttoned the top buttons of his shirt. The scent hung in the air, so similar to the way he smelled when she'd placed her lips against the warm skin of his throat.

She swallowed.

"The name is what's bugging me. Obviously, they put thought into the name, but Censured?"

He quickly typed on his keyboard and then read off his screen. "Express severe disapproval of."

"What is that supposed to mean as a scent? Not that we need to go with the literal meaning, but how do we make that sexy? Or do we just disregard it and go with what we think will work? I love what we've come up with, but it's fairly generic."

Drew put his feet up on the coffee table and leaned his head back to stare up at the ceiling. "Most cologne ads are sexy and sophisticated, but yeah, ours isn't anything that might have been done before."

She picked up the cologne bottle and this time sprayed it on her arm. Closing her eyes, she inhaled deeply. The scent reminded her of Drew. Subtle strains of sandalwood. Hints of cedar. The way her bedsheets had smelled after he left them. "Decadence. Silk sheets. Darkness. Candles. Even the word is soft and almost forbidden. Censured."

She opened her eyes and met Drew's. His pupils were dilated and his lips slightly parted as he looked at her.

"Here." She passed him the bottle with a hint of challenge in her eyes. "You try."

He raised his eyebrow, but he took the bottle and sprayed it on his arm.

"Close your eyes."

He gave her a doubtful look but did it.

"Inhale and say what comes to mind."

"Incense?" He opened his eyes and frowned. "It smells like every other cologne out there."

"Maybe to you, but to me, it smells like warm nights with the windows open. With two lovers, uncaring of the heat, pressed up against each other. Maybe with a fan on, making the candlelight flicker. The room dark with only a few candles to add depth to the exposure. Even the sheets are dark. They drape over the couple in strategic ways to hint at skin without exposing them fully. A voice-over whispers, 'censured.'"

Drew swallowed. "That would definitely make me want what they're selling."

"Personally I think they should change the name, but. . . ." She shrugged and inhaled again. She'd been smelling Drew on her sheets for the past few nights. It was one of the reasons she hadn't slept well. Her body hadn't received the memo it wouldn't happen again. Even though he gave her exactly what she asked for in the beginning. Sex, no strings, no talking about it. But after Friday night and Saturday morning, it had felt like there might be something more there. At least more than a physical connection. Which made his leaving that much harsher.

"Why don't you write it up in an email to art to add and we'll move on to vodka or the diamond ring?" He held up both. "Eternal love or eternal damnation?"

He wiggled his eyebrows like he'd just strapped the heroine to the train tracks in a silent movie.

"Damnation for sure." She pulled her computer onto her lap and kicked off her heels to put her feet up on the couch. She wrote up a quick note to art on the secondary concept for Censured. "Without the design team staying this weekend, we won't have much to bring to the client on Tuesday besides ideas."

"I could do some storyboarding," Drew suggested.

"We could find some stock photos similar to what we are going for."

"We could steal a camera from art and make our own ad," Drew said. Her eyes shot over to Drew who held up his hands in surrender. "Just a suggestion."

"I'm not about to get naked with you." She tried not to sound like a prude because he knew she wasn't, but right now, she needed as much armor or clothing as possible to keep from wanting more from him. She needed to focus on the promotion.

"I was merely suggesting positioning ourselves in the photo, not pretend to be models. I can't do that pouty lip thing anyway." He stuck his lip out, trying to achieve a model pout.

"The only thing you have going for you is that Muppet hair and your pretty face." She hit a few keys on her keyboard to see what a search result might render on images similar to what she was going for.

"You think I'm pretty," he teased.

"You know you are. It's part of your problem." She didn't look up from her laptop.

"Only part? What, do you have a list?" Drew chuckled.

She rolled her eyes and closed them to take a deep breath. "It would take all weekend and we have other things we need to do."

"Foxx Vodka." Drew set the bottle on the table between them. "All I can think of is that viral video from a few years ago. What does the fox say?"

"I don't think that's the type of class they're going for." Morgan set her laptop on the coffee table and covered her eyes, trying to think of something different to do for vodka. "Parties, high class, tuxedos and fancy clothes."

Her eyes popped open at the sound of the seal breaking on the vodka bottle.

Drew held up the bottle and poured some into the Solo cups. "Research."

She opened her mouth to tell him they couldn't, but he held up his finger to stop her.

"It is officially after working hours and there is no one else in the office." Drew held out the cup to her, shaking it temptingly. "Come on. Live a little."

She tightened her lips and looked at the cup. This had

Bad Idea written all over it. But if it helped her relax a little, maybe she wouldn't compare Drew's abs to the stock photos as much. "What the hell. For research."

"That's my girl." He winked and drank his vodka.

Her insides surged into a riot at his words. To cover her sudden flush of warmth, she drank the vodka like a shot. "Oh my."

"That whole flavorless thing is a myth. Why do I taste bread?" Drew smacked his lips a couple times.

"I only tasted the leftover Mountain Dew. Sweet and sticky." Morgan put her cup on the coffee table. "So we're going for high end clientele for this. Do they want print or commercial?"

"Let me check." Drew clicked on his computer. "Commercial."

"All right." Morgan closed her eyes to concentrate. "Vodka is supposed to be pure. So things that are pure."

"Water, glaciers."

"Ice, unicorns."

Drew laughed. "Wait, unicorns?"

"It's called brainstorming." Morgan opened one eye and gave him a glare. "Yes, pure equals unicorns."

He held up his hands. "Sorry I questioned."

She closed her eyes again, trying to get back in the zone, but the sound of him pouring more vodka made her sit up and open them. "What are you doing?"

"Making Friday evening interesting." Drew poured the cups halfway. "A drinking game if you will."

"I'm pretty much a lightweight when it comes to drinking." She eyed the cup with distrust. "If I get drunk, you'll have to make sure I get home. . . "

He raised his eyebrows and held out a cup.

"Alone," she added.

"Fine, but I think it'll make the evening more interesting.

Not that the cologne wasn't fun this morning, but it'd be a shame to waste this very expensive bottle of vodka. We'll only take sips."

"What are the rules?" Morgan sank her toes into the carpet under the coffee table and took the cup.

"What are the main things that you see in alcohol ads?"

"Partying, water, the color blue, ice."

Drew scrunched up his face. "Yeah, if we pick those words, we'll be drunk within the first hour."

"Oh, I have an idea."

"I'm all ears."

"Let's do our research on the smart board. We'll watch old commercials together." Morgan scooted to the edge of the couch.

"When anyone drinks, we drink." Drew connected his computer to the smart board.

"We'd be drunk in no time." Morgan shook her head. "As much partying happens in vodka commercials, the ads are usually about dancing and flirting. Not kissing. How about whenever someone kisses, we drink?"

"Sounds good."

She walked around the coffee table so she could see the smart board better, and instead of sitting in the armchair, she sank down on the plush carpet and leaned back against the chair.

Drew pulled up YouTube and typed in "vodka commercials" before sinking down to the carpet in front of the other chair. He handed her a cup.

"Good luck." He tapped his cup against hers.

"Just so you know, and so I can say tomorrow, I told you so. . . this is a bad idea."

～

"Oh my God, why, Absolut, why?"

Drew held up the bottle. "Half the bottle is gone."

His smile was loose, and the words slurred slightly. His stupid hair fell into his stupid pretty eyes.

"That's probably a good thing because I don't think I could drink anymore." She set her cup on the coffee table, but it fell over. She righted it and let her head loll to the side to look at him. "That was pretty smooth vodka."

"Smooth is us trying to get to the elevator later." Drew leaned back on the chair, and it slid backward. He went down laughing his ass off.

"Are you okay?" Morgan leaned over to check on him and ended up falling half on him. "See, bad idea."

"Are you I told you so-ing me?" He placed an arm over her which wasn't helping her get up. "Already?"

"Why are you so warm all the time?" she complained but didn't try to move away as she rested her cheek against his chest.

"To melt those pretty icy princess eyes of yours." His hand rubbed her back.

"We shouldn't be doing this." Again she didn't move. Didn't think she could if she wanted to. The room had stopped spinning, and she was pretty sure the minute she tried to get up, it'd start spinning again. Besides, he was warm and solid beneath her cheek, and she could hear his heart thudding rhythmically against her ear.

"We're not doing anything, except laying down on the job." He snickered.

Her hand grasped his shirt. "Stop moving the world."

"I blame Absolut and their kissing video." Drew gestured at the smart board. "We get it, you like kissing."

"We probably should have stopped watching it after the fifth kiss." Her eyes felt heavy and she let them close.

"Don't fall asleep, Morgan. I can't carry you anywhere in my current state."

"I'm not going anywhere in my current state." She snuggled tighter up against him and reached up to put her hand in his hair. She rubbed it like the silky binding of her blanket from her childhood.

"I thought you said my hair was stupid." His hand kept rubbing her back, helping her sink further and further into relaxation.

"It is. But it's also really soft. It reminds me of my blankey." She smiled.

"You had a blankey?" His voice was incredulous.

"I suppose you got through childhood without any sort of emotional support item?" She gave a curl a tug.

"Hey! Don't make me tickle you." Drew paused in rubbing her back.

"You wouldn't dare," she called his bluff.

"Right now? Probably not. I'm too comfortable." Drew let out a deep breath.

Morgan started giggling.

"What?" Drew rubbed her back.

"This isn't very professional."

"No. No it isn't." He sighed. "I suppose we should say work ended about thirty minutes ago. Start again tomorrow."

"Good. I'm going to sleep then." She snuggled in tighter, letting his warmth be her blanket.

"Nope." He stopped rubbing her back and shifted.

"Stop moving."

"Morgan, we need to get up. We can't sleep in the office."

"But I'm comfortable," she whined.

"Up." His hands moved to her shoulders and pushed her to sitting.

She pouted down at him.

"With those eyes, it's a wonder you don't always get your

way." Drew shook his head and sat up. "I'm going to order us a Lyft."

She stood, weaved a little, and his hands caught her hips to keep her upright. "I'm okay. I just need to make a trip to the ladies'."

"Shout if you have any trouble," he yelled after her. He still sat on the floor, now with his cellphone in hand. His hair was wilder than she'd ever seen it and it made her giggle as she made her way to the bathroom.

When she returned, he'd straightened everything and stood waiting with her purse.

"Thank you." She took her purse and they headed for the elevators.

"I don't think we need to worry about passing out or anything. I'm pretty sure we didn't drink *that* much." He leaned against the back of the elevator.

When she joined him, she rested her head against his shoulder. "I'm feeling pretty good."

"Are you now?" His smile softened when he looked down at her.

She nodded against his arm and felt the ridiculously goofy grin on her face.

"Tomorrow we'll have to get up early to work." He took her hand in his, entwining their fingers.

"Ugh." She didn't want to think about tomorrow. She just wanted to sleep.

The elevator dropped them off at the ground floor. He held her hand as they crossed the empty lobby and out into the street, where their ride waited for them.

He opened the door for her and followed her into the back seat. The driver and Drew made some small talk. She leaned her head against Drew's shoulder and watched the lights streak by the windows. His low voice rumbled softly next to her. A little part of her flashed warning signs, but the rest of her was so relaxed it barely noticed. Drew radiated warmth and he would keep her safe.

The car stopped and Drew thanked the driver before they both got out. At the door, she dug in her purse for her keys, nearly dropping her purse. When she finally got the keys out, she dropped them.

"Somehow I think I'm less drunk than you," he said as he bent to retrieve her keys and unlocked the front door.

"They say women get drunk on less than men." She went through the door, and he followed her to the elevator. "Less mass, or something."

"Leave it to you to know random facts and be able to recite them when drunk." He took her hand again as they entered the elevator and pulled her to rest beside him against the back wall.

"Sometimes you make me feel warm and fuzzy." She closed her eyes as she rested her head on his shoulder.

"You make me warm and fuzzy too." He squeezed her hand.

Her face melted into a smile as the elevator reached her floor. He helped her to her door and used her keys to open it. "You going to be okay?"

Her lower lip jutted out and she grabbed both his hands to pull him into her apartment. He didn't even try to resist. "You can't go anywhere. You're drunk."

"Is that so?" He grinned.

"We need to make sure neither of us stops breathing." She nodded as she kicked off her shoes and waited for him to kick off his. "It's only reasonable given how much we had to drink."

"Only."

She pulled him into the kitchen and handed him a bottle of water and took out a couple of Advil pills, handing him one. "Time honored tradition after drinking too much. A bottle of water and an Advil before bed."

She took her pill and drank and encouraged him to do the same. Then she took his hand and pulled him into the bedroom. "No hanky panky."

"If you insist. . . ." He sat on the edge of her bed.

Seeing him in her bed did odd things to her insides. She shook her head and mumbled to herself, "No hanky panky."

His chuckle raced down her spine.

"I'm going to change into pajamas. You stay there."

He held his hands up in surrender and leaned against the headboard, after setting his water on the nightstand.

She went in the bathroom to change and when she came out, she caught his sapphire eyes. She swallowed and climbed onto her bed. He lowered himself to lay down beside her on top of the covers. It was cold on her side, so she moved closer to him.

"Why are you always so warm?" she whispered as her eyelids started to droop.

As she drifted off to sleep with his hand rubbing her back and her face pressed against his chest, she thought she heard him say, "For you."

CHAPTER 11

DREW WOKE up to sunlight in his eyes and soft snoring in his ear. Morgan draped half over him. Her hand seemed to be permanently attached to his hair. His arm wrapped around her shoulders, holding her close. It felt so natural, like they did this every night instead of just twice. Her softness and his sudden wakefulness had woken other parts of his anatomy as well.

Thankfully, he was fully clothed in his business wear. Her pajama top had ridden up as she slept, and his hand rested on the warm skin of her waist. He pulled her shirt down and smoothed it over her skin to take away the temptation. They couldn't go down this road again.

As much as sex with her was one of the most enjoyable things he'd done recently, they both needed to focus on the goal, which was to get the promotion. Given his discussion with Thomas, he really shouldn't be with Morgan. If she ended up his assistant, it made things ten times more complicated. Not that it hadn't been complicated before, but. . .

He should have gone home last night.

"Morgan?" He tried to shift her to the other side of the

bed, but her grip tightened on him. "Morgan, I need to go home and change."

"Ten more minutes," she grumbled.

"If we wait ten more minutes, we'll be doing more than sleep." He slipped his hand under her top and toyed with the elastic of her pajama bottoms to make her take his threat seriously.

"Fine." She snuggled down.

He laughed. "I thought empty threats would work."

"I haven't slept this good in almost a week."

"Maybe you should get heated blankets." He tried to sit up, but she was immovable.

"Nope, I'll just keep you." Morgan sighed.

A tightness filled his chest. She didn't know what she was saying. Sleep fog and all that. He took a deep breath and inhaled the incense smell of Censured. They had both sprayed it on themselves. Smelling it on Morgan wasn't helping the situation in his pants.

"We still need to come up with an idea for the vodka," he said.

"No more vodka. Vodka bad." She buried her face against him.

"Agreed, no more partaking of vodka." He brushed her hair away from her face. "But I really need to get home and change so we can get started this morning."

Her fingers in his hair flexed and her hand on his chest drew a circle over his heart.

"You're going to have to let me go, Morgan."

She gave a huge sigh. After disentangling her fingers from his hair, she rolled onto her back away from him. She took in a deep breath and let it out. "Thank you for not taking advantage last night."

He moved to the edge of the bed and sat up. "You were drunk and asleep really quickly."

"I mean it." She swiveled her head to look at him. Her eyes, always so huge, this morning in the sunlight filtered by the drapes, were the color of the sky.

He had to leave before she tempted him even more to stay. "I'll see you in thirty."

~

WHILE IT WASN'T TECHNICALLY a walk of shame, Morgan repositioned her sunglasses as she strolled into Hart Association's building. She flashed her badge at the security officer and took the elevator up to their floor. All the while, she kept thinking how stupid it had been to drink so much. How stupid she'd been to invite Drew to spend the night. How stupid she'd felt when he'd left.

Had she really wanted something to happen? Had she been hoping something would happen? Something taken out of her hands where she didn't have to admit she wanted him again? Because that ship had sailed when he'd walked out after the last time. And it should be over.

They were competing for the same job. There would be no happily ever after. One of them would get the job and the other would have to decide whether or not they could work for their nemesis, AKA the person who'd seen them naked.

As complicated as that may be, this weekend they had to prove their worth as a team to Thomas. If they succeeded in wooing this company, there would be no stopping them. She entered Allison's office and breathed in. Last night, the room had seemed cozy and intimate with the darkened cubicle farm beyond the door and the darkness outside the windows closing them into a little box.

The harsh light of morning glared off the coffee table, practically blinding her. That was about par for the course. Morgan set her purse down and went into the breakroom to start some coffee. Beating Drew to work had been the goal. Mission accomplished.

Her gray T-shirt and jeans were comfortable and a nice change from her pencil skirts. She liked casual. It made her more at home and relaxed. Her usual office wear was armor to deflect the glancing blows that happened all too frequently during the workdays.

The coffee finished, and she poured herself a cup. She'd opted to make a pot instead of an individual cup, since liquid caffeine would be necessary to get through the day with Drew. She wouldn't be drinking any more Mountain Dew. Or vodka. Ever.

Fortunately, she only had a slight hangover, which the steaming cup of coffee should fix. She returned to Allison's office and pulled up their brainstorming sheet from last night. Yeah, brainstorming slightly tipsy-to-drunk was not a good idea.

One of the ideas was just kissing, written over and over and over. She shook her head.

She grabbed a dry erase marker and started a new list on the white board. A few good ideas were buried in there. As she finished, Drew came in. He wore jeans and a black T-shirt today. She hated to admit it, but Drew looked good in his casual wear. Almost as good as he looked out of it.

"There's coffee in the breakroom."

He nodded and went there. Obviously not much of a morning person. Though neither was she before coffee. She'd already finished one cup and already felt more human.

He returned with a steaming cup in his hands. "Ready to get busy?"

"Yes." She raised an eyebrow at the innuendo but let it go. She turned to look at the white board. "I think if we spend the morning on the vodka campaign, we will be able to crank out the diamond ring after lunch. We might be able to be done before dinner time and then we can work on the presentation Sunday."

"Seems doable."

When she turned to have a seat, she caught Drew looking at her ass.

He had the decency to look embarrassed at being caught. "Sorry. Haven't seen you in a pair of jeans before. May I just say, well done."

It was her turn to flush with warmth. He flustered her so much she couldn't think of a comeback and the longer she took, the more awkward it got. Finally she cleared her throat and picked up her laptop before sitting on the couch.

"So, we came up with quite a list last night. . . ." He held up the handwritten list. "Whose idea was 'a handsome man riding a unicorn with really good abs'?"

She shook her head. "Don't look at me. I'm pretty sure that was one of yours. Though I remember giggling at the thought of a unicorn with really good abs."

"I noticed you didn't add it to the board." He gestured with the paper to the board.

Her brows drew together. "Honestly?"

"Why not? It's surreal and would capture attention. It's different." He shrugged. "If we went with the same old, same old, we'd have an attractive couple going to a party where everyone is good looking and rich and drinking vodka while dancing provocatively."

"I guess there are no bad ideas in brainstorming." She stood and added it to the list. "Though if we add that one, we should probably add the one with the T-rex who can't open the bottle by himself."

Drew cracked a grin. "Sure. Add it up there."

"I guess our clients sell to people with senses of humor." She wasn't sure this was the smartest route. It might just distract from the core ideas and wouldn't get them closer to done.

"Think about it. The gecko ads, the ad campaign with the guy on a horse, the butter ads with Fabio. When someone goes to work, that's what they talk about. Not the ad where these people were at a party drinking some alcohol."

Drew had a point, but Morgan didn't think this would land the client. They had been fairly picky the first time around. "They didn't go with us the first time because we played it safe. They went with the company that gave them an orgy, but it didn't pay off. What if they are looking for a safer campaign and that's why they came back to us?"

Drew shrugged.

Morgan had an idea. "Why not blend it a little bit."

"Continue."

"If you're expecting partying with the vodka ad and we show up with some odd ball premise totally outside the box, they'll laugh us out of the conference room. But if we take a little of what they expect and a little of the surreal, we might be able to come up with a concept that sells them and still be talked about at the water cooler."

"Interesting. Maybe getting drunk wasn't such a bad idea." He looked up at her through his lashes with a flirtatious smile that made her stomach do a flip.

"No repeat performances, though. I don't think my stomach could handle it again." She tried to make the situation less than it was. She'd asked him to stay with her last night. She hadn't thrown herself at him, but she definitely hadn't been unwilling. But she'd just wanted to be close to him, to sleep with him, and let him make her feel safe and cherished. This morning it just felt awkward. Almost more awkward than Monday morning.

"Drinking." His smile didn't change. "No repeats of drinking."

She met his eyes. "Right, no drinking."

Dangerous to be with him in any capacity. She could write off last night as them being out of their mind drunk. Friday through Tuesday, she could write off as just a flash in the pan. She just needed him out of her system.

Now they were working and getting things done. They needed to focus on this project and the promotion. And not on how he made her feel inside or the fact her body didn't seem to be done with him yet.

She broke the eye contact. "A masquerade party." She started writing notes into her computer.

"Perfect. Not your classic party with all the right people." He pulled out a sketchpad and quickly made a drawing of a woman in an elegant white gown with a unicorn headdress on.

"Exactly. With pale blue decorations and gold. Wealth and clean." She pulled up color choices and attached them to the file.

Meanwhile he sketched a few more party goers. Elegant figures each with a distinctive animal headdress. He turned to a new page and drew a man in a tux with a fox's headdress. When he finished, he spread them out on the coffee table.

Morgan connected to the smartboard to throw her design scheme up on the board. She gathered up the sketches and took them to the copy room to scan into her computer. They weren't the best drawings, more like hasty sketches, but they gave an idea of what she and Drew were going for. Drew really had a talent for art no matter what he said. She'd never been any good at art in school. His drawings, while maybe not on scale with the art department's work, would definitely be enough to sway the client. When she returned to Allison's office, Drew added a few pictures, like a chandelier and an interior of a museum with a white marble lobby, to her digital sketch board.

"Good idea." She sat beside him on the couch. "The museum is the perfect place for the party. It'll give it a regal feel. I think the clothes should be the vivid colors in the space. The decorations the palest blue and gold and white. So you have these colors swirling around in the space and then the fox and the unicorn dancing in the center."

He slid her laptop to her, and she added the sketches to the board, filling out the idea board with different fabrics for the costumes. The fox in an orange-red suit and the unicorn in a white and gold dress. Vivid blues, roses, greens, purples, and yellows filled out the palate.

They leaned back on the couch, shoulder to shoulder, and stared up at their creation. It would be different with the figures moving.

"All we need is music." Morgan pursed her lips. "Classical or contemporary?"

"What if it started out with something classical before changing to something upbeat? Kind of like a dichotomy of two worlds coming together."

"I like that, but what's going to be the story of the commercial?" She gestured to the screen. "We have a beautiful graphic, but how are we going to sell Foxx Vodka?"

They both stared at the board. Awareness filled the silence. His heat flowed over her with him so close. It used to bother her, but now it made her want to snuggle closer. The walls between them were too blurred right now, and she didn't know how to put them back up or even if she wanted to.

"The fox and the unicorn are our key players." Drew broke her out of her thoughts. "So it's their story."

"We could do something fairy tale-ish." She leaned forward to grab a notepad and pen off the coffee table and returned to her place next to him. She wrote Fairy Tale at the top of the page. Then she wrote true love and villain with a question mark.

"I don't know if we'll have time for a villain or even if it's needed. Keeping with the party theme, maybe this is the ball where they first meet. A look from across the room. Their eyes meet and there is an instant connection."

She wrote down *eyes meet*. "Maybe the fox is at the bar having vodka, so you see the bottle and then he sees her."

"She comes to him?" His breath tickled her ear as his voice caused shivers to run down her spine.

"I think they should meet in the middle, but how do we work the vodka into that?"

"What if it's not eye meeting, but they are both at the bar and order vodka and their hands touch reaching for the same one?"

She wrote down the many ideas. "I like the idea of the instant connection across the busy dance floor and meeting in the middle to join the dance. At which time the music changes to the faster paced modern music."

"What if. . . ." He held his hand out for the notepad and she passed it to him. He wrote as he talked. "He's at the bar to order a vodka. Our bartender pours him a Foxx Vodka and as our hero turns to look out over the dance floor and sips his drink, his gaze collides with our heroine, who is also enjoying a Foxx Vodka—"

"How do we show that?"

"Hmmm. We'll have to work that out. But then they both finish their drinks and make their way across the dance floor and into each other's arms. They do the dance that everyone else is doing. Some sort of Jane Austen-like dance. And then the music changes to a modern dance and everyone starts club dancing. The fox gets the girl. We close with an image of the Foxx Vodka bottle against a pale blue background with gold accents around it."

"I like it." She smiled and her stomach growled.

Drew glanced at his phone. "It's already noon."

"Do you want to break for lunch, or you can start sketching the storyboard while I run out to pick us up something?"

"Does that make me the lead since you are running out to get me lunch?" He nudged her with his shoulder.

"You wish. I think that makes me the lead. While you do the grunt work, I'm making sure your base needs are met." The minute she said it she wished she could rephrase.

"Base needs, huh?" The words were soft and low and did funny things to her insides.

"Food," she clarified, refusing to turn and meet his gaze. "I'll get us food."

"Honestly, even though I'm in the flow, I think I could use a quick break." He set the pad down on the coffee table and stood. He reached a hand down to her. "There's this place I like around the corner. It's quicker than the bar."

She debated taking his hand, but it would be rude not to and they were working so well together. She slid her hand in his, and he helped her stand. For a moment, their bodies were close. Her breath caught. He dropped her hand and stepped back, breaking the spell.

"You like sushi?" Drew closed the laptop.

"Sure." She grabbed her purse and followed him to the elevators. They were just two colleagues going out to grab a bite. Just because they'd known each other intimately didn't mean anything really. She glanced at him on the way down. Physically they'd been intimate, but she knew next to nothing about the man beside her.

"Do you have any brothers or sisters?" she asked as they walked out of the building.

"A younger sister."

"Where are you from?"

He gave her a funny look. "Suddenly interested?"

Her cheeks burned, but she kept going. "I just think if we are going to work together, I should know more about you."

"Fair enough. I'm from Chicago. My parents are still living in the suburbs and my sister is at college. What about you?" He grabbed her arm to steer her around a puddle.

"Only child. Mom and Dad are in Pittsburgh." When he didn't let go of her arm, she found she didn't mind.

"Dogs or cats?" He released her arm to open the door to the restaurant.

"Neither. I don't have time to devote to a pet with my work hours."

She waited while the hostess sat them at the counter and the waitress took their order before asking, "How about you?"

"I'd love a dog, but I'm in the same boat. Too much work to be a responsible pet owner."

Sitting at the counter, she didn't have to look at Drew while he talked. It made it easier. His eyes were a huge distraction. Instead she could watch the chef create sushi rolls in front of them.

"What else do you want to know?" Drew's voice was soft and low.

She knew her next question wouldn't be work related or even any of her business, but she couldn't help it. "Any serious relationships?"

"Not since college." He took a drink of his green tea. "You?"

Turnabout was fair play. "Define serious."

He chuckled. "You define it. It was your question."

"I dated a guy for a few years, but I don't think it was ever serious."

"A few *years* isn't serious to you?"

She could feel the heat of Drew's stare. The waiter set their plates in front of them. They'd both ordered a mix of different sushi rolls.

"Well?" Drew asked before using his chopsticks to eat one of his rolls.

"I don't think he took the relationship seriously, and I knew he wasn't a keeper." She shrugged and ate a sushi roll to keep from having to say more.

"How do you know someone's a keeper?"

She glanced at him before tucking her hair behind her ear. She'd left it down today. Something she never did during work hours. "I don't know. We were both really focused on our careers. We barely saw each other, and when we did, we didn't talk much. I don't think we ever got real close emotionally. The relationship just kind of fizzled out."

"You didn't answer my question."

He noticed that. Damn.

She sighed and stared at the sushi roll being made in front of her. "*If* I were to want a lasting relationship, the guy should be someone who makes me laugh. Who I have fun with even out of bed. Someone I'm excited to see. That would make him a keeper. Satisfied?" She gave him her best cold stare.

"Hardly." He smirked before he ate another sushi roll.

CHAPTER 12

"You know something I've been wondering about?"

Drew looked up at Morgan from the sketch he worked on for the storyboard. He was skeptical about what she wanted to know now. Lunch had been a checklist of different things. Everything from favorite movie to favorite music type. Surprisingly, they both liked alt rock and had a few favorite bands in common. Not surprisingly, they had different tastes in movies. He was a Marvel fan and she preferred period dramas.

"What have you been wondering about now?" Drew set his pencil down.

She leaned back in her chair and pursed her lips. She did that when she was thinking. It lit a fire in his belly every time. "You mentioned Jane Austen style dancing. . . ."

He brushed his curls back. "I did."

She lifted a brow quizzically. "Does that mean you are a secret fan of Ms. Austen's?"

He laughed. "Do I have to be a fan if I've seen some movies? Mostly by force. My little sister and my mother are huge fans."

"Hmmm." She sat back and tapped her pen against those lips. He definitely didn't need any help to think about those lips. They were a soft natural pink today. Had it been days since he'd kissed them? "I think maybe you secretly liked them."

He shrugged. "Maybe. Maybe not." He returned his focus to the sketches. They needed to finish working while it was still light out. With the windows streaming in daylight, the office was just the office. The place where they worked, except that one time in the breakroom. . . . But when the night sky closed in, it was too easy to get lost in her eyes. Too easy to think of other things they could do in the dark. Last night, holding her had been nice, but it hadn't been close enough. Not when he'd held her skin to skin.

"Why do you want the promotion?" Her soft words pulled him from his thoughts.

"Better pay. Better job. Another step up the corporate ladder. Promotion or opportunity to be promoted was the reason I switched jobs. Probably the same reason you want it." Drew kept sketching the scene where the fox and the unicorn start across the dance floor to each other.

"Probably."

That word was loaded. He let out an exasperated sigh, set his pencil down and looked into her huge eyes. "Why do you want it, Morgan?"

Curled up in the chair, she shrugged, dropping her gaze to her laptop.

"Morgan?" Drew put a coaxing tone to his voice. She obviously wanted to tell him.

She cleared her throat and met his eyes. "I want to make a difference. I want to prove I can do this job. Even though I don't have the necessary years of experience, I deserve it. I love doing this." She gestured to her laptop and his drawings. "And if you get the job, the opportunity to stay in this line and take the Creative Director position will vanish. I'll have to wait until someone else quits or retires to move to another division's Creative Director and be up against someone like me but with all the knowledge of that line. And I'll be the one lagging."

She dropped her gaze again. "I love my job. I love luxury goods. I like the sophistication that comes with this division. I won't get that in the beverage division or the food division."

Drew studied the top of her blond head. Everything she said made sense. It could be years before another opportunity like this became available. He didn't want to wait any more than she did. "What happens if I get the job?"

She shook her head and very quietly said, "I don't know."

"I'd hate to lose you."

She lifted her head and met his eyes. Her blue eyes had a hint of sadness about them.

The words he said penetrated his brain. The vague implication that he didn't want to lose her in ways beyond just working together lingered in the air between them. Something he wasn't ready to look into too closely. He cleared his throat and tried to clarify. "You have real talent."

A shadow seemed to drape over her face, hiding her emotions. "Thank you. You aren't so bad yourself."

He picked up his pencil.

"I'm almost done with the storyboarding and then we can move on to the diamond engagement ring." He wanted to ask if she was okay, but what would be the point? They both knew the score on this game. One of them would get promoted and the other would be the assistant. Unless the other transferred or quit. Neither of them wanted to do that. At least he didn't think she did, but if he got the promotion, she might feel forced to leave.

They worked in silence while he fleshed out the storyboard and she started adding colors to his earlier sketches using her computer. When he finished, he went to the copy room to scan in the storyboard. On his way back to the office, he almost ran into Morgan coming out of the break room with a cup of coffee.

"Sorry," he said.

She smiled and said, "It's okay." But something about her expression made him think she was sad.

Every fiber in his being wanted to do something to cheer her up as they walked back to Allison's office. "So next up, marriage?"

She stumbled a little. "Excuse me?"

He grabbed her elbow to help her. "You know, first sex, AKA cologne, then true love, AKA vodka, now marriage, AKA diamond engagement ring."

She gave him a look that made him sorry he tried to put a spin on it.

He held up his hands in defeat. "Honestly, that just came to me. I'm flying by the seat of my pants here."

They made it back to the office and he let her lead the way in.

"Any thoughts on what type of ad we should do?" He picked up the box from the table and opened it, revealing the square cut diamond with sapphire triangles on the sides. "For a fake, this is pretty damn shiny. Do you think it might be real?"

"Probably glass."

"Still very pretty." He looked at her, but she occupied herself opening a new workspace on her laptop. This would be a tough one. He didn't have any experience in matters of the heart, either in real life or in advertising. Sex was easy. He knew sexy. He could even fake romantic for ads, but love. . . . That was the real shit.

"Okay. Diamond ring. We need a print ad for this one." Morgan finally looked up at him.

He snapped the box shut. "Wedding. Couples. Forever. True love. Best friend. Commitment."

"Honesty, trust, love, together, proposal." She typed all the words into the blank page and up on the smart board.

"What's the most common type of ad for this?" Drew sank into the chair and placed the box back on the table.

Morgan quickly threw a few ads up on the screen. "Mostly it's about the ring. Well-lit on a black background with some phrase about love or eternity."

She changed the screen to another. "Couples in love. Weddings. The first kiss as a married couple."

"Last but certainly not least"—she changed the screen—"the ring again. This time on a white background. Or the ring and a happy couple sharing the page, either newly engaged or at the wedding."

"Not a lot of options."

She shrugged. "It's print. Likely the ad will be in a bridal magazine or some other magazine. It needs to be simple and catch the eye. The words have to inspire the gentleman or the lady to want this particular ring. Saying, 'it's unique like your love,' can also earn brownie points in an ad campaign."

"We just need a fancy tagline about love, then? And a pretty picture of the ring?" Drew opened the box and left it on the table.

"Have you ever been in love?" Morgan met his eyes. He couldn't read her emotions on this. She added, "In love enough to propose?"

"The only time I was in love, I was too young to consider marriage. I was just starting my career and we were going separate ways. Timing, I guess." Drew thought of his college girlfriend. College was all they'd really had in common. That and both being really driven to succeed. For a moment, he'd considered asking her to marry him, which would have been the only reason she would have considered staying here with him instead of taking her job in L.A. But he didn't want to add that pressure to their relationship. Asking someone to give up on their dreams to follow yours? It would have been over in a heartbeat. Better to get it over with while not screwing up each other's futures and career potential.

"What about you?" Drew watched her icy eyes. "Ever been proposed to?"

"Does kindergarten count?" She smiled a soft little smile. His pulse picked up its pace.

"Was it true love?" He waggled his eyebrows at her.

"Me and Tommy could have lasted forever"—she sighed for dramatic effect—"but he refused to share his brownie with me." She shook her head. "It just wasn't meant to be."

He returned her smile. "All this talk of brownies is making me hungry."

"We just ate lunch." She glanced at her phone. "Two hours ago? Time flies."

"Vending machine run?" The vending machines were on the fourth floor of the building. They had practically everything there. He stood and reached his hand down to her. "Come on. It'll be an adventure."

DREW'S EYES sparkled with mischief in the sunlight, brighter than the sapphires on the ring. Or rather the fake sapphires on the ring. Sending the actual ring would be insane.

"Only if there is chocolate involved." She took his hand, expecting him to pull her up and release her. Instead he helped her up but didn't drop her hand, curling his fingers around hers. Her heart kicked up a notch. She didn't know what to think. He'd built a wall around him after their last time together, but maybe it had started to crumble.

"There's always chocolate involved." He wiggled his

eyebrows like a mustache-twirling villain and pulled her along behind him.

She didn't know how she'd work with him after they found out who got the promotion. While she didn't want to leave Hart Association, it wouldn't be long before she would want to succumb to temptation again. She actually liked Drew. Not just his body either. He was fun to be around. Which surprised the hell out of her. It also surprised her how easy he was to work with.

But she also wanted him.

The company policy against fraternization reared in her head. It was bad enough when they were equals and in separate departments, but if one of them was the other's boss, no way would corporate be cool with them dating or whatever this was. If he wanted her still.

Instead of the elevator, he led her to the stairwell.

"To burn off some calories before the chocolate binging begins," he explained.

It was only two floors down and since she wasn't wearing her typical heels, she was willing. She normally stayed away from the vending machines. She'd been trying to eat healthier which meant bringing in snacks and a nutritious lunch... for Drew.

She stopped on the steps in the concrete stairwell, pulling Drew to a stop with her. "Why did you keep eating my lunches even when I changed to kale and the most disgustingly healthy foods I could think of?"

He stepped on the step directly below her, bringing their faces in alignment. His closeness sucked all the air from around her. A dark ring of blue circled the sapphire blue of his eyes and on his left eye a black mark like an ink spot hovered in the blue. Like a lone island in a vast ocean. He entwined their fingers. His warmth flowed over her, making her want to sway and close the inch separating them.

His exhale touched her lips. The anticipation in this moment was like waiting for Santa on Christmas Eve, thinking you can stay up. Feeling wide awake, but then falling quietly into sleep. She was falling into something, but whatever it was, it was sneaking up on her. Hopefully the presents would be worth it.

"I did it because you were so uptight. Your name was written in Sharpie on your lunch. Maybe the first time was a joke, but then you didn't do anything. You barely reacted except to give me those glacier stares during meetings. I kept waiting for a response. It became part of my routine. Because I knew you'd look at me. Otherwise you ignored me."

"You made it impossible to ignore you." She could practically taste the mint he'd eaten after lunch. "The things you said while in meetings. . . . The way you looked at me. . . . Every time you were close, I felt your heat."

"But. . . ." His eyes dropped to her lips.

Her lips parted as if welcoming him. "But?"

"You didn't want me. You just wanted someone to have sex with." His eyes flared.

She squeezed his hand. "You have no idea how relieved I was when you showed up. Phoebe had convinced me to have a one-night stand with that guy, but he wasn't who I was trying to get out of my system."

"Am I?"

"Are you what?"

"Out of your system?"

She shook her head. "But we have to work together. It's against corporate policy and if we get caught, it could mean our jobs. And forget about finding new jobs because we got fired."

"Who's going to tell on us?" His words caressed her lips.

And then his mouth closed over hers and everything inside her cheered. She welcomed his kiss, finally feeling complete. She let his warmth cover her. But it ended too quickly.

When he pulled back, he smiled at her and pressed a quick kiss against her lips. "We need to get back to work. We can continue this when the work is done."

She followed him down the stairs in a daze. What did "this" mean? Did it mean anything? Did it have to mean anything? She could just let *this* be and worry about the fallout when the promotion happened. She could spend a week in his arms with him in her bed.

That would have to be enough.

She might want to explore the current want ads though, in case Drew's sucking up to the boss resulted in him winning the promotion over her. Though working with him this weekend hadn't gone as bad as she thought it might.

They entered the vending machine room, and he released her. A chill flowed over her and she almost snatched his hand back. He gave her a cocky smile like he knew what she was thinking. One thing was certain, she was out of her depths with him.

"What's your pleasure?" he said.

She had to blink a few times, still disoriented from his kiss.

"M&Ms, Reese's Peanut Butter Cups, Snickers?" Drew walked over and slid his credit card into the machine.

"You pick." She suddenly had a craving for things that had nothing to do with chocolate. But he was right, they had work to do and a promotion to secure. He made a few selections and gathered up the goodies from the bin.

"You want a drink?" He headed to the soda machine and again inserted his card.

"Water."

He brought his prizes over to her and gave her the chocolate to carry upstairs, while he went back for her water and his Diet Coke. "Elevator back?"

She nodded and followed him to the elevators. He leaned against the back of the elevator and whistled along with the elevator Muzak. His eyes never left her, and a warm feeling tingled through her.

When they got back to the office, she placed the candy on the coffee table. He'd picked out four things: Snickers, Reese's Peanut Butter Cups, Twix, and a brownie. She held up the brownie and raised one eyebrow.

"I promise not to end things over a bite of brownie," he said.

"Things" implied they had something to end, but the sentiment hit her straight in her heart. He remembered her little story.

He handed her the bottle of water. She drank to settle her nerves before placing it on the coffee table. Her head still spun, trying to make sense of what was happening between them.

"Do we need ground rules?" she asked.

He opened the brownie, broke it in two and offered her a half. His eyes glittered. With a smile, she took it.

"The only rule is that we need to do work when we're at work." He sat and picked up his laptop. "We need to focus on working right now."

"So. . . later?"

He met her eyes. A promise lingered there. "Later."

CHAPTER 13

"WE ARE NEVER GOING to figure this out." Morgan pushed her laptop away and stared out the windows at the darkening sky. She stretched her arms over her head.

"All we need is some cheesy romantic saying to put above the ring." Drew pushed his hand through his hair. He pulled the ring from the box and held it out to her. "Why would you want this ring?"

She eyed it like he held out a snake. "You mean what would make me accept this ring from someone?"

"It's supposed to be a promise, right?" He held it up to the light. "This is supposed to signify an undying love that I'll be with you until the end of our days. That's romantic, right?"

She laughed. "I think we are definitely not qualified to talk about love."

"Maybe not." He set the ring back in the box. "But we are really good at bullshitting."

"That we are. But for an engagement ring, the bullshit has to ring true."

"Do you think if we sleep on it, we'll figure something out?"

She lifted her gaze to his and her breathing went shallow. "I thought the plan was to not sleep?"

"I'm sure we'll sleep at some point." Drew closed his laptop. "Fuck it. We need fresh brains. It's dinnertime and we've gotten nowhere. I'd say we should break open the vodka again, but as amusing as it was, I think it would interfere with 'later.'"

Warmth crept up her chest. "We wouldn't want that."

"Close up shop. It's time to call time of death."

She closed her laptop and stood up. "Seven twenty."

"What do you want for dinner?"

Would it be too forward to say, him? "I'm okay with whatever you want."

He reached out and tucked a strand of hair behind her ear. "Some place close and quick?"

She nodded as shivers spiraled down her spine to settle low in her abdomen. She grabbed her purse and took his hand as they walked to the elevator. He didn't release it during the ride down, but she let go as they reached ground floor. He seemed to understand that the night security officer would see. Especially after last night's escapade of drunkenness, they didn't need to stir up rumors.

No one else needed to know.

Whatever this was, it was temporary, and they couldn't get caught.

They crossed the lobby and went out the doors.

"Where to?" She turned to face him.

"I wish I had food at my place." Drew didn't touch her, but she could tell he wanted to, and she desperately wanted him to touch her. "I suppose all you have is kale?"

He made a face that made her laugh and his eyes went soft.

"What about the burger place a block away?" she said.

"I don't know if I'm strong enough to watch you eat a burger again."

She gave a quizzical look, but he didn't elaborate.

"There's a chicken place this way." He reached out his hand to take hers but didn't. Their coworkers frequented the restaurants in this area. Most everyone knew they were working the weekend, so being out to dinner wouldn't be suspicious. But most people thought they didn't like each other. The only time they'd be safe to touch would be in one of their apartments.

They walked to the restaurant.

"Do you live in this area?" she said as he held open the door for her.

"I actually live not too far from you." Drew winked at her.

They ordered at the counter and sat in a booth across from each other.

"Now what?" she said.

He shrugged. "We wait for the food and then head back to your place."

Her insides were pure mush at this point. One giant raw nerve ending needing to be touched. "Shall we set up terms?"

"My vote is for no rules besides the obvious one about work."

"There's an obvious end date too. We can't continue this if one of us reports to the other."

He leaned forward with a very serious face. "Afraid of losing control?"

She leaned in too and maintained eye contact. "We both know I can make you lose control."

His pupils dilated. "I'd love to see you try."

"A number three." A teenager wearing a striped shirt with a chicken on the shoulder held out a plate of food.

Morgan sat back as Drew raised his hand. "That's mine."

"And a number five." The teenager looked at her and waited.

"Mine?" Morgan said.

The teenager put it down and said, "Enjoy." And he left as quickly as he'd arrived.

They exchanged a look that said *what the fuck* before laughing.

"How are we going to come up with a tagline for the engagement ring?" She sighed before she picked up her chicken sandwich.

"We could always brainstorm more."

"I think we'd need a brain hurricane to get anywhere on it. Everything has already been done. I don't think there's a new phrase to figure out," she said.

"Maybe that's just it. Maybe we don't need to go with something new, but something old. What was the line Darcy says that makes Lizzie go all medieval on his ass?"

Morgan scrunched up her eyes. "I don't recall a scene where Lizzie goes medieval on Darcy's ass. Is that in a version I haven't seen? Maybe *Pride and Punishment*, the porn version?"

He shook his head. "Do you own a copy? I'd pay good money to see that, but no. . . . When she's out in the rain at the round building and he comes up on her and startles her."

She pointed at him with a fry. "Admit it. You like it. You've seen it more than once and you secretly love it."

"Never." He stole the fry from her fingers and ate it.

"I think I know what you're talking about. It has the line about him most ardently loving her?" She scrunched her face up trying to remember the exact lines.

"Maybe. I'll look it up." He didn't move to grab his phone. "Later."

"It's a good idea though. Maybe we could do a couple of ads with famous quotes of love from movies and books."

"That's better than us trying to wrack our brains figuring out what would make someone want to declare their love for someone for the rest of their lives." He ate his chicken tender.

He was right. She had no real experience with love and hadn't met anyone she'd want to spend the rest of her life with. Not to mention spending thousands of dollars on a party to celebrate that love. She'd never wanted to spend that much time with someone before.

Even Drew was just lust right now. It was new and shiny, and the ways he moved made her brain explode. Not really her brain but. . . . It would pass. Hopefully quickly. They'd be out of each other's systems by Friday when Thomas decided the promotion.

They chatted about different movies that might work for the ads while they finished their dinner. Some were good ideas, like *Princess Bride*. Others were questionable, like *Rocky*.

"Are you finished?" Drew grabbed his dishes and when she nodded, grabbed hers to take to the trash.

As they went through the door, his hand touched the small of her back and a bolt of electricity passed through her. He hailed a cab and when it stopped, he held the door open for her. It was odd, but she kind of liked that he opened doors for her. It made her feel special and cared for.

"Your place or mine?" she asked. She didn't care either way as long as they got there quickly.

He gave her address to the driver. He took her hand. "I'm assuming you have coffee. I ran out this morning."

She looked at where their hands connected them. No one would see them in here. At least not their interlocked hands. This was insane. She never should have started this, but it was like trying to stop a snowball rolling down a hill. The farther downhill it got, the larger and harder it would be to stop.

"Are you sure this is a good idea?" Morgan couldn't make out his whole face in the streetlights as they passed into the residential area.

"It's a risk. But one I'm willing to take. Are you?"

She wished she could see his eyes. The answers usually lurked in the vibrant blue. The risk was high. Her job, her promotion. The reward. . . . She glanced down at their hands. The intense attraction made her willing to try. She could admit, at least to herself, she wanted more of it. More of him.

The taxi stopped in front of her apartment building.

He squeezed her hand. "Well?"

She inhaled and nodded. "Let's go."

DREW WOKE up with Morgan's hand wrapped in his hair, but this time her naked body spread over his. He grinned. Not a bad way to start the day. Unlike the previous night, they'd made it under the covers. The plan was to not overthink things. He wanted her. She wanted him. And in a few days one of them would get promoted, but until then he planned to make the most of his access to her body. Knowing what Thomas had implied, Drew should never have started this back up, but he couldn't seem to help himself.

However, today was a workday. He didn't want to move but needed to see what time it was.

His phone hadn't made it out of his pants and without charging, it would likely be dead. He glanced around for an alarm clock, but it didn't surprise him when he couldn't find one. Even he used his phone as an alarm. The light coming in through the curtains was faint, so it was potentially early or an overcast day.

Morgan's golden hair tickled his chin as her head rested on his chest right above his heart. Her face was peaceful in sleep. He couldn't believe this was the same woman he'd considered icy.

Somewhere the sound of electronic chimes went off.

"If I could find it, I'd hit snooze." Morgan didn't even open her eyes.

He tracked the phone by the continued sound and found it on her nightstand plugged in. Not surprising considering how controlled Morgan generally was. She must have plugged it in one of the times he'd been in the bathroom. When he reached for it, she clung to him and growled in protest of him moving. He let out a chuckle. So different from the first night he'd stayed when she'd practically tried to kick him out of bed.

He grabbed her phone and hit the snooze. It was still early, and he didn't want to move from the warm bed and Morgan's warm body.

"Snooze achieved." He let his hand trail down the smooth skin of her back. "We do need to get moving though. We have to find famous quotes, put together the ring ad sketches and then create the presentation."

"You're such a bummer in the morning." She didn't even open her eyes. "Your Muppet hair looks ridiculous by the way."

"I'd believe you minded if you didn't always end up with your hands in my hair. I think you like it ridiculous." Drew kissed the top of her head and drew out the dyed streak. "You never did tell me about the blue."

She shrugged and stroked his hair between her fingers. "I've always loved the color blue and would have gotten more if it hadn't been for the company policy for natural hair colors only. So I settled for one streak that most people can't even tell is there."

"A little act of rebellion?"

"You ought to be grateful I'm a rebel, otherwise what

happened last night wouldn't have happened." She stretched her body along his.

He had been half aroused when he woke, but the longer they stayed like this, the more aroused he became. "If we don't get up soon, we'll be staying in bed for a while."

She moved to straddle his waist and propped herself up to look down at him with wickedness in her eyes. "I don't think it will put us too far behind."

"I never refuse a lady."

Her smile was mischievous. "That reminds me." She trailed her fingers down his neck and over his chest. Her eyes were all innocence when they met his. "Do you always walk around with a condom in your pocket at work or did you think something would happen with me that day?"

"I always like to be prepared for any eventuality." His breath caught as she lowered to kiss his jaw. Her breasts skimmed his chest as she moved down his body. Her lips continued to kiss and suck and lick his flesh on his neck and shoulders.

"So it wasn't just for me?" Her teeth scraped his nipple.

He sucked in a breath at the rush of desire coursing through his body. "Only for you."

She glanced up at him with her huge pale blue eyes. "Good answer."

As she moved lower, he lost all rational thought. He was hers to do with what she pleased. When she took his cock in her mouth, he almost lost it. He held on by a thread as she pushed him past the breaking point. What she could do with her tongue and teeth. . . .

When he knew he couldn't take anymore, he lifted her from him and slid her up his body. He rolled them both over until she laid on her back. Her eyes were dilated and partially closed. This woman drove him crazy.

She reached down to stroke him while he reached for one

of the condoms on the nightstand. He ripped open the packet with the help of his teeth. He couldn't wait to be inside her again. When she took the condom to put it on him, he took his turn to drive her crazy.

His hand trailed over her body, teasing her nipples and massaging her breasts. Then his hand found her softness between her legs. She opened up for him like a flower, and the look on her face made him want to wake up like this always. Her soft smiles. Her warm body. Her eagerness for him.

Finally, he slid into her and they both let out a breath. For a second neither of them moved. Perfection achieved.

"If we don't want the promotion, we don't have to leave here," she whispered in his ear. "We can spend all day in bed."

He kissed her ear as he pulled out and buried himself deep within her. "We both want that promotion. But I'll be working hard today to get back here quickly tonight."

"Better make this count then."

He moved again and she let out a groan in his ear.

"I like that sound."

"You like all the sounds," she said.

"When you make them."

Unable to keep the tempo slow, he picked up the pace. She rose to meet his every thrust until they moved in tandem. He slipped a hand between them to rub the place he knew drove her crazy. When she came, the pressure surrounding him intensified. In a few more strokes, he let himself go.

With her in his arms, he lost track of time and all presence of mind. It was frightening and exhilarating. He wanted her over and over again. He wished they had today off so they could spend the day in bed, finding all the spots that drove each other insane.

"Good morning," she said, as he slid off her and the bed.

She smiled at him and stretched her gorgeous body. Her hair framed her face in a messy golden halo.

"Good morning to you, too." He took care of things in the bathroom. When he returned, she hadn't moved and that soft smile remained on her face. He was sorely tempted to climb back in bed with her.

"I have to get dressed and get home for a shower." He started tugging on his clothes. "Would it be too forward of me to ask to bring a change of clothes and some things for tomorrow?"

She sat up cross-legged in the bed. "Phoebe lives down the hallway. We're lucky she hasn't caught us yet. Maybe I could come to your place with a bag."

He buttoned up his jeans and winked at her. "Do you think you're ready for my apartment?"

"I'll even bring coffee." Her smile would be the only thing he would look at if she weren't still completely naked and tempting.

"Deal." He pulled on his T-shirt and found his shoes. He walked over to her and kissed her. "I'll see you in thirty."

"See you." She tweaked one of his curls before sliding off the bed and crossing to the bathroom.

He was in deep doo-doo if he would risk this promotion to take a shower with the woman he was up against. That thought didn't help as he wanted to be up against her, taking her against the shower walls while her wet body slid on his. Because sex in the shower would lead to more sex that would keep them from getting to work and finishing this project on time.

He shook himself free of the fantasy and made himself walk to the door of her apartment. It was self-locking, so once he left, she'd be safe. He needed to go, but part of him wanted to stay and see if she'd try to feed him kale for breakfast.

He had to go. He forced himself to leave her apartment and head for the elevators. As the elevator arrived, he glanced down the hallway wondering where Phoebe lived and how good a friend she was to Morgan. After all, they were all in the same division right now, and if he weren't around, Phoebe would have likely moved into Morgan's spot when Morgan got the promotion. Thomas had implied the Assistant Creative Director position would be the title of the person who didn't get Creative Director, meaning she would keep her title or he would become her Assistant Creative Director.

Sleeping together was dangerous for both of them, but the sex last night and this morning had been worth it. It was a risk worth taking. *Here's hoping we won't get caught.*

CHAPTER 14

"'In vain I have struggled. It will not do. My feelings will not be repressed. You must allow me to tell you how ardently I admire and love you.'" Drew read the quote from online. His laptop was propped on his lap. They were once again in Allison's office, soon to be either his or Morgan's office.

"Doesn't she reject him for that one?" Morgan kept scrolling through the script she found of *Pride & Prejudice* online. "What about at the end?"

"You mean the field scene?"

"This is your favorite movie, isn't it?" She stopped scrolling to look up at him with a gotcha grin.

He didn't say anything.

She looked down and found the quote. "This one. 'You have bewitched me body and soul and I love you. And never wish to be parted from you from this day on.'"

"Maybe we could use both, because damn, that's better than anything I could come up with." Drew leaned back in his chair. "Should we check for other Austen proposals or devotions of love?"

"Why not? She's good at them." Morgan worked on her computer. Today, she'd pulled her hair into a ponytail. Her blue streak winked at him. Had she done it on purpose for him? A warmth flooded his chest. She had on a blue T-shirt and a pair of jeans that definitely shouldn't be legal to wear. They fit all her curves like they were made specifically for her.

She'd managed to beat him to the office again and had a cup of coffee waiting for him. He could definitely get used to this.

"Oh, here's one from *Emma*: 'If I loved you less, I might be able to talk about it more.' And one from *Sense and Sensibility*: 'I come here with no expectations, only to profess, now that I am at liberty to do so, that my heart is and always will be yours.'"

Had Morgan always been so beautiful to him? When he first saw her in the conference room at his initial meeting, she had been perfectly put together, from her hair pulled back in a bun, hiding that fabulous blue streak, to her perfectly pressed white shirt, to her curve-catching black pencil skirt. She'd been presenting some figures that had gone over his head since he'd just joined the team. Her huge pale blue eyes made her seem otherworldly. He'd admitted that she was pretty, but way too uptight and high-strung for him. High maintenance, which was definitely something he couldn't handle.

"Oh, this is a good one. 'You pierce my soul. I am half agony, half hope. . . . I have loved none but you.'"

"*Persuasion*," he said.

Her mouth dropped open and she stared at him for a good half minute. "I swear if you tell me one more time your sister forced you to watch these movies, I'm going to find her number on your phone and call her to discover the truth."

He smirked at her. She could think what she wanted.

"I think we have enough quotes and can move on to lighting and how we want to showcase the ring." He set his laptop on the coffee table and picked up the ring box. "Do we know if this is a unique design or if anyone can walk in and buy a copy?"

"I think it's a signature design they've made duplicates of, but no two are alike." Morgan set her laptop down on the couch beside her and scooted to the edge to look at the ring. "It's a really gorgeous ring."

"I'm sure some woman would be happy to receive it. How about you?" He glanced up at her face.

"How about me what?" She met his eyes suspiciously.

"If you could have any ring in the world, would this be your pick?" He took it out of the box and held it out to her.

She cocked an eyebrow. "I'm not looking for a proposal."

"But if you were." He shook the ring in front of her until she sighed and took it from him. "Slip it on."

"No." She shook her head as she looked at the ring. "I love the setting. It's simple and clean, and it's got one of my favorite colors." She glanced up at his eyes.

"I have an idea for the picture." He took the ring from her and held her hand with his other. "What if we combine the two concepts and just have a photo of him putting the ring on her finger, but only show the hands." He demonstrated by slipping the ring to her first knuckle. He glanced up at her face.

She stared at his hand holding the ring on hers, with a slightly panicked look.

He cleared his throat and she pulled her hand away. She slipped off the ring and handed it back to him.

"I think that would look good." She picked up her laptop and wouldn't meet his gaze.

He put the ring back in the box and snapped it shut.

"How about we combine the backgrounds?" She showed him her screen which had a black background covered by white bridal lace. When she lifted her gaze to his, the panic had vanished.

"Great idea. Let's put together the concept." He glanced at the time on the computer. It was only ten. "Give it an hour, then an early lunch to figure out how to put our presentation together?"

"Let's get delivery and keep working through lunch." She was already sorting through stock imagery.

"We could use my phone camera to mockup the picture using their ring," he suggested.

"Yeah, okay." She set her laptop back down. "Let me go and get the menus for delivery, so we can get that done first."

He watched her walk stiffly out of the office and wondered what just happened. They'd been working fine today with none of the pent-up frustration that had plagued the last few days. But maybe the tension between them was more than just sexual.

He stood and followed her out, but she had disappeared. The breakroom seemed the logical choice. There was a drawer full of menus in there, but she might have some at her desk, which was on the way. He passed by her empty office, still dark, and headed to the breakroom.

She stood by the drawer and startled when he came in.

"Are you okay?" He started toward her but she flinched and turned away. He stopped.

"I'm fine." Her tone said she wasn't fine.

"Is this about the ring?" He lowered himself into one of the chairs and waited for her to reply.

She shook her head and then shrugged. She sighed and turned around to face him. "I've never wanted a ring before. I never even considered it an option until I reached the top of my career."

He remained quiet.

"It's a truly beautiful ring, and if I ever am ready, I imagine that would be the type of ring I'd want."

"So what's the problem?" he asked gently.

She threw her hands up. "I don't know. Maybe it's these campaigns with sex, true love, and marriage. It's all hitting a little close to home. And we're. . . ." She gestured between the two of them. "I don't even know what to call this, but I know that it doesn't have a future."

He stood and slowly walked toward her.

"But I don't care because I want to be with you." She paused as he closed the distance between them and then she looked up at him with a disgruntled look. "I like you."

She said it like it was the worst thing in the world.

He pulled her into his arms and hugged her, resting his chin on top of her head. "I like you too."

She returned his hug and the tension slipped from her body with a sigh.

"I don't know what this is either." He shrugged but didn't release her. Her hair smelled like sunshine. "I know that I like being with you. I also know things will change with the promotion. And this can't continue after."

Her arms tightened around him. That was all he could say. They both knew what would happen. All they could do was enjoy the time they had left together.

❧

"AND THAT'S THE LAST SLIDE." Morgan saved the presentation on the shared company drive.

"And it's only four in the afternoon." Drew closed his

laptop. "We'll have to show Thomas what we've come up with first thing tomorrow morning."

"What should we do with the rest of the day?" She closed up her laptop and started to straighten Allison's office. She really ought to stop calling it that, even mentally. By Friday it would be someone else's office. If someone had asked her a week ago, she would have said hers, but after working with Drew, she'd understand if he got the position. It wouldn't make it any easier, but at least she would know he got it because he worked hard and was competent. And not just because he had seniority and a penis.

"I have a few movies to help us get in the mood for tomorrow." He gave her a sly look.

"Though I have nothing personal against pornography—"

"I was thinking more along the lines of *Pride & Prejudice,* but if you want porn, I can give you—ow!" Drew rubbed his shoulder where she'd thrown a dry erase board eraser at him. "I could have HR write you up on that."

She laughed. "Who'd believe you?"

"I'll have you know those ladies in HR love me." Drew repackaged all the ad samples in the box they came in and picked the eraser up. "I'm one of their favorites."

"Everyone loves Drew." She made air quotes around "loves." "Why is it so important to you to be loved by everyone?"

He set the box on the coffee table and came over to her, until his toes practically touched hers. She strained her neck to look up at him.

"You don't love me," he said quietly. "You barely like me."

"Only because you made it your personal mission to be everyone's best friend. It's rather pathetic if you ask me." She did her best to look down on him, while looking up at him.

"It's better to be liked than to be so serious that one wonders if you could even laugh."

"Respect versus friendship. I'll take respect every time."

"Well, I respect the hell out of you and can't wait to respect your brains out tonight." Drew's voice dropped a little deeper.

Shivers chased up her spine. "See, and if we were friends, we couldn't do what we're doing."

"And why is that?"

"Because it would ruin our friendship."

"I don't know." His eyes flicked down to her lips and a jolt of desire sliced through her abdomen. "I think it might enhance a friendship."

"Sex complicates things."

"It's as natural as breathing."

With him, it was. But it wasn't always that way for her. Enough banter.

"We should probably finish up here." She gestured toward the coffee table.

"My apartment is ten minutes away."

She wanted a kiss. She wanted a hell of a lot more than a kiss, but this was work and kissing at work was off limits. "Quickly?"

He nodded and backed off. He lifted the box and headed down the hallway to his office. She took a deep breath and looked around. Their computers and notes were the only other thing they'd left in here. The remains of lunch were in the breakroom trash so they wouldn't stink up the office.

She picked up an eraser and cleared off the dry erase board. Then she replaced all the pens in the holder. It was odd to think how well they worked when they put their heads together. They'd fleshed out the cologne ad a little more, and with the vodka and ring, they even had a story to their presentation.

Sex, then true love, then marriage.

It rang a little more realistic these days. Well, maybe not

the true love part. She'd actually felt a pang of sadness when she realized she and Drew would never make it past the sex stage. The sex stage was worth it though. But at least after this, they might be friends.

Because however it ended, they'd be working together for at least as long as it took her to get a new job if she didn't get the promotion. If she got the promotion, and he didn't intend to quit, things would be awkward for a while, but eventually they'd find a way to go forward.

"Did you bring your overnight bag?" Drew stood in the doorway in his T-shirt and jeans. Tomorrow he'd be back in his business casual. But today he was the Drew who showed up at her door and kissed her senseless. Maybe that was why this weekend she'd found it so much harder to resist him. He seemed more real in his casual clothes.

She tucked a stray lock of hair behind her ear. "Yeah."

"Careful. The way you're looking at me, I'm not sure I'll make it ten minutes."

She smiled. She couldn't stand the wait either, but she turned and picked up her laptop and their notes. "My stuff is in my office."

He grabbed his laptop and walked across to secure it. She retrieved her tote bag and met him to head to the elevator. Once inside the elevator, Drew took her bag from her hand and dropped it on the floor.

"What are you—"

He drew her into his arms and kissed her. Not a sweet peck on the lips, but a hot, "oh my goodness, I'm going to make you worship me" kiss. When Drew kissed her, she lost her grip on reality, every time since that first night. She'd thought the text had been a mistake, but maybe it hadn't. Maybe the universe had wanted him to kiss her, and this had been their opportunity.

The floors dinged by. As they approached the ground

floor, somehow Drew was aware enough to set her away from him, before readjusting himself. She smiled at the obvious effect she had on him. The doors opened and the sunlight in the lobby blinded her for a second. She grabbed her bag quickly.

"Come on." He pressed his hand into the small of her back to lead her out.

They were in an Uber car within seconds of leaving the building, and she only partially registered Drew's address when he confirmed it with the driver. Drew took her hand in his, and her heart settled as she threaded her fingers through his.

She didn't want to look closely at this. At the emotions welling up in her when he was near. It was only lust. They'd burn through it this week and be done with each other. Then they could proceed as coworkers, who'd once seen each other naked. . . . And did things that coworkers probably shouldn't do to each other.

The car stopped at an apartment building similar to hers. Drew thanked the driver and helped her out. She followed him through the lobby to the elevator. Up a couple of floors and then down a hall to his apartment. Nerves tickled her stomach. He opened the door and let her through, clicking on the lights.

He had a decent-sized apartment. Comfy looking furniture with a nice TV. A small kitchen off to the side. Even a table with four chairs. It had a lived-in feel. Cozy, comfortable, home.

He dropped her bag in another room she assumed was the bedroom. "Scared, yet?"

She looked at him. "Should I be?"

He shrugged. "Can I get you something to drink? A snack? Chocolate?"

"Water."

"Make yourself comfortable." He disappeared into the kitchen and she heard the fridge open and close.

She took a deep breath and sat on the edge of the couch. Being here felt awkward because they'd only been at her place. But being with Drew made it easy at the same time. Her insides were a knot, and she couldn't figure out why. They'd had sex, multiple times on multiple occasions. Sure, she'd never been to his place before, but how was this different?

Maybe, because since last night, she'd known they were going to end up here. They had finally acknowledged this attraction between them and planned to see it through.

But they'd never really hung out before. Not alone. Not without being naked.

"Here you go." He handed her a bottle of water and sat next to her on the couch.

She held it with both hands, not quite sure what to do with herself.

"I'm serious about a movie. If you're interested." He set his Diet Coke on the end table beside her. "Unless you'd rather. . . ."

He didn't have to finish the statement. Why was this so awkward? They'd been all over each other minutes ago and the tension had been palpable.

"Morgan?" He used a finger to turn her chin to him. His beautiful eyes were full of concern, but his silly hair dispelled the effect of his eyes. She reached up and tweaked a curl. His eyes went soft, and he leaned forward and pressed his lips against hers. A tenderness filled her and made her feel strange inside.

He ended the kiss. "So? Movie?"

She nodded, not sure what to say. He grabbed the remote and after a few minutes of pressing buttons, the familiar strains of piano from the beginning of the *Pride & Prejudice* from 2005 came on.

"I knew it!" She pointed at the movie and then at him. "I knew it!"

"If you say anything, I'll deny it." He put his arm around her and drew her against him. "Now shh, watch the movie and I'll tell you my favorite parts."

THE CREDITS ROLLED and Morgan sighed with happiness. This movie was one of her guilty pleasures and now that she knew it was Drew's, too, she wanted to torment him with it.

"Okay, you promised me your favorite parts." She turned to look at him. They'd shifted into a more comfortable position during the viewing. He sat wedged in the corner of the couch, and she rested against him with her head on his chest. His heartbeat had been strong and steady under her during the whole movie. Helping to settle her initial anxiety.

"I only watch for the horses." He smiled at her.

She shook her head. "You're an idiot."

"Okay, I like the men's fashion. I think they should bring back formal attire. It's so refined." He lifted an eyebrow as if daring her to believe him.

"Now you're just baiting me."

"Maybe. Maybe not." Drew laughed when she gave him an exasperated look. "Okay, okay. I like when Darcy helps Lizzie into the carriage, and she looks at him like she felt something and as he walks away, he flexes his fingers. It says so much without saying a word. It's beautiful."

Her mouth had dropped open about halfway through that speech.

"I swear I will deny it if you try to spread it around." He pressed a hard kiss to her lips. "I'm not sure why you're so surprised."

"Your frat boy reputation is safe with me. No one would believe me anyway. They wouldn't believe you and I survived a weekend together without killing each other."

"The weekend's not over yet." His hand skimmed her back and down to hold onto her ass. "Have I told you how much I enjoy your jeans?"

"My jeans?"

His eyes held her captive as his finger traced the seam of her jeans. Her body tightened. "They've been tormenting me all day, showing me what is just out of reach."

"Is that so?" She used her hands on his chest to sit up. "So you are saying I should keep them on?"

"Hell, no." He lifted her so she straddled his lap, her hands braced on his shoulders to steady herself. "But maybe for a little while."

His fingers dipped under her T-shirt along the edge of her low-hung jeans, leaving a trail of fire in their wake.

She leaned in and kissed him properly, not like the chaste kiss he'd just given her. His hands curved around her hips to hold her against the hardness behind his zipper. She moved her hips against him and they both groaned into each other's mouth.

Any awkwardness she'd felt earlier had faded during the movie. The second he touched her, she melted. Something about him made everything in her sit up and take notice. Maybe it was the whole package of him, from his physical attractiveness, to the banter that made her laugh, to his ridiculous hair.

He lifted her T-shirt and she broke off the kiss long

enough to let him take it off over her head. She made short work of his T-shirt as well before returning her mouth to his. The heat of his skin stroked against hers. Her breasts strained against her bra, but his hands stayed occupied with controlling her hips.

She broke off the kiss and gave him a look that said he should be doing more to help, but he just smirked at her with that look that drove her crazy. She rested her head against his shoulder for balance as she unhooked her bra and threw it across the room. She sat back feeling pleased with herself.

His gaze dropped to her breasts, and she wasn't the only one pleased. She tipped his chin up and claimed his mouth again. When her breasts stroked against his chest, she slipped a little in the kiss at the sensation coursing through her.

His hands dropped lower on her jeans to the seam, and he stroked along it again, reaching as far forward as he could, tormenting her with just enough pressure but not enough contact. She stroked his tongue with hers in response, needing him as turned on as she was. She rubbed herself against his hardness again. If he kept this up, she'd come before she got her pants off.

One of his hands grabbed her ass and the other braced her back as he stood with her still attached to him. Her legs wrapped around him, and her arms latched behind his neck. He took advantage of her gasp against his lips to explore her mouth with his tongue for a few seconds before he pulled away from the kiss.

"If I could move blind through my apartment, I would, but I'm afraid I'd run you into a wall. So please forgive me." Drew wiggled his eyebrows at her.

She shook her head. "And here I thought you'd be perfect, but I guess it was too much to hope for."

"I'm still waiting for you to magically get these jeans off so we can just get on with it."

She laughed. "Wow. You want me to snap my fingers so we can be done faster?"

"Never faster." He moved through his living room and into the bedroom, flipping the lights on as he entered. "Just on to the next phase."

"Sure," she said sarcastically.

He dropped her on the bed and pushed her to lie back. She got a quick image of a mostly masculine colored room and heavy wood furniture. His bed was nice sized with a soft, dark purple comforter. Then Drew sucked her breast into his mouth and nothing in the room registered.

Her eyes flickered shut as she let herself revel in the soft warmth of his mouth and the torment of his teeth against her nipple. His fingers went to work on the button and zipper of her jeans. His lips trailed down over her trembling stomach. Her breath caught as his lips and teeth brushed against the skin exposed by the opening in her jeans.

Every touch made her climb higher. Made her want him even more.

He slid his hands into the back of her jeans and underwear, cupping her butt.

"Okay, now I wish I could snap my fingers to get rid of the jeans," she whimpered.

"Your wish is my command," he said against her stomach. He slid her jeans and underwear down slowly, kissing every inch of skin revealed. Though not where she needed him the most. She burned for him, knowing he would quench the fire in the best way possible. He kissed the inside of her thighs and behind her knees, torturing her. His teeth scraped against the back of her calves down to her ankles.

By the time her pants were off, her breathing was chaotic, and she couldn't think of anything but his lips and where they'd go next. He followed his route back up until his mouth settled over her sex.

The sensation was too much. She hung by a thread, barely keeping herself from falling over. When his tongue penetrated her, he pushed her over the edge, and she cried out. He didn't stop to let her come down. His mouth continued to torment her tender flesh until she found herself going over the peak again. This time she came with laughter. Her body was so sensitive every touch felt like feathers tickling her skin.

He released her from her torment for a moment while he took off his jeans and boxers. When he joined her on the bed, his warmth and touch were soft and coaxing. He stroked her gently, waiting for her to catch her breath.

She met his eyes. His were dark pools of blue, begging her to dive in. And she wanted to. She wanted him to be part of her. To mark her as his forever. She ran her hand down his abs and closed her fingers around his cock. He was steel in her grasp.

She explored him, all the while holding his gaze.

"I . . . can't. . . hold back. . . much longer." His breath was ragged.

"Then don't." She reached over to his nightstand where a couple of condoms waited. She grabbed one, opened the package, and pushed him flat on the bed.

She made short work of the condom. Straddling his hips, she lowered herself onto him, controlling the pace. Easing down and filling herself with him.

When she was fully seated, she squeezed her muscles around his cock.

"That's not fair," he groaned.

"It never is." She lifted until he almost fell out of her and then slid all the way back down.

His hands found her breasts as she continued her slow dance. She felt an orgasm building again but she wanted to hold it off. She tried to slow down, but he wouldn't let her.

His hands slid to her hips, stilling her movements, and he thrust up into her. She moaned. The overwhelming heat engulfed her, consumed her.

They rocked together. Him thrusting up. Her grinding down. Until they both couldn't hold back anymore. Their movements became frantic until she couldn't stop from falling into the abyss. He followed her over the edge.

She collapsed on his chest. Heart racing, breath chaotic. His chest rumbled beneath her as he let out a laugh.

"Holy shit." Drew took a deep breath. "I didn't think you were literally trying to kill me, but. . . . Damn, Morgan."

She didn't have the energy to laugh. "I don't like to do anything half-assed."

"Thankfully." He took another deep breath and patted her ass. "I'd love to stay like this, but I need to take care of. . . ."

She squeezed his cock inside her, and he groaned. But she slid off him and watched him go into the bathroom. She fell back on the bed and looked up at the ceiling. How was she going to get him out of her system when every time they had sex, she became a little more addicted to him? She might even start to care for him. It was bad enough she kind of liked him.

He returned to the bed and pulled the covers down so they could slip under them. She found her spot in the crook of his arm against his chest. The spot better than any pillow she'd ever had.

"We should probably eat something for dinner," he said.

"Probably." She reached up and wove her fingers into his hair.

He chuckled. "Don't go to sleep."

"I'm not," she said, closing her eyes. "I'm just resting my eyes. It's been a long weekend."

"It's not over yet." He stroked his hand down her back. "What should we have for dinner?"

"Something we can eat naked and in bed," she said.

"Well, in that case." He started to roll her onto her back.

"Whoa, a girl needs a break and some food for energy before another round. Unless your intent is to kill me by orgasm." She pushed up to look into his eyes. "In that case, do your worst."

"How would that look come Monday morning?" He patted her hip. "Sorry, Morgan wasn't able to come in today. I killed her, but she died happily ecstatic."

She chuckled. "I'm sure a full-scale investigation would be launched as no one would believe I'd sleep with you willingly."

"Little do they know." He shifted her up his chest enough so he could kiss her. Slow, lingering, sated. Tender. Which didn't make any sense to her. This was only about sex, right?

She pulled away and looked down into his eyes trying to see if something had changed. Because it felt like something was changing, which would be bad. It was all well and good if they were just having a little fun, but if their hearts got caught up in it, they'd be in trouble. They couldn't have each other and their careers with Hart Association at the same time.

"Food?" She rolled onto her back and sat up, suddenly very conscious of her nakedness and that her clothes were scattered throughout his apartment.

"All kinds of delivery available or there's a grocery store around the corner." He grabbed a button-down shirt from a laundry basket and tossed it to her before pulling on a pair of sweats.

Even though the shirt was freshly laundered, it smelled like him. Probably because she smelled like him. Her heart warmed. She almost finished buttoning it up when Drew leaned over and kissed her.

She moved onto her knees to take the kiss deeper and to

press her body against him. This was about sex and not tenderness. She needed to reestablish that. His hands played with the edge of the shirt which came down to about mid-thigh on her. She threaded her fingers through his curls. Would a few days be enough when she had been completely satisfied a few minutes ago, but now, she wanted him again?

He pressed his forehead against hers. "We'll order and then we'll see where that was going."

He helped her off the bed. She started toward her jeans and underwear, but he shook his head and gave her that grin that tied her up inside. "Leave them off."

She flushed with heat, but shrugged.

He led her to the kitchen and pulled some menus out of a drawer. "Pizza, Chinese, Thai, fried chicken, pizza."

"I don't think I can handle any more pizza. How about Thai?"

Using his phone, he ordered quickly and waited for the confirmation.

"Twenty minutes," he said.

She started to do the calculations in her head for how long sex had taken them before. When he lifted her onto the counter, she squealed, startled. "What are you doing?"

He started unbuttoning her shirt. "Not wasting any time."

"Do you even have a condom in—"

He paused to pull one out of his sweatpants pockets and put it on the counter next to her. Then he resumed unbuttoning her shirt.

"Always prepared." She ran her fingers through his hair as he reached the bottom button and opened the shirt like a present.

"That's my motto." He claimed her lips with his and used both of his hands to torment her body. His fingers played with her breasts until her nipples were so hard they ached.

She had thought his lips and mouth were divine, but when his fingers caressed her lower, she forgot to breathe.

If he told her he played an instrument, she'd believe him. And that instrument would be her. Each stroke brought forth a new chord from her. A new sigh. A new moan. A sound that only he could make her create. He played her higher and higher until she felt like a string about to snap.

His hand was replaced by his cock. She wrapped her legs around his hips, and he moved within her, catching that string and winding it tighter and tighter. Until it snapped. She didn't recognize the sound coming out of her as her own. Her brain was fully melted. He continued to fill her, thrusting in and out, and she held on as if her life depended on it.

He caught her mouth and surged into her one more time. An aftershock hit her, and she sighed into his mouth. He continued to kiss her slowly as he withdrew from her and made sure she was stable on the counter.

When he lifted his head to look at her, she saw eternity in his deep blue eyes.

He took care of the condom, dropping it in the kitchen trash before pulling up his sweats and washing his hands. He came back to her and started buttoning her shirt.

"You are one hell of a temptation," he said, looking into her eyes.

"I think you truly are trying to kill me." She grinned at him. "But what a way to go."

"Why, thank you." He lifted her off the counter and straightened the shirt, drawing up the collar and holding her by it while he kissed her again. "I actually hate waiting."

"What?" She opened her eyes and tried to clear the cobwebs from her brain.

"Waiting for anything. Food, sex, cabs." Drew tugged her

after him out of the kitchen and onto his lap on the couch. "You are my favorite way to pass the time though."

"I'm not sure that's a compliment." She brushed his hair out of his face. "I mean, we could have played Go Fish if you just wanted to pass the time."

"Go Fish wouldn't have been nearly as much fun." His hand slipped under her shirt to rest on her hip.

"I think I'd better get more clothes on." She started to get up, but he pulled her back down on his lap. She laughed.

"Trust me. I'm not going to be a threat for at least an hour." Lifting her hair, he kissed the back of her neck.

"My sanity is definitely being threatened." But she didn't move away as his lips explored the nape of her neck. Waves of electricity sparked from his lips down her spine.

His doorbell buzzed.

"Saved by the bell." He lifted her and set her on her feet. She tucked the shirt under her as she pulled a blanket from the back of the couch to cover her legs when she sat. Bare chested with his sweats hanging on his hip bones, he strode across his apartment barefoot.

His work clothes truly did not do his body justice. Yes, he looked good in them, but he looked far superior out of them. Those arms though. She sighed. It only took a few minutes to let the delivery guy up, pay him, and bring the food over to the end table beside the couch.

Drew clicked on the TV and picked another movie to watch. This time: *Iron Man.*

"Just in case you thought I lied about being into Marvel." He handed her a Styrofoam container of Thai goodness and a plastic fork.

"Classy." Holding up her fork, she winked at his offended look. "I've always had a thing for Robert Downey Junior."

Drew hit pause and gave her a look that said he didn't want to compete with RDJ.

"What are you worried about?" She ate a bite of food. "That he'll get me all revved up?"

He raised his eyebrow.

"Who do you think is going to benefit from that?" She pointed at the screen. "That guy?" And then she pointed at him. "Or that guy?"

"When you put it that way. . . ." he grumbled and pressed Play.

"Are you feeling inferior to RDJ?" she mocked while continuing to eat her food.

He shrugged and shoved a forkful of noodles into his mouth.

"I don't think you have to worry about him." She turned to watch the movie. "The likelihood of me running into RDJ and him actually being interested in me—"

"Oh, he'd be interested or he'd be a fool." Drew continued to stab at his food.

She blushed. "Still the chances are so low as to be laughable."

He grunted and gave her the side-eye.

She laughed. "I'm sitting on your couch. My bra is hanging from your lamp. I'm wearing your shirt and no panties."

The heat in his next look scalded her.

"I'm here. I'm yours."

"Are you?"

Her heart pounded. She wanted to say yes. Instead, she said, "For now."

"Watch the movie."

CHAPTER 16

At the end of *Iron Man*, Drew clicked off the TV and stared down into Morgan's sleeping face. She was curled up against him under the blanket. *Take that, RDJ; you put her to sleep.*

The curtains were drawn back so the city lights sparkled and added a glow to the room even though it was dark. He couldn't imagine not seeing her like this. Peaceful, sleeping, completely at ease in his arms. It would be over soon.

But, would it?

He couldn't seem to get enough of her. Her laugh. Her sweet smiles. Her fingers in his hair. Her making fun of him.

She was gorgeous and smart and so talented at work. If he got the promotion, she'd be too offended to sleep with her boss. If she got the promotion, she would never sleep with him again. At least not while he worked under her. He could transfer back to beverages, but even then, she might not risk it. It was still against the rules of the company. *She might not risk her job for us.*

But right now, she was in his arms. Right now, she was his.

He rearranged her on his lap so he could carry her to his

157

bed. Her sleepy arms wrapped around his neck as he cradled her against his chest still sitting. The balloon in his chest that always seemed to expand when she was near filled him so much it was hard to breathe. When had that started happening?

Had it always been there? Inflating and deflating with every look, every dismissal. What would it be like when all the air in the balloon was gone? When she was gone?

He lifted her and carried her into the bedroom. He pulled down the sheets and lowered her to the bed. She protested briefly when he unwrapped her arms from his neck. He quickly discarded the sweats and crawled under the covers with her, pulling her into his warmth.

She snuggled back and let out a deep sigh, wrapping her arms around him.

"Oh, Robert," she said with a giggle.

He rolled his eyes and plotted his revenge. He smiled as he released her so she could roll to face him. Laughter sparkled in her eyes.

"I bet. . . ." He started undoing the buttons to her shirt. "That I can make you scream *my* name."

Her eyebrow lifted as if to say she'd like to see him try.

"Challenge accepted."

MORGAN COULD BARELY BREATHE by the time Drew finally left the bed. She held her hand to her chest and willed her heart to slow down. He'd made good on his threat. Even the neighbors knew his name by now.

He smiled as he lay down beside her. "Bet you won't forget my name now."

She patted him on the arm and let out a shuddering breath. "If I don't make it to morning, tell Phoebe she can have my coffee mug that says, 'Eat Like No One is Going to See You Naked.'"

"So dramatic." He rolled to his side and leaned up on his elbow to look at her. "You were the one who played with fire."

She opened her eyes and sighed. "We should watch *Iron Man* more often. Apparently he does it for you too."

"Do I have to start over—"

"No." She shook her head and patted his chest with the back of her hand. "No, I'm good. You're good. We're all good here. No need for any sudden movements or really slow ones and definitely no tongues."

He started chuckling. "You're insane."

"Takes one to know one." She smiled at him.

He leaned down and kissed her.

"I'm going to need to invest in some Chapstick." She touched her lips.

His eyebrow cocked up. "Did you want me to kiss somewhere else instead?"

"Fine! Kill me now and be done with it." She threw her arms out to the sides, smacking against his chest with the one closest to him.

"Oh, I'm not going to kill you. I'll keep you in my bedroom for a while though. Maybe occasionally in the kitchen and we haven't even tried the couch yet." He twirled a fake mustache.

"No one's going to take you seriously as a killer with your Muppet hair." She ruffled his hair.

"Should I just shave it all off?" He pretended to start to get up, but she grabbed his arm and pulled him back down.

"No." She rubbed a strand of it between her fingers. "Mine."

He cupped the back of her head in his palm and brought

his face down to hers, so close their lips brushed when he whispered, "Mine."

His lips touched hers with a softness and tenderness that shook her to her core. What was worse was she wanted it, longed for it, returned it. And that word, *Mine*, echoed in her chest until it filled her.

He pulled her into his arms and closed his eyes. She could hear the rhythmic beat of his heart beneath her ear, and she wondered if he could feel the scared pitter-patter of her own. Something had changed. Something wasn't quite the same. A shift in the dynamic between them. A shift in what they meant to each other. It frightened her, but made her feel whole at the same time.

As she drifted toward sleep, he squeezed her tight and she thought she heard him whisper, "Mine."

"I SWEAR to God I will lock you out of this bathroom if you take one more step toward the shower." Morgan was sore in places she normally didn't think about. And while Drew was only half awake, she wasn't about to let him into the shower with her because they would only end up doing the dirty again.

"Fine." He grabbed a towel and draped it over his naked lower half and sat on the toilet lid.

"You're going to watch?"

"Definitely." He gave her a smug smile.

She shrugged and placed her shampoo, conditioner, soap, and her razor in the shower before turning it on. She'd wrapped a towel around herself when she'd come in here. The air chilled her after being wrapped in his furnace-like warmth all night.

"How are we going to do this?" she asked as she stepped into the shower.

"Well, I was hoping to help, but I guess I'm waiting my turn."

"I meant at work. Are we going to arrive together? Take separate cars?" She washed her hair and put the conditioner in it.

"I don't think we need to go too cloak and dagger on it. I doubt anyone would even notice." He shrugged.

"I'd notice," she grumbled as she washed her body.

"You sure I can't help in there? Get those hard-to-reach spots." He started to stand, but she held her hand up.

"I'm not going to be late for work." She rinsed off the conditioner and soap. Then lathered up her legs to shave.

"We need to get the presentation ready for Thomas to review, so if anyone questions, we can just say we coordinated to arrive at the same time." Drew stood and leaned his shoulder against the glass shower door. "Are you sure—"

"Yes. I'm sure." She tried to keep from smiling but he made it damned hard to stay mad at him. Even pretend mad. "When I'm finished, I'll start the coffee."

"I'd rather skip coffee and maybe wake up a better way."

"I swear I will use up all your hot water, since you desperately need a cold shower."

"You're no fun."

"But you respect me, remember?" She turned off the water and pulled her towel in to dry herself.

"So fucking much." His eyes tracked the progress of the towel, turning her on a little bit.

"Stop it." She wrapped the towel around herself before she got out of the shower. "Be a good guy and take your shower."

"You know, good guys generally finish last." He dropped a kiss on her shoulder before slipping into the shower.

"I don't know how you can still have an erection after last night." She towel-dried her hair as she watched him shower. The water coursed over all those muscles, lovingly following his sculpted abs.

"I thought you were going to make coffee." He opened the shower door. "Or you could join me. I can be quick."

She shook her head. "No you can't."

He gave her a fake sad look and closed the door.

In the bedroom, she slipped on her clothes, a blouse and a pencil skirt, before heading into the kitchen to brew the coffee grounds she brought with her. His refrigerator was shockingly bare, with the exception of a six-pack of IPA beer with one missing. His freezer on the other hand was a teenager's dream, with frozen pizzas in various forms, a bag of chicken nuggets, French fries, and three kinds of ice cream.

"If you look hard enough, you might find Narnia in there."

Caught snooping, she closed the freezer door and spun to face Drew. "I figured ice would be the quickest way to cool you off if the shower hadn't done the trick."

"I used to think your eyes were icy pale blue." He had dressed, ready for work. His hair appeared still damp though. It curled up even more.

"And now?" She started toward the bedroom to blow-dry her hair but stopped at his words.

"Now, they remind me of a spring day when the sun has just come over the horizon and the sky is this soft, pale blue."

She turned to look at him, but he got down two coffee mugs and watched the coffee drip. He was an enigma. Every day she learned something that shattered her illusion of him. She shook her head and went to dry her hair.

As she finished her makeup, Drew came into the bathroom and set down a steaming cup of coffee. "I'd offer you toast, but you've seen everything I have for breakfast."

"I'm good with a cup of coffee. Thanks." She applied her lipstick and tucked everything back into her makeup bag. She'd already repacked her overnight bag, even the bra left on the lamp all night.

"You can leave it here." Drew leaned in the doorframe watching her with those intense blue eyes.

She lifted the cup of coffee and blew across the surface. She looked over the edge at him. "I'll have to take it home tonight to repack it if I'm staying here again."

"Unless you want me to come to your place. . . ."

It was almost like they were feeling each other out. This weekend had been amazing. Not only had their work gone great, but the sex was on the next level. But it would have to end. Every molecule in her body said they would get caught if they kept this up.

Especially if they went to her place and Phoebe saw Drew. Phoebe would say something. Not to corporate, but to Morgan. She'd be the voice of reason Morgan didn't want to hear right now.

"I think it's safer if we come here tonight." She took a sip of coffee. She wasn't ready to give him up just yet.

"Yeah, you will." He gave her a dirty smile, but she just rolled her eyes and shook her head.

CHAPTER 17

THOMAS LOVED THEIR PITCH IDEAS. He wanted them to get some concepts through art that morning and give the copy department their quotes to double check. But overall, their work weekend was a success. Drew sat at his desk and looked out the open door toward Morgan's office.

The personal aspect of the work weekend had also been a success. Though what type of success, he still didn't know. This thing between them had changed ever so slightly. She had wanted it to just be sex, but he could feel more there.

They were supposed to be ready to present to the client tomorrow morning. If they could get Bradbury to sign on, their future with the company would be solidified. The problem was they did it as a team, so how would Thomas sort out which one of them would get the promotion? Unless Thomas was always going to give the promotion to Drew.

That thought gave Drew pause. Was it because he had the experience or was there another reason for Thomas wanting Drew to win?

"How was your weekend?" Robin came in carrying a few files. As an associate in the luxury goods division, Robin knew he and Morgan had spent the entire weekend working. But as one of the office gossips, Robin probably wanted more than just a recap. Most of the staff were aware of his baiting Morgan and her dislike of him.

"It went fine." Drew reached for the files, but Robin held them back.

"I would have happily worked all weekend with you. I was surprised Thomas asked you to work with Morgan since everyone knows she doesn't like you." Robin sat in the chair without being asked. Her legs crossed, raising her pencil skirt just a little. "What was that like?"

Drew took in a deep breath and considered everything he chose to say carefully. "Morgan and I are professionals. We can put aside our disregard for the betterment of the company."

She leaned forward and glanced over her shoulder. "You didn't hear it from me. . . ."

Drew managed to keep a straight face and not roll his eyes as she turned back to him.

"But I heard Morgan was going to try to sabotage you. I was shocked when I heard."

"Really?" He tried to sound like he cared, but he didn't put a lot of stock in office gossip.

Robin nodded seriously. "She was going to post a profile on Tinder that you liked furries."

Drew laughed, trying to imagine Morgan's face if she ever looked up furries on the internet. "Furries? Really?"

He glanced across to Morgan's office as she walked out. Those pencil skirts drove him fucking nuts. When he got her to his place tonight, he couldn't wait to pull her hair out of that bun and mess up that perfect lipstick. He'd make her leave on the skirt and blouse though.

"That's what I heard, of course. But no one would believe you needed to be on Tinder. You could have your choice of dates anywhere." Robin started to turn to see what had drawn his attention.

He held out his hand for the files to distract her. "I'll keep an eye out for people in costume. Thanks, Robin."

"Of course, you could be into furries." Robin's eyebrows shot up.

Drew shook his head and laughed a little. "No. Definitely not."

"If you wanted, I could let slip what you really like?" She pursed her lips together.

Drew's gaze drifted over her shoulder to Morgan. He knew what he liked and he already had it. Robin started to turn again, so he held out his hand again. "The files?"

She stood and placed the files in his hand. "I just wanted to let you know I support either you or Morgan for the Creative Director position. But I think you would be perfect for it. I will keep doing a great job for you both."

He nodded. "I appreciate that."

He ushered her out of his office and went to the break room, where he was pretty sure Morgan had headed.

She was busy refilling her coffee cup when he came in. No one else was in the break room.

"Did you really sign me up as a furry on Tinder?" He could tell he'd startled her.

"What if I did?" She turned with her coffee, blowing gently across the surface. Her huge eyes made her seem innocent, but he knew better.

"Not very professional of you. Which isn't in character at all." He stayed by the door so she'd have to pass him to get out. That and he could block the door if someone tried to come in. Giving them a second to pretend nothing was happening.

"I heard of a new site I could sign you up for." She tapped

a finger against her lips as if thinking. "What was it called again? Something catchy. Oh, I remember. . . FetLife?"

He leaned against the wall and crossed his arms over his chest. "And what exactly would you have signed me up for?"

"Maybe a furry." She took a sip of coffee and regarded him with a critical eye. "Though I could imagine maybe a kinkster."

"And what exactly is a kinkster?"

She crossed the room to the door like she was going to leave but stopped in front of him. As she spoke, she gave him a long and thorough once-over, not skipping an inch, heating his blood. "According to the website, a kinkster is someone who doesn't want to define themselves as just one thing. They like role play, master or submissive, sadomasochism, fetishes, and even sometimes cross-dressing. I bet you'd look stunning in a dress with that hair."

She raised a challenging eyebrow and took a sip of her coffee.

"Hmmm." He didn't quite know what to say which was unusual for him. Listening to her list kinks and look at him like he would be her next hamburger had caused a rush of blood to head southward. Her gloating made him want to do some pretty naughty things to her. Some of which might have been on her list. He took a turn at giving her a slow perusal.

"Any you'd like to try?" he said.

Her eyes went wide, but someone opened the door before she could say anything.

"Hello, Robin," Morgan said brightly. "Thanks for holding the door for me." She gave him a wink behind Robin's back before slipping out.

"Robin," he acknowledged before following Morgan out. She had already made it halfway to her office. There seemed to be an extra sway in her hips just for him. She would be the death of him.

"Hey, Drew." Thomas walked up to him. "I was thinking of golfing this weekend again with Zack and he said you'd had to reschedule this past weekend because of work."

"We haven't firmed up a new tee time yet, but I'm looking forward to it." Drew turned all his focus on Thomas. Being from the same fraternity had bonded them in his interview and may have had a bearing on him getting the position here. But he'd also like to think his qualifications solidified that decision.

"Why don't you join us this weekend?" Thomas patted him on the back. "Let me know if you have a fourth you can bring in. Dr. Lowry is busy this weekend."

"I will." Drew glanced over at Morgan's office. "What about Morgan, sir?"

"I don't know." Thomas looked down at his phone screen. "Sometimes the language can get a little. . . too much for a lady, if you know what I mean. I was thinking of one of your frat brothers. Maybe someone around my nephew's age. He could use some new connections."

"Sure. I'll see what I can come up with."

"See you in the meeting this afternoon." Thomas walked away.

Drew reeled from the *too much for a lady* remark. He had Thomas pegged as slightly sexist but that might have been more of an age thing. He just hoped that wasn't a factor in his decision-making when it came time to promote. Drew wanted the promotion because he had the talent and more experience, not because he was a man.

He had to get ready for the meeting with art in a few minutes. Morgan was supposed to meet him in his office in fifteen minutes to head down together. What would she think of Thomas's brush-off? He probably shouldn't even tell her. It would just upset her.

~

"Earth to Morgan?" Phoebe waved her hand in front of Morgan's face.

"What?" Morgan shook herself back into the present. She'd been thinking about Drew's expression when she'd explained about a kinkster. She was pretty sure she was in for it tonight, which sent a delightful shiver down her spine.

"Did something happen this weekend?" Phoebe looked very suspicious, snapping Morgan out of her daydreams fully.

"Like what?"

"Like did you do Drew again?" Phoebe wiggled her eyebrows.

"What?" Morgan tried to keep the panic out of her voice. Had Phoebe seen Drew leave her apartment? Oh God, he'd left there twice this weekend.

"The doctor, not Drew, ew." She stuck a finger in her mouth as if to induce vomiting and made a gagging noise. She glanced out the window and looked at Drew's office. "Though he is looking pretty hot today. And I could totally get behind some hate sex to screw with him so he didn't get the promotion."

Oh, the doctor. That would definitely lead Phoebe down the wrong track. "Yup, I even spent the night at his place last night."

Morgan hadn't even registered the last half of Phoebe's words until Phoebe's eyes got wide and she pointed from Morgan to Drew's door and squished her fingers together.

"No. The Doctor Drew," she hurried to clarify.

Phoebe grinned. "So it got better?"

Morgan could feel the flush in her cheeks. "Yeah, it definitely got better."

"Sweet. Is the doctor kinky? Oh wait don't tell me, I don't want to know. But I do. But I don't." Shaking her head, Phoebe sat in one of Morgan's chairs. "I bet this weekend sucked otherwise. How's working with ew Drew going?"

"Actually not bad. He had some really good ideas and we put together an awesome pitch." She glanced at the time. "Which I have to go to art to see what they did with our vision."

"I'm still rooting for you, Morgan," Phoebe said as she stood. She went through the door thrusting her fist into the air. "Girl power!"

Morgan smiled and collected her preliminary sketches and the printed storyboards from this weekend. She headed to Drew's office and knocked on his open door. He looked up from his computer and his eyes softened when he saw her. Her heart leapt to her throat.

"Ready?" he said.

She held up her laden arms. "Ready."

"Give me just a sec." He typed something on his keyboard and then stood. He'd put on a pale blue shirt today, not unlike the one he'd let her wear last night. She needed to keep it together. People would start wondering about her if she kept flushing like she was coming down with something. She'd be especially in trouble if people figured out the root cause to the warmth was Drew King.

He picked up a few things of his own and gestured for her to proceed. She felt horribly self-conscious of Drew following her through the office and to the elevator. Everyone's eyes seemed to be on them. What if they knew just by looking at them? What if Drew checked out her ass and everyone saw? Would that be so different than normal? At least for Drew.

When the elevator opened and was empty, she breathed a sigh of relief as they got on. He pressed the floor for the art department.

"Are you okay?" he asked.

She nodded. "Just nervous."

"We put together a strong pitch. I'm sure art will come up with some fantastic things for us." He leaned against the wall of the elevator.

"I'm not nervous about the pitch," she mumbled. Should she tell him about Phoebe? About how Phoebe thought she was still sleeping with Dr. Drew?

"No one suspects a thing, Morgan." His voice was low and quiet.

"I know." At least she wanted to think she knew. The elevator arrived at their destination and they fell into business professional silence again.

IT WAS six thirty when Morgan finally stood up from working and stretched. Across the way, the only other light on in the office shined from Drew's office. She respected his work ethic. A smile crossed her face. She couldn't wait to respect the hell out of him tonight.

Drew lifted his head and looked at her. Her heart skipped a beat.

She walked across the deserted office and leaned in his doorframe. He tilted back in his chair and put his hands behind his head. His slight smile made his dimple wink in and out of existence.

"Everything ready for tomorrow?" she asked.

"I think so. We should do a run-through tomorrow morning before the client arrives." His eyes never left hers, sparking her memories of this morning. Of him standing under the stream of the shower and all those hidden muscles under that shirt. She'd love to follow that same path with her fingers and then maybe her tongue.

"I think that's wise." She wet her lips. "We should probably get in early then."

"We can definitely do that." He pushed away from his desk and stood. "Do you have anything left to do?"

She shook her head. "Just grab my stuff."

"Shall we?" He picked up his laptop bag.

Champagne bubbles raced through her veins as she stopped at her desk to grab her purse and computer bag. With both their lights off, only the dim overhead lights provided a shadowy path through the desks. Even though she was sure they were alone, she wasn't willing to risk being caught by holding his hand or kissing him.

"You get so nervous," he whispered behind her.

"Only because it's my career on the line if we're found out," she whispered back.

They entered the elevator and he said, "Worth it."

She got caught in the facets of his sapphire eyes for a moment. The look in his eyes scorched her and would be enough to tempt a saint.

"Still at work," she reminded.

"Fine." He winked at her as he moved to the corner of the elevator.

"I should have brought my bag, then I could have taken it home to refresh. Now I have to go get it and then go home." She shook her head.

"Wouldn't an overnight bag have been a little obvious?"

She swallowed and looked at him out of the corner of her eye. "I may have let Phoebe believe I was screwing around with the other Drew. The doctor."

"So it's okay to have sex with the doctor?" Drew walked over to her as the floors ticked by.

"Sex with the doctor won't get me fired." She stood her ground. She wouldn't feel bad for telling a lie that would prevent them from getting caught.

"Sex with the doctor would be subpar to sex with me." He'd closed the distance so she could feel the heat of his body.

"Have you had sex with the doctor then?" She cocked her eyebrow up at him.

He chuckled low and rich. "I don't have to."

She searched his eyes, knowing he was right. Sex with Drew was on a whole new level. There had been a little interest with the doctor, but not this intense pull like when she was with Drew. It was almost as if she needed him as much as she wanted him. She parted her lips and his gaze dropped to them.

The elevator dinged and the doors slid open.

He stepped back, and she drew in a shaky breath. The lobby, usually bustling with people early in the day, seemed almost empty. A few people walked by but no one they knew. He held the doors as she walked out of the elevator. Her heels clicked on the tile floor, echoing the beating of her heart.

Music and voices echoed in the lobby from the bar at the far end. She didn't know if any of their coworkers hung out in there or could see them leaving. Again, nobody would think anything of it. They were working on a project together. An important one at that. It made sense for them to leave at the same time. She was just being paranoid.

He walked behind her as they made their way outside. While she looked around one last time to make sure no one saw them, he hailed a cab.

"If you keep looking suspicious, people will wonder what you're up to," he said into her ear.

"One of us has to be on the lookout," she muttered as he held open the door of the cab for her.

He climbed in next to her and gave the cabbie her address. "You need to calm down. No one is going to turn us in. You must have been squeaky clean in high school."

"What makes you say that?" She watched the cars going by as they made their way through traffic to her apartment.

"You have no guile." He relaxed against the taxi seat, watching her.

"I skipped classes occasionally."

"Did your mother know?"

"Yes. So what?"

"Doesn't count." As the cab stopped at her apartment, he leaned forward and paid the guy. He got out and held out his hand for her. Even when he was a bit of a dick, he still took care of her. She took his hand to let him help her out.

"I'm sleeping with you, aren't I?" she said in a huff.

He held her hand for a second longer and then turned to walk to her building.

She hurried to catch up and unlock the door. He held it open and followed close behind her like a force of nature bearing down on her.

"You don't have to come up," she said.

"Yes, I do." The tone of his voice sent delicious shivers down her spine.

She pressed the elevator button and it opened immediately. She took a breath to calm the beating of her heart. As she stepped in, Drew followed her and pressed her floor button. They were the only two on the elevator and his silence started to make her nervous.

As the doors closed, he pulled her in close.

"We shouldn't—"

"We most definitely should." His lips captured hers, and she forgot to breathe. How had she gotten through the whole day without his lips on hers? The world faded into slow ticks as floors went by and his lips and tongue removed all her doubts and fears. Her thoughts scattered until all she could think was that he wasn't close enough and there were too many layers between them.

When the elevator jerked to a stop, he stepped away with a cocky smile.

Heat swamped her face. "You're impossible."

The doors opened, and she fled into the hallway and down to her door. He caught up to her just as she opened the door. His breath teased the hair on the back of her neck. As soon as they walked through the door, he closed it.

"Now what were we talking about earlier. . . ." He was undoing his cuffs and loosening his tie as he slowly stalked her.

"Um. . . . That I need to grab a change of clothes and then we'll go back to your place?" She dropped her things by the door and backed away from him until her spine was up against the wall. That feeling of being hunted and trapped made her heart clatter with anticipation.

He unbuttoned his shirt and shrugged it off, draping it with his tie on the armchair. She swallowed as she took in his arms and chest.

"That wasn't it." He tapped his finger against his lips. "I'm sure it will come to me."

"I should. . . ." She gestured toward the bedroom and made to slide along the wall, but his hands went on either side of her head, effectively trapping her in.

"I remember now." He rubbed his nose against hers. "Something about kinks."

She inhaled and her nostrils filled with his sandalwood scent, overflowing her mind with memories of him and what he did to her. Her body softened as her heart sped up. "Kinks?"

"I can tell you one of mine." He reached his hand into her hair and started pulling out pins, one by one.

Her chest rose and fell heavily as his eyes held her captive. "Which one?"

"It's definitely not furries." When he pulled out the last pin, her hair fell around her shoulders. He ran his hands through it and sparks tingled through her. She closed her eyes briefly at the sensation.

"Good, because I'm all out of mouse costumes," she whispered against his lips.

He cradled her head in his hands and he kissed her, a little harder than normal. When he lifted his head, he studied her face. His thumb brushed along her bottom lip. "That's what I wanted all day."

"What?"

"To mess up that tight knot of hair and those red lips." He pressed his lips against her jaw, encouraging her to lift her chin to give him better access.

"What else?" she said, breathless.

"This shirt. . . ." His fingers worked the buttons loose as his lips worked her neck.

The wall held her, the only thing keeping her upright at this point. His mouth was liquefying her joints. His hand slipped into her bra to stroke her nipple. She pressed her knees together to try to ease the ache he created.

He finished unbuttoning her blouse and pulled it open. "Nice."

"What else?" she whispered.

"I've wondered all day what was under this skirt." He started hiking her skirt up inch by inch.

"You saw me naked this morning."

He lifted his head and met her eyes. "Oh, I know what's beneath all these layers, but I was wondering what layers you might have left off this morning."

She blushed. "That's one fantasy that's not going to happen. I will always wear the proper undergarments to work."

He kissed her. "A guy can dream, can't he?"

His fingers met the skin of her thighs as her skirt continued its journey upwards.

"Fantasy is part of our work after all." His words tickled her ear as she waited with bated breath for him to finish what he'd started. "Creating desire for products. With images and sounds. You wrap yourself up so tight and straightlaced every day from your hair, to your makeup, to even your clothes."

Her skirt bunched up around her hips and his fingers caught the edges of her panties.

"It just makes me want to fuck with you." His lips turned and latched onto her earlobe.

She let out a breath she hadn't realized she'd been holding. Her insides had turned into molten desire, willing to let him do with her what he would.

"To mess it all up." He slowly inched her underwear down. His mouth trailed along her neck and over her chest, pausing to put his mouth on her breast through her bra before releasing her panties to fall on the floor. His hand slipped between her thighs, caressing her, driving her mad. His fingers pressed into her and she caught her bottom lip in her teeth.

She watched in a haze of need as he undid his belt and pants with his other hand while stroking her higher and higher. His mouth teased her breast through the lace of her bra. Gah, she wanted this man.

Her hands held on to his shoulders, molding his muscles with her fingers, trying to stay in one piece. Knowing it wouldn't take much to push her over the edge. Realizing he had the power to shatter her into a million pieces and she needed him to do just that.

He released her breast and straightened, leaving her aching as he drew his hand away to finish undressing himself. Her chest rose and fell in shuddering waves. He stood before her naked, while her shirt hung open with her bra still on, and her skirt wrapped around her waist. The wall and the look in his eyes held her upright, even though she felt boneless.

"To see that look in your eyes, right before you fall apart. When you need me so much that you would do anything for me." He grabbed a condom out of his pants and put it on. "That's my fantasy. That's my kink."

He grabbed both her hands and pressed them against the wall near her head. He leaned in, pressing his bare skin against hers, and whispered in her ear. "You are my kink."

She bit her lip as the heat rose within her.

He thrust into her, shredding any thoughts she might have gathered, and her legs wrapped around his waist.

"Look me in the eyes, Morgan," he commanded.

She opened her eyes. His blue eyes were almost pitch black.

He thrust again, hitting her deep. She moaned and her eyes tried to slip shut.

"Keep them open." Drew gave her a half smile. "I'm not finished with you yet."

His movements were small and then hard. All the while he maintained eye contact.

"That's my girl," he said. Her insides were all aching to reach the summit. She needed him to move faster. "Tell me what you need."

"I need. . ." she said between breaths. "I need you, Drew. Faster. Harder. Now."

He lifted her from the wall, still a part of her, but not

doing a damn thing to finish. He carried her into the bedroom and turned to sit on the edge of the bed. "You do it."

She pushed her knees onto the bed and lifted off of him slightly before coming back down. It felt so damn good.

"Look at me," he whispered.

She opened her eyes as she moved. His face twisted as if in pure torture. She did this to him. She wasn't the only one that shattered with every touch. She leaned forward and brushed her lips over his. "Move back," she said.

He moved onto the bed more. Leaning back against the headboard, he grabbed her hips. "Show me what you need."

She rose and fell on him, taking him deep and hard. Over and over. Losing herself in his eyes. Sweet torment.

"Touch me," she whispered. Needing that push over the edge that only he could give her.

His fingers slid over her sex as his other hand slipped over her nipple, brushing back and forth over the satin cup of her bra.

Her breath stopped as she came. Her focus narrowed to his eyes. Reading pleasure and triumph in his before he took hold of her hips and finished with a few more deep thrusts. His eyes filled with satisfaction as his mouth opened in a groan. She slumped on him. Willed this to never end.

His hands stroked her hair and her back.

She laughed. "Wow."

His chest rumbled with his chuckle. "It was a long day," he said, apologetically.

"It was." She let out a sigh and hugged him. He snuggled her to him.

"Get your clothes and we'll get some dinner on the way to my place." He gave her a playful tap on her bottom.

"Hey," she said. "I thought you weren't into spanking."

"I'll try anything once." He winked at her.

She shook her head as she got off the bed and pulled her skirt off.

"If you are going to walk around half naked, we won't be leaving anytime soon." He shouted as he walked into the bathroom.

She laughed as she slipped on a new pair of underwear and a pair of jeans. She buttoned up her shirt and went into the living room to pick up his clothes for him. Someone knocked on her door.

"Shit," she said under her breath. She chucked Drew's stuff in the bedroom and closed the door. She yelled at the front door, "Just a second."

She grabbed a tissue and wiped what remained of her lipstick off and checked her appearance in the mirror. Her hair was a disaster. She finger-combed it as best as she could. Glancing down, she saw her discarded underwear. She grabbed them and stuffed them in her pocket.

There was another knock.

"I'm coming." She glanced at the bedroom door, hoping Drew would take the hint and stay in there. She threw open the door to find Phoebe.

"It's about time." Phoebe came in before Morgan could stop her.

CHAPTER 18

"WHAT TOOK YOU SO LONG?" Phoebe finally stopped and looked at Morgan. "Wait? Did I interrupt. . . ." She put her hand over her mouth.

"No." Morgan shook her head. Praying Phoebe wouldn't notice.

"Is he here?" Phoebe stage whispered. "Dr. Drew?"

"Uh. . . ." Morgan glanced at the bedroom, right as the toilet flushed. Fuck.

"You naughty minx. On a school night even." Phoebe backed away until she was against the door. "Have fun. Definitely do what I would do."

Morgan heard the doorknob of the bedroom turning. *Please don't come out.* If Phoebe saw Drew, she'd flip out. She'd be convinced Morgan had thoroughly lost her mind. Morgan's eyes widened. *Please don't come out naked.*

"I'll see you tomorrow at work." Phoebe slipped into the hallway, but before closing the door, she yelled, "Have fun, Drew."

When it closed, Morgan spun to make sure Drew hadn't

emerged yet. His curly dark hair popped into view at that moment.

"Are you about ready to go?" Drew said as he walked out buttoning his shirt. He stopped when he saw her expression, which was probably a mix of surprise and horror. "What's wrong?"

"That was too close." She shook her head.

"What was too close?" He closed the distance between them.

"Phoebe." She gestured toward the door. "If you had come out any sooner, she would have seen you."

"Phoebe's your friend, right? She wouldn't go to HR. She wouldn't make you lose your job." Drew pulled her into his arms and rested his chin on her head.

"I don't think she would, but. . . ." Morgan buried her face in his chest. Her heart was pounding so hard. Phoebe was her best friend. But she would have lectured Morgan about the right thing to do which definitely wouldn't include Drew. She didn't want reality yet. She wanted to stay in the fantasy. Morgan shook her head against his chest. "You're right. She would have been surprised, but she wouldn't rat me out."

"Should we head to my place then? Or do you want to wait?"

She took a deep breath. "Let's wait. Just to make sure."

"What should we do while we wait?" He lifted his head and when she looked up, he wiggled his eyebrows at her.

"Honestly?"

"You know how I hate to wait."

She rolled her eyes. "How about some TV and a little computer time instead? I have a couple of emails for work to finish."

He gave a heavy sigh. "Fine. I have a few things to finish up, too."

She grabbed her laptop bag and sat on the couch. After

turning on the TV to some sitcom reruns, she pulled out her laptop. He joined her. Within moments, they worked side by side with their feet up on the coffee table.

She just checked out an attachment from art for one of their projects when Drew bumped his foot against hers. She looked over at him and he was busy typing on his laptop. Must have been an accident.

When it happened again, she glared at him until he looked up with a suppressed smile.

"Can I help you?" he said.

"Can you stop playing footsie with me?"

"I can." He lifted an eyebrow. "But I won't."

She shook her head. "You really are impossible."

"You look so tense." He bumped his toes against hers.

"If this is your ideal of flirting, it's a wonder you get dates at all."

"I don't need to date. I've got all the sex I can handle right now."

She managed not to crack a smile. "Only for a little while longer."

"Then I better not waste time." He set his laptop on the table as both of their laptops sounded an email notification. He groaned. "Saved again."

Morgan opened the email. "Shit."

"It looks like we'll be working tonight," Drew said as he read the email.

The email was from Thomas. Their client, Avalon Jewelry, wanted the preliminary mockups as soon as possible for their Christmas jewelry ad for the necklace and bracelet campaigns.

"I have the information from art and copy writing." Morgan opened the file.

"Why don't we order takeout for dinner and go to my place? We can work on it there."

Morgan took a deep breath and looked at Drew. "No distractions?"

"Scout's honor." Drew held up his hand.

"Were you even a Boy Scout?" she asked, suspiciously.

"No." He grinned at her. "But I do know how to behave, and this impacts both of our jobs right now."

"I'll go grab my stuff. You order a pizza and be a little more creative than pepperoni." She waited for him to nod before heading into the bedroom to grab clothes for tomorrow. All of her toiletries were already at Drew's, so it made sense to go over there. She just hated wasting time when a job needed to be done.

This was the reason she didn't date. Work took up all her time. It was ridiculous to think she'd be able to maintain a relationship while working as Creative Director. Allison had done it, but even she'd realized the job didn't mesh with having a family. Morgan glanced out of her bedroom door at Drew. This was the perfect situation. Sex. No commitment.

If only they weren't up for the same promotion and that job would make one of them the boss. Not to mention the company's policy.

Two hours later, they had finished the pizza and created more than half of the client presentation for the account while sitting at Drew's table. The half a pot of coffee stayed warm on the coffeemaker. Each of them had a mug beside them as they worked.

"It doesn't look like there will be an end in sight." Drew rubbed the back of his neck. "Do you need a refill?"

Morgan was completely focused on the task at hand. She reached out, grabbed her cup, and held it out to him. Then went back to typing on her keyboard.

All the research and materials were in the folders; they just had to consolidate it into a presentation for the account manager to give the client. Drew filled up their cups and returned to the table.

Without even breaking stride, Morgan took her coffee mug and drank half of it while pasting and cropping a photo. Drew glanced at the time on his laptop. They were approaching midnight and probably had another hour or two to work.

"Do you want to take a break?" Drew pushed back his chair.

Morgan finally glanced up at him with a vacant stare. After a minute, she finally registered what he'd said. "Break?"

"What people do to maintain their sanity?" He lifted her hands off her mouse and keyboard and kissed her knuckles. When her look turned suspicious, he chuckled. "Not sex. I swear, that's all you see me as."

She shrugged. "Sometimes I think that's all you see me as."

"Okay, so we need to do something other than sex. . . ." He pulled her out of her chair and gave her a quick kiss.

She opened her mouth, most likely to tell him off, but before she could utter a sound, he said, "Let's go for a walk."

That stunned her into silence, but she nodded and put on her sneakers. He held her hand as they rode down the elevator and walked out of his building. The night air was crisp, and no one was around. The city was quiet with a soft whir of activity unlike the bustle of the day.

"What made you go into advertising?" Drew asked as they walked.

"Fame and money." She gave him the side-eye.

He laughed. "Wow, you picked the wrong career track."

"I like the elegance of a good campaign. Almost all advertising is positive. Whether it's 'have a better day with our product,' or 'look at what you could do if you used our product.' I like when a campaign comes together, and how it feels to see something I created on TV or in a magazine. We bring products to life for consumers."

"I like that thought." He smiled down at her.

She blushed and turned to look away. "We have a knack for putting things together. For creating a desire where there might only be an inkling of a spark. That's the fun part. The long hours and lack of personal life are the rough part."

"No other guys in your life besides the one for a few years?"

She shook her head and lifted her eyes to him. "No other women besides your college sweetheart?"

"Most women won't put up with my schedule." He shrugged and turned them down another street so they could circle back. "It seems pretty impossible to have a relationship and a career in this business. Take tonight. . . ."

"If we hadn't left the office, we'd still be there," she said, nodding.

"What woman will be happy if her man doesn't come home until two in the morning?"

"That's why Phoebe says doctors make great boyfriends. They have crazy schedules too." She leaned into his arm and wrapped her other hand around it.

"Still wishing the doctor had shown up instead?" Drew didn't feel the bite anymore. The doctor didn't have her, and while Drew didn't technically have her, he had her right now.

"It would have been less complicated, that's for sure." She glanced up at him with her pale blue eyes dancing in the moonlight.

A fist wrapped around his heart and squeezed. "You like complicated."

She gave him a soft smile and a shrug. "Maybe."

～

"ARE YOU READY?" Drew stood in the doorway of Morgan's office. His smile was casual, but his eyes swept over her with longing.

A pulse of heat flooded her. They'd finished up last night and then crawled into bed and fell asleep quickly. When morning came, Drew woke her up in a very mutually pleasing way. Way better than any alarm clock. She couldn't hold back her smile all morning.

"Is everything set up in the conference room?" At his nod, she closed her laptop and stood. She straightened her skirt, drawing his gaze down. The appreciation in his eyes sent little thrills through her.

"Time to go." Drew held out his hand, indicating she should lead the way.

Normally her stomach would be filled with butterflies before she presented to a new client, but even her butterflies felt calm, cool, and collected. Morgan and Drew had this one in the bag. Bradbury Industries would be insane not to go with their ad campaign.

His hand brushed her low back as they entered the conference room. The butterflies went haywire at his touch and then settled. Drew and Morgan were the first to arrive.

"Let's run through the slides one last time," she said and took a seat.

He gave her a smile. "We've got this."

"Humor me."

"Only if you humor me later." He winked but ran through the presentation slide by slide.

"I'll 'humor' you when the client says yes." She flipped open her notebook to a blank page. "Are you going first or should I?"

"You aren't nervous, are you?" He sat in the chair beside her and waited for her to look him in his eyes. "Honestly, we've got this. We've created a campaign they'd be crazy to pass up."

Every time she looked in his eyes, she felt this tug deep within her. It wasn't necessarily sexual, but part of her recognized the same thing in him. Maybe it was their competition for the same job or that connection they'd made while pulling this campaign together. But something there was more than sexual. It would frighten her if it didn't feel so natural.

"How are my stars?" Thomas said as he walked in the door.

Drew stood and offered his hand. "Doing well. Prepared for anything."

Thomas took Drew's hand and looked at Morgan. "Everything ready?"

"We're going to make them wish they'd chosen us the first time around." Morgan stood and took Thomas's hand. He held hers for a beat longer than was necessary.

"I'm glad I put you two together. It was time to shake up the luxury goods line." Thomas took his seat at the head of the table.

Morgan tried not to read too much into Thomas's comment, but her mind kept working on the "shake up" comment. She, Allison, and the department had done some great campaigns before Drew arrived. They'd scored some key accounts in the business. The only difference now was Drew, who happened to be male and buddy-buddy with the boss.

The receptionist brought in the representatives from Bradbury Industries, and they took up the other half of the table.

"I'm so glad you've decided to give Hart Association another chance to service your advertising needs," Thomas said, as soon as greetings finished and everyone had found their seat. "I put my best and brightest on the team to bring you our best concepts for your products. We will tailor them more once we are awarded the account, of course."

Thomas gestured to Drew and Morgan. They stood and pulled up the first slide.

"When we received your products, we immediately found a story in what you gave us," Drew said.

Morgan pulled out the cologne out of the box. "Desire." Next, she pulled out the vodka. "Love." And then, she pulled out the ring box and opened it to set next to the others. "Forever."

"We started with the cologne and came up with two distinct ideas for you to choose between." Drew forwarded the slide to a mockup of the man sitting in the chair with the barefoot, elegantly dressed woman bent behind him, her hands on his chest. "Cologne ads are dominated with a good-looking man and an elegant woman. We wanted to convey a feeling of sensuality without going over the top with this particular ad."

The representatives from Bradbury nodded as they stared thoughtfully at the slide.

"We also wanted to give you something that was evocative of the name and scent." Morgan nodded to Drew, who forwarded the slide. Here was the erotic picture Morgan had painted when she'd smelled Censure. The image was dark but it highlighted the tangle of flesh beneath the satin sheets, the moon captured in the window, and the candles playing shadows over them. "With its rich tones of sandalwood and cedar, Censure made us want to show that desire as well as the elegance."

The Bradbury team made some notes as they nodded.

"With Foxx Vodka"—Drew changed the slide to a random picture of people partying in the club—"we wanted to encapsulate the experience of vodka without giving in to the expected party scene most high-end vodka commercials run. Instead. . . ."

Drew's storyboard sketches came up and he clicked through as he talked about them. "We wanted something people would talk about. Elegance with a throwback party to the Regency period clothing and music. Couples in costumes dancing in a museum. The eye grabbing color of the dresses. We have our Fox, drinking Foxx Vodka. He sees his Unicorn across the party. The unattainable, unless you are a Foxx drinker. They come together and for a moment, dance to the strains of violins, before things change tempo to a modern dance."

"Last, but not least." Morgan waited for Drew to advance the slide. "It isn't every day you ask someone to spend the rest of their life with you, and love like that doesn't come often." She glanced at Drew and ignored the tidal wave in her stomach. "We wanted your diamond ring to stand out, and what better way than with the most well-known proposals."

She presented the slide. The ring being slid on a hand against a backdrop of lace over black with the lines from Darcy's speech at the end of Jane Austen's novel.

"Jane Austen is a far superior writer than we are," Drew said. He glanced at Morgan and gave her a smile. "And we pulled some of her finest lines to help represent your ring and its promise of love and forever after."

A warmth surrounded Morgan and she had to look away from Drew to collect herself. The clients took down some notes and Thomas smiled.

"Thank you, Drew and Morgan." Thomas gestured for them to sit. "Any questions or thoughts?"

CHAPTER 19

"I THOUGHT for sure they were going to say no. Did you see that one guy's expression during the slide show? His face was stuck in a frown." Drew followed Morgan into her office and closed the door.

Morgan set her notebook down and grinned at Drew. "We did it."

Drew stepped forward and lifted her off her feet into a hug and then kissed her. She didn't think, just reacted and kissed him back. When he set her down, she was dizzy like he'd spun her around a dozen times.

"That definitely wasn't work safe." She leaned against her desk.

"Sorry, I got carried away." His eyes flashed with heat and desire and she doubted he was even a little bit sorry.

She struggled to feel a little guilt but couldn't manage it. "What do we need to work on next? We have to finish out the Avalon Jewelry campaign for Thomas to present to the client."

"It's almost finished. We're just waiting on the final copy with our changes from art—"

A knock on her door made her scurry around her desk and check her hair before saying, "Come in."

"Oh, good, I hoped to find you two together." Thomas stood in the doorway. "They are definitely excited about the campaigns and have another product they want you two to work your magic on."

"Okay," Drew said with a glance at Morgan.

Thomas handed Drew a perfume bottle. It was tiny with a diamond-like top. "They want to introduce this at Christmas, but they want something different and over the top. Not the naked orgy they got from R&F Group. The perfume is called 'Désir.'"

"Any notes?" Morgan asked, grabbing her notepad and pen.

"Commercial, approximately 30 seconds to 60 seconds long." Thomas leaned against the doorframe. "They want something original like you did with Foxx Vodka. Something within the normal, but a little out there to create a good buzz. I want the whole department to be part of this since one of you will be expected to lead them."

"No problem. I'll send out a notice." Morgan sat at her desk to start typing the email.

"One more thing." Thomas was already out of her office. "I need it by tomorrow afternoon."

Pulling an all-nighter was nothing new to advertising. But they didn't get much sleep the night before, so it would be a little rough. Between Drew and Morgan, they notified everyone who needed to stay and a few who could go home but be on call if they were needed. Mostly it would be Robin and Phoebe, along with Brad from art and Tina from copywriting. Morgan talked to Phoebe to get pizza ordered and to set up the larger conference room. It was going to be a long night.

The large conference room had some distractions in it to promote brainstorming. A ping pong table sat in one corner and a foosball table in the other.

Drew stopped her on her way to the conference room. "Would you please come to my office for a second?"

Her heart picked up the pace as Morgan followed him into his office and sat down. He closed the door, trapping them in. She noticed in a distracted way as she jotted down notes and ideas for the perfume. She couldn't let their attraction interfere with their work. That was part of their deal after all.

"Do you think we should avoid the super sexy ads like the one with Alice and the Hatter?" She glanced up to see him leaning on his desk in front of the other chair.

His focus on her was intense and she couldn't quite read what went on in his head.

"What?"

"I'm going to have to behave badly in there." Drew tapped a finger against his lips.

Images of him and her behaving badly filled her head, but she pushed them away. She leaned back in the chair and crossed her legs. "What do you mean?"

"I have to antagonize you."

"I don't have any clue what you mean—"

"We're going to be with our colleagues." Drew ran a hand through his curls. "If we want people to not suspect anything is up between us, then I'm going to have to act like I always have."

"Oh." They hadn't had to work with others much, and they'd missed a few meetings because of their busy schedule. She'd almost forgotten about his incessant teasing during meetings. It had been one of the things she disliked about him. It was unprofessional and unnecessary.

"I'll try to go easy on you." He gave her a wink.

"By all means, I'd hate for people to believe we are getting along to do actual work." Without expression, she stood and gestured to the door. "Is it okay if I go now? I have a job to do."

"No." He looked down at his feet and rubbed the back of his neck. "I don't know why I said any of that."

"What?"

"I just wanted to get you alone before we spent all night with our team instead of each other." His dimple flashed and one of his curls fell over his eye when he peeked up at her, chagrined. "That's one less night."

She flushed with heat and gestured with her thumb at the door. "We need to work."

He closed the distance between them until not even a paper's thickness separated them. "All I need is you."

Her heart filled her throat as she stared up into his beautiful eyes. The company could fall into shambles around her feet at that moment and she wouldn't notice. Here was this crazy foolish man with his ridiculous hair and pretty eyes telling her he needed her, and it made her insides melt.

He dropped his forehead to hers and her breath caught in her throat. His hands settled on her hips. "Have I told you how amazing you were today?"

"No, you haven't." She swallowed. Everything in her begged her to kiss him, but that one stubborn part of her brain kept her still. Whatever was between them would end. Work would not.

"You were amazing." His lips dropped and brushed gently across hers. Too brief and wonderful at the same time. Her chest flooded with warmth. He lifted his head and smiled at her.

She cleared her throat of the lump in it. "You weren't so bad yourself."

~

DREW FLIPPED his pen in his hand again. Morgan sat across the conference table from him. Her large icy eyes locked on her computer screen as Phoebe droned on about something to her, but not loud enough for him to hear. Every now and then Morgan's eyes would flick up at him and catch him staring. Her cheeks would glow pink, and she'd give him a cut-it-out look.

He couldn't play the game much longer, though, as the last stragglers came into the conference room. Robin had a couple of boxes of pizzas in her arms, and Phoebe stood to help her put them on the table.

Giving him a chastising look, Morgan mouthed a stern "stop" at him but her soft smile ruined the effect.

Drew took a deep breath and stood up. "We have a long night ahead of us, so let's eat and then we'll get to talking about the perfume. You guys help yourselves. Morgan and I will go get some sodas."

Robin, Tina, Phoebe, and Brad all gathered around the pizza while Morgan led the way out of the conference room and over to the break room. Drew felt a jolt of desire when they entered. Images of the time they'd had sex against the break room door flooded his mind. He'd never been more grateful to have a condom handy.

He attempted to slow his breathing and focus on the present work goal. "What do you think—"

Whatever he'd been about to ask completely left his head as Morgan leaned over to grab some bottles from the refrigerator. She held them out behind her, waiting for him to take them. When she looked at him, he happened to be admiring the shape of her ass and hips in her pencil skirt. He shrugged at her pinched lips and narrowed eyes.

She rolled her eyes and shook her head. "Get your head in the game, Drew."

He smirked. "Sorry, boss, thinking of the wrong game."

"There's only one game at work," she reminded him. Her huge eyes made her words less effective. It was like being chastised by a Disney princess.

He took the bottles from her and she stacked a few more on top.

"There are only six of us." He nodded toward the bottles, which had ended up totaling ten.

"Selection, and it seems the only way for you to keep your hands to yourself is to keep them occupied, so. . . ." She grinned.

He just shook his head as she held the door for him. "I can behave."

She raised an eyebrow in doubt as they crossed to the conference room.

"I can," he grumbled. "I may not want to most times. But I can."

"We'll see." She held the door to the conference room for him.

They settled in and everyone talked quietly while eating. Morgan had chosen to sit as far away from him as possible it seemed, but that just meant that she was always in his sight-line. If she thought to remove temptation, she'd failed.

After everyone finished with the pizza, it only took a few minutes to clean up.

"I hope you've all had time to read the file on the client and review our presentation to them this morning." Morgan leaned back in her chair as she talked. "They want something 'different and the same' for their perfume. Something that will catch people's eyes and have them talking about it."

"We have tonight to come up with a concept to wow

them," Drew added. "We'll use tomorrow morning to finish up the pitch."

"The perfume has a few different notes, but for the most part it's fairly subtle." Phoebe put up a slide on the smart board. "While it has some hints of floral notes, the vanilla note gives it a richness without overpowering it."

They passed around the bottle so everyone could smell it. Drew had it last and when he inhaled, it triggered memories of Morgan, warm and sated, curled in his arms. He smiled as he set it in the middle of the table.

Robin picked up the perfume bottle and dabbed a little on her wrist while her eyes met Drew's. "It's really nice. Do you want to...?"

She held her wrist toward Drew but he shook his head. So she held it out to Brad, who leaned forward slightly to whiff it and nodded his head.

"What about getting a celebrity endorsement?" Robin asked. Even though the rest of what Robin said wasn't a question, each of her statements ended as if they were or as if she wasn't sure of herself. "We could build it around an actress that would be suitable for the perfume. Someone who is light and breezy. Natural maybe."

"They haven't given us a specific budget yet." Morgan tapped her finger against her lips. "We can definitely make that an option, but I think we should also have one in case they don't want to spend the money for a household name. The previous ads didn't include a celebrity spokesperson."

Drew shifted to get more comfortable. Every move Morgan made distracted him. "I agree. We need to have something that will go viral. Preferably without having a cat video attached to it."

A few people chuckled, but Morgan looked serious. "Don't underestimate the cat angle. Remember, no idea is a bad idea during brainstorming. That's how we came up with the Foxx Vodka ad."

She didn't glance over at Drew, but he noticed a slight smile at the corner of her lips. Was she remembering their drunken night of crazy brainstorming? Or the night after?

Phoebe shrugged and pulled up a list for brainstorming and added cat video.

"However, we should definitely make it sexy," Drew said. Morgan's gaze slipped to him for a moment. "After all, the perfume is called the French word for desire."

"Definitely sexy." Robin sounded a little breathless, but Drew didn't look back at her. Morgan held his attention with ease.

"Let's go back to basics." Morgan stood and grabbed a dry erase marker. "Perfume ads already are pretty absurd. Nonsense fantasy. A lot of people have been bucking the trend of soft music and an upscale function with a romance plot thrown in."

"True. We want to buck the trend, but if bucking the trend is the trend. . . ." Phoebe shrugged. "How do we find something unique?"

Robin added, "The themes tend toward sex, beauty, freedom, individuality, and distinction."

Morgan added those to the board. She moved with an unconscious grace that always captivated him. Her hair was pulled back and up, but he could catch a few blue strands mixed in the gold.

"Grace," he said, and she added it to the board.

"Allure," she said as she wrote it.

"The obvious one, desire," Brad threw out.

They kept adding different adjectives along the same theme to the board until they had a pretty hefty list.

Morgan sat down and contemplated the list. "How do we make this into a commercial?"

"Why don't we consider ultimate fantasies? What are common fantasies we can build on for the commercial?" Drew looked around at the others before settling his gaze on Morgan. "What are your fantasies?"

She blushed and looked at Phoebe. "You're good at fantasies, Phoebe."

He couldn't help but wonder what Morgan thought about and if he could make it come true for her. After all, he'd shared one of his fantasies with her.

"Oh sure, put me on the spot. That'll make the ideas flow." Phoebe didn't really look annoyed though. She glanced at the white board. "Okay, how about we forget about the standard ads. What if we did go into a fantasy, but not with the normal absurdity?"

"We can always add nonsense later if we need to," Morgan acknowledged.

Phoebe leaned back and looked at the ceiling. "Did everyone else have a chance to see the print ad for *Joli*?"

"Was that the Mad Hatter?" Robin asked. She fanned herself with a stack of papers. Her gaze landed on Drew. "That male model definitely changed my fantasies for a while. I never thought of the Mad Hatter as sexy before that."

Tina nodded. "The final product you guys put together was definitely different but the same."

"What about fantasies like that?" Phoebe looked to Morgan.

Drew could tell Morgan remembered their reenactment of the Mad Hatter and Alice against the wall when she glanced at him with heat in her eyes.

Morgan looked away and cleared her throat. "Yes, let's explore things like that."

"What about the doctor/nurse fantasy?" Phoebe started typing to add it to the brainstorming ideas. "We could make the doctor the woman and the nurse the man."

"Would it be at a hospital?" Tina asked. "Because I can't imagine perfume at a hospital. Let alone sexy times in such a sterile environment."

Everyone chuckled. Morgan held up her hand to stop them. "Remember no bad ideas during brainstorming. While I agree hospital does not equal sexy necessarily, we might be able to incorporate the basics into the final product."

Phoebe gave Tina a vindicated look before continuing. "We all have seen those dramas with the doctors and nurses in the lounge or wherever they can find space. Obviously, people like watching those shows because they have high ratings."

"Doctors are highly overrated from what I've heard." Drew lifted an eyebrow when he met Morgan's eyes. She narrowed them slightly at him.

"I think in today's political climate, we should probably steer clear of the boss/secretary romance." Robin glanced at Drew when she said that. "Even though it's a good one. I think people are a little more sensitive about it."

"Good point, Robin." Morgan added some notes to her notebook before glancing up at Drew. "Boss and underling romances are off the list."

"What about coworkers?" Drew gestured to Phoebe to write it down. "Without the undertones of authority, a forbidden work romance might be exactly what our commercial needs."

"I don't think—" Morgan started.

"No bad ideas." Drew lifted an eyebrow to challenge her to say more. She tightened her lips, but he just gave her a smile.

"I like it," Phoebe said. "We could set it in a conference room like this one with the windows looking out over the rest of the office."

"They could get close, but not too close, for fear of being

discovered." Drew shifted in his chair, casting Morgan in the scene with him.

"To bring in the perfume, we could have her start out her day applying the perfume before getting dressed," Tina added as everyone seemed to jump on the idea.

"Or she could reapply in the bathroom before the meeting," Phoebe added.

"He could notice it as he walks behind her," Robin said. "Maybe it's new. Something he'd never noticed before. Maybe he's never noticed *her* before."

"Oh, he could make a comment about the something different about her," Phoebe added.

"They could share a look while they set up for a meeting," Brad kicked in.

"After the meeting, everyone leaves except the two of them," Tina said.

"And he walks over to her and presses her up against the outside window," Phoebe said.

"And he drops his head to sniff her neck," Brad said.

As they worked through the commercial, Drew held Morgan's eyes. The heat in hers had to be reflected in his. He had to admit he'd had similar fantasies about Morgan since starting at Hart Association. He'd never imagined actually getting to fulfill any of them with the ice queen.

But now he knew. She wasn't an ice queen at all. She was molten silver that coursed through his veins and made him want nothing more than her. Their time together might be ending, but he'd never forget the feel of her beneath him. The way her eyes widened slightly, as if in surprise, every time she orgasmed. The way her lips parted, and her lids fell heavy afterwards. The way she claimed him as hers when they slept, wrapping tight against him and threading her fingers through his hair to keep him close.

She had become a part of his world. Even if she wasn't

sleeping with him, at least he'd get to see her every day. Make her smile at his jokes. Roll her eyes at his innuendos. Chastise him for not paying attention.

"Earth to Drew!" Phoebe laughed. "Hello, space cadet, welcome back to Earth."

Everyone chuckled as Drew blinked and looked at the screen with the fantasy themes written on them.

"Sorry. Long day." He met everyone's smiles with a chagrined smile of his own. Too few days remained until they knew where he and Morgan would land. "Coworker fantasy. On board."

"Unfortunately, here that type of romance would get you fired." Robin sighed wistfully and again her gaze flicked over to him.

"Maybe we should explore forbidden," Brad said. Everyone nodded. "That can make a fantasy hot. Like that one ad a few years ago with the woman on a train and the stranger. The misconnections until the very end."

"That was good." Phoebe tapped her fingers against the table. "There was a recent ad for headphones where strangers danced together."

"We played with that for Foxx Vodka," Morgan said, brushing a lock of stray hair behind her ear. "That first look across a crowded room. What about an elevator?"

"Go on." Phoebe leaned forward on the table.

Morgan took a sip from her soda and her gaze flicked to his before going back to Phoebe and the rest of the group. "A crowd on the elevator. So there is this feeling of closeness. The first scene he's behind her and notices her scent, kind of like the train ad. Maybe the elevator is mirrored, so she sees him notice and their eyes meet in the mirror, but he has to get off at the next stop."

"Keep working it," Drew encouraged.

She took a deep breath. "The next scene is her getting

into the crowded elevator and he's there too. They stand next to each other, arm against arm because of the crowded elevator. He brushes the back of his fingers against hers. Our camera focuses in on that slight touch. Then we go to her indrawn breath and his slight smile."

"What if this were an apartment building elevator or hotel?" Robin said.

"I like hotel. It gives it an immediacy as if these two might not meet again and have limited time." Phoebe added, "Definitely not work."

Morgan nodded. "That way we could get different outfits and different days."

"I like that," Drew said, already sketching a storyboard on his notepad.

"Then the next scene, she's coming back from some event and so is he. Tuxedo and fancy dress, but something flirty and pretty for her, not sexy and slinky like the normal." Morgan bit her bottom lip as she thought. No one wanted to disrupt her flow. "They enter with maybe one or two other people, who get off together on a floor below their stops."

"As they move together, our tagline is voiced over," Drew said. "More than just a fantasy. Désir."

"Oh, I like it." Phoebe frantically typed to catch up with the fantasy as Morgan had laid it out.

"Why don't we do a storyboard of both?" Morgan said. "Brad, will you work with Drew on them? Robin, would you look to make sure neither has been done before? Tina, I like Drew's tagline, but we need some music and maybe more words in the commercial. Phoebe and I will work on the presentation and background for the commercials."

Everyone followed her orders without question. A warm sense of pride rushed in Drew's chest. She was already a leader. She'd do well as the Creative Director if he didn't get it. Even though Thomas had stated the job was basically

Drew's, Drew should let him know he'd be making a mistake not considering Morgan seriously for the position. The only problem with her getting the job would be to convince her to continue with whatever was happening between them. Because he wasn't sure he'd be able to stop wanting more after Friday.

CHAPTER 20

IT WAS one a.m. before they had the concepts in a form worthy of the client and they decided to take a break. Morgan stretched her arms above her head. Tina and Robin were playing ping pong in the corner. Brad and Phoebe were out making copies and walking around. Drew had disappeared.

Even though he was being respectful, Morgan was sure at least Phoebe thought something was up. She kept glancing between them with a suspicious look. The risks were high, but was the reward really worth it? It was just sex. Obviously the sex was amazing, but was it any more than that? Not that it could be. Her insides churned.

She closed her eyes to rest for a few minutes. The smell of fresh coffee tickled her nose. She opened her eyes and a cup of coffee and half a brownie sat in front of her.

Drew sat down in the chair beside her and bit into the other half of the brownie. "You looked like you could use a pick-me-up."

"Thank you." Something warm and sparkly filled her when she looked at him. She'd known it would be dangerous to let him in that first night, but she'd figured it was a danger she could handle because she didn't like him. It would be one-and-done and they'd both forget about it. But they hadn't really worked together before. Just for the same company.

Now seeing his crooked smile with his dimple, she knew there had been a point where she should have stopped this and things would have been fine. It was long past that point.

She took a sip of coffee and a bite of brownie. It would hurt when it ended, but she'd take now. His sapphire eyes sparkled in the overhead lights.

"I really like when you take charge," he said softly. A mischievous smile played on his lips.

The ping pong ball kept going in the background. No one paid attention to them.

"The sooner we get done, the sooner everyone gets to go home." Morgan turned to look out the door as Brad and Phoebe did another lap around the office.

"Unfortunately, I think the only thing we'll have time for is sleep when we get home." The look of false disappointment on Drew's face made her laugh.

"I'm sure you would find time," she said softly and looked up at him over her coffee cup.

"For you?" He gave her a thoughtful look before giving her a naughty wink.

Her insides flushed with warmth. She shook her head and tried to restrain her smile. He really was impossible. He gave her one last smile before heading over to his computer.

They were almost at the end of the break. Tina and Robin had abandoned their ping pong game, muttering about a search for some chocolate. Drew worked on his computer across the table from her. She didn't know what to make of him. Just being in the moment with him was nice, calming. Sleeping in his arms would be enough tonight.

Which if this were only about sex, that might be a problem. . . . She drew in a breath and decided to make a trip to the bathroom.

When she came out of the enclosed stall, Phoebe stood leaning on the counter of sinks. Her arms crossed and her expression thoughtful.

"So what's going on with you and Drew?"

Morgan delayed by heading over to the sink and washing her hands. "Are we talking about Dr. Drew or ew Drew?"

Phoebe handed her a paper towel and raised her eyebrow. "Ew Drew."

Warmth rushed through Morgan's body. What had Phoebe noticed? Had she seen him at Morgan's apartment? Could she trust Phoebe not to rat them out? "Work? Is that the word you are looking for? So, we're getting along. It's better we put aside mutual hatred for the project."

Morgan glanced at the enclosed stalls. She hadn't heard anyone else since she came in, but she hadn't heard Phoebe come in either.

"Is something going on with you two?" Phoebe raised an eyebrow.

"Besides working?"

"Yes, besides working." Phoebe rolled her eyes. "I know you haven't been seeing Dr. Drew."

Morgan's chest tightened. "How would you know that?"

"Alex told me Drew called you, and you blew him off. And not in a good way."

"I thought you weren't seeing Alex."

Phoebe shrugged. "Only occasionally. But that's not the point. Who flushed your toilet the other day, and why are you and your arch nemesis smiling at each other? You do remember you're going for the same goal, right? There can be only one."

"We've been working together as adults do." Which was

true, except they were also seeing each other naked a lot more than work associates were supposed to.

"That's the other thing. Don't you think it's odd Thomas has you guys working on the same projects together instead of seeing what you guys would come up with on your own?"

Morgan stared off into the distance. It hadn't exactly escaped her attention. "He said we'll be working together no matter who ends up with the promotion, so it makes sense."

"Yeah, makes complete sense the boss's golf buddy gets to ride your coattails to the promotion." Phoebe jumped up to sit on the counter. "You should get the promotion, but I'm worried your head isn't in the game."

"What do you mean?"

"I think Drew is being nice and flirty to get you to lower your guard around him. Keep you off your game."

Morgan pressed her lips together. It hadn't been Drew who had started this whole thing. "I've got my head in the game."

"Okay." Phoebe smiled and slapped her hand on the counter. "So let's post that Tinder profile and blow his phone up so he's off his game."

Morgan shook her head. "I can't do that."

Phoebe smiled and bumped Morgan with her knee. "That's what you have me for."

"It's complicated now." So fucking complicated it was ridiculous, but she couldn't share that with Phoebe. The whole thing was a secret and she had no one to talk about it with except Drew. And when he was around, she felt safe and warm and forgot all her concerns.

Phoebe got quiet and thoughtful. "Who was at your place the other night?"

"I can't say." She dropped her gaze to her hands.

"Morgan?"

Morgan inhaled and met Phoebe's eyes and said softly, "It was a mistake."

"Okay," Phoebe said slowly. "What or who was a mistake?"

Morgan glanced around at the full stall doors in the bathroom. She definitely didn't want everyone to know what she was about to tell Phoebe. She shouldn't even be talking about this at work, but she needed to tell Phoebe. She needed someone else to wake her out of her weird and twisted reasoning. She returned her gaze to Phoebe's face. "Drew."

"Wait? What?" Phoebe scrunched up her face, trying to piece together everything. Morgan had obviously looked like she'd been screwing around with someone and then her toilet had flushed. Morgan knew the moment Phoebe made the connection because her face transformed to a shocked expression. "You and—"

Cringing, Morgan held up her hand. "Don't."

"But. . . how did. . . when. . . how long?"

"Since that night when you texted him."

"But. . . ." Phoebe clapped her hands over her mouth. "Oh, man, I was pretty toasted. And he just showed up?"

Morgan nodded her head.

"And you just let him in?"

She nodded again.

"And you. . . ." Phoebe made a crude gesture.

Morgan grabbed Phoebe's hands to stop her. "Yes."

Phoebe smirked. "And it was good?"

Morgan cringed and nodded.

"Nice." Phoebe bumped Morgan's arm with her hand. Her face fell and she jumped down off the counter. "Wait. No. This is no good. He's trying to throw you off your game. You're totally being played."

"It's not like that." Morgan shook her head, but she was beginning to have her doubts. He seemed really into her, but it's not like they'd discussed a future, because there wasn't a future where they stayed together. One of them would be the other's boss. They were lucky they'd gotten this far without being discovered.

"Dude. Come on. You both happen to be up for the same position and he just happened to give you his number which was the first text box in the messages?"

"It was before we knew about the promotion." It wasn't Drew's fault. She had been the one who initiated with her text, and they both kind of kept whatever this was going. Though it had been Drew who initially wanted things to keep happening, and that had been after they'd found out about the promotion. It had seemed so simple. Yes, there was risk, but it was fun being with him.

"The sex can't be that good."

Morgan met Phoebe's eyes. "We shouldn't be talking about this at work."

"Okay. But we're going to talk about this later. I think you should stop seeing him." Phoebe patted her hand. "Cold turkey. Focus on work. On the promotion."

A chill flowed through Morgan and her insides clenched. Phoebe was right. The risk was so high. What she couldn't tell Phoebe was it had become more than sex for her. She liked being around Drew. Loved how he made her smile. How he teased her. How even at night he pulled her in close and made her feel protected and safe. How she couldn't wait until they were alone so that they could be themselves around each other.

"Morgan?" Phoebe said.

Morgan blinked. She nodded. Phoebe was right. This was why Morgan hadn't wanted Phoebe to find out. Phoebe would bring reality crashing back in.

Better to end it now. They would have to end it soon anyway. Why not today? So why did it feel like Morgan couldn't catch her breath? Like she was making a huge mistake. She met her own eyes in the mirror and stiffened her resolve. It had to end.

DREW DIDN'T KNOW what had happened, but something had changed during the break for Morgan. Hell, something changed in the last ten minutes. She'd been fine when she left the conference room, but when she came back in. . . . Her face had been a mask of indifference and focus.

She paused in the doorway for a brief second next to him before heading to her spot. She announced to the group, "It's late. Let's wrap things up so we can get some sleep before finishing in the morning. Let's take the next hour to make sure all our ideas are on paper."

Her voice wasn't any different, but there was an edge. Had someone said something to upset her? Had he upset her in some way? He went through their last conversation, but nothing jumped out at him. Maybe she was just tired.

"Sounds good." He moved to his workstation. He'd find out when they were alone together.

Robin scurried in a few seconds later. Her gaze went to Morgan before bouncing away. "Sorry."

"We're finishing up for the night. Whatever we can get done in the next hour." Drew nodded to her area.

Robin gave him an odd look before going to her place. He glanced over at Morgan. She wouldn't meet his eyes. Maybe everyone just needed sleep. His brain was definitely fried.

Everyone settled in and got to work. Morgan continued to ignore him, but that shouldn't bother him. She hadn't paid him much attention prior to the break when they were all working. He couldn't help but feel like she was off, but he wouldn't know anything until they finished work. The minutes seemed to tick by slowly. Until the hour was finally up, and everyone busied themselves with packing up.

"See you tomorrow," Tina said to him as she and Brad left with an armful of stuff to take down to their work areas. He smiled at her and thanked them for their work.

Robin collected her stuff, and with a quick look at him, headed out to her desk. Phoebe and Morgan headed out together, leaving him alone. Again, Morgan avoided meeting his eyes.

Phoebe hadn't even given him a snide look. Something had definitely happened.

He hurried to put his things in his office. Phoebe and Morgan stood waiting at the elevator. He managed to catch up to them as the elevator reached them. Robin also walked over to join them.

He couldn't exactly ask Morgan what had happened with two of their coworkers in the elevator with them. And with Phoebe there, he wouldn't have an excuse to ride with Morgan. Fuck this night.

"See you tomorrow," Robin said as the rest of them left the elevator. She had to ride down to the parking garage under the building.

He shouldn't let her go by herself. He took a deep breath and tried one more time, unsuccessfully, to get Morgan's attention. She glanced up at him, but her expression was blank. Not questioning. Not longing. Just blank.

A rock fell hard in his stomach.

"I should walk Robin to her car."

"You don't have to—" Robin said.

"Yeah, I do. You two have a safe trip home." He nodded to Phoebe and watched Morgan walk away from him as the elevator doors shut. Fuck.

Robin fidgeted with her keys. "I really appreciate it. But there's a security guard down there."

He smiled. "I'd feel better to know you got home safely."

She blushed. "Thank you."

He leaned against the back of the elevator until the doors opened. His heart raced as much as his brain as he tried to figure out how to salvage tonight. Morgan's stuff was still at his place, so there was that. Maybe she would go home and get a change of clothes, and he could pick her up to take her to his place. He gestured for Robin to lead the way. She hurried out and glanced at him several times as they made their way to one of the last cars in the parking garage.

She opened her door and said, "Do you need a ride home?"

"No thanks. I have an Uber waiting for me." That and he had no intentions of going to his place. Morgan may have been able to avoid him here in the office, but she couldn't avoid him at her apartment.

"Have a good night." Robin closed her car door and he watched her pull out and drive away.

He took out his phone as he headed back to the elevators.

I'm on my way, he texted.

I've got a bit of a headache and just want to sleep tonight. See you tomorrow at work?

Was that why she had been acting weird? She had a headache.

That rock felt a little lighter.

The elevator stopped at the lobby, and he walked across to his Uber ride.

Hope you feel better. Sleep tight. Night.

Night.

CHAPTER 21

IT HAD BEEN SURPRISINGLY easy to avoid being alone with Drew all morning as the team worked to get the proposal finished in time to present it to Bradbury. The presentation went smoothly, and everyone was satisfied with the results. The client gave them the usual we'll get back to you speech, but Morgan had a good feeling about it.

Now she worked in her office sorting through some of the Avalon Jewelry files for the Christmas advertising campaign. They had enough time to work on it, but she'd rather cut down the amount of time she had to work on it with Drew. Some prep should do the trick.

She was surprisingly well-rested. Fortunately, lack of sleep and too many late nights had caught up to her, and she'd dropped right off. Even without Drew keeping her warm.

Phoebe tapped on her doorframe.

Morgan gave her an encouraging smile, and Phoebe closed the door behind her.

"How are you this afternoon?" Phoebe sat in the chair

across from Morgan. Her eyes narrowed, probably looking for any cracks in Morgan's armor today.

"Good." Morgan could breathe a little without worrying about Drew stopping by or walking by. But even with the threat of him, she hadn't closed her door. She'd missed him last night. More than she wanted to think about. She'd missed his arms around her, holding her while she slept. She'd missed waking up entangled together.

"Have you talked to him yet?"

Morgan looked at the ceiling and pushed a little back from her desk. "No, and I know I have to, but not at work."

Phoebe nodded. "You could just text him."

Morgan had thought about that too, but the thought alone made her chest ache. Yes, it was only supposed to be sex, but. . . . They knew each other now and would have to continue to work together afterward. "I can't do that."

"I still can't believe you and Drew. It's crazy. I mean I could imagine him with other people. He's the rule-breaking type. But you aren't." Phoebe shook her head and stood. "Rip the Band-Aid, Morgan."

Phoebe waited until Morgan nodded before leaving her office. The door stood open once again, and across the way she could see Drew in his office. Not all of him because of the walls, but enough to know he was there. She had to call it quits with him. Her breath caught in her throat, almost choking her. Her whole body seemed to be rejecting the idea, but Phoebe was right. The stakes were too high and so far, they had been lucky. She didn't need to push that luck right out of a job. Her career with Hart Association was her life. It was what she'd sacrificed and worked hard for.

Settling back into work for the afternoon, she barely registered the noise from the office slowly dying down as computers were shut off and people left for the day.

"Hey." His voice sent shivers down her spine with dread

from having to face him finally, while warmth filled the rest of her at him being close.

She raised her eyes to meet Drew's smiling face. "Hey."

He leaned in the doorframe, relaxed and at ease like they had all the time in the world and not only a few days left. No days left if she could rip the Band-Aid off.

"How's Avalon Jewelry going?" He didn't move from his spot. His presence filled her office but not in an intimidating way.

"Well. The initial artwork and copy for the Christmas pendant are what you and I talked about. We should be ready to present our ideas to the client next week." She didn't know if anyone else remained here, so now wasn't the time to talk about what they did outside of work. Or get one last mind-blowing kiss before she ended it.

Drew nodded. "Interviews are tomorrow."

A lump settled in her chest. She nodded. She couldn't help saying, "Won't be long until you are reporting to me."

"Or vice versa." It didn't hold any heat anymore. In fact, it almost sounded sad. He glanced toward the elevators.

"Did you need something or are you just checking in?" Morgan folded her hands on her desk.

He stepped inside the door and said softly, "I missed you last night."

She swallowed and closed her eyes. She wanted to say, "me too," but that wouldn't help matters. Not in the long run. She opened her eyes. "I have a few things to wrap up still."

He smiled. "Later?"

She nodded. She could do this. Rip the Band-aid off, get the pain over and done with, and hope her heart wasn't as involved as she suspected it was. She couldn't fall in love with Drew.

~

DREW WORKED at his desk while he watched for Morgan's light to go off. When it finally did, he shut his laptop and headed out to the main area. She joined him in the empty office. As they walked to the elevator, she didn't talk. It was like the ice princess had reemerged and he didn't know how to handle that anymore.

"Want to share a cab?" He hoped it was all in his mind and things weren't starting to crash down around him. He wasn't ready to let her go. Sure, he wanted her. That wouldn't change. But not just for right now.

It wasn't about lust anymore. He couldn't imagine not having her with him. Making her laugh and smile. Spending time with her in and out of bed. An end date was rapidly approaching. It made him want to grab her and hold her until she admitted she didn't want to let go either. Convincing her to continue with him after Thomas announced the promotion would be near impossible. But he wanted to try. No matter who ended up on top.

Even if he couldn't have her forever, he wanted these last few days. Maybe with them, he could show her that they were good together and worth the risk.

She nodded as the elevator opened. "I need to grab my things."

No one was in the elevator. He breathed out. "So do you want to stop by your place first?"

She patted her hair, near her ear. As if a hair would dare to get out of place. He reached out and threaded his fingers through hers. Her hand closed around his and she squeezed her eyes shut. A wave of relief crashed through him. She was still his.

She opened her eyes and met his. "No."

"No?" He released her hand. She clasped both of hers together in front of her. The numbers disappeared quickly, counting down to the first floor. "Not your place first?"

"I need to get my bag from your place." She dropped her gaze from his.

"Okay." The elevator doors opened, and he followed her out. Now wasn't the place for a conversation about them. The bar was hopping tonight, and at least a few of their coworkers hung out in there.

He pushed open the door to the outside and hailed a cab. Everything felt wrong. Morgan was closed off, more so than she was when they first met. And he couldn't talk to her about it. Not here. He was willing to gamble a lot to be with her, but he didn't need to be stupid about it. He wasn't sure he wanted to know what was happening in that brilliant mind of hers, but he knew he had to find out what went wrong. Where he had gone wrong.

He gave the driver his address and entangled his fingers into Morgan's cold ones. Again she closed her fingers around him like nothing was amiss. Habit maybe? Or maybe he was reading too much into her distracted attitude? Maybe this was all about work and the stress they were under to perform. They both had a lot on the line tomorrow.

"Are you ready for your interview?" he asked.

"As ready as I can be. I put together my portfolio and updated my resume." She continued to look out the window at the passing buildings.

"I'm sure you'll kill it tomorrow." He gave her a grin, but she didn't turn to see it.

She fell into silence. As much as he wanted to pry, he didn't want to do it with an audience. He'd have her to himself in a few minutes. Fucking waiting. Obviously, something was wrong, whether it was nerves or more. . . . A dull ache throbbed in his chest.

The cab finally arrived at his place, and he paid the guy and followed Morgan to the front door. The words stuck in his throat as he tried to find a way to penetrate the walls she'd put up. Maybe it was all in his imagination. He led her to his apartment door and opened it, letting her precede him.

He shut the door and took a deep breath. "Are you okay?

She shrugged.

He closed the distance between them and lifted her chin with his finger. Her eyes finally met his. "You can tell me."

He leaned in and pressed his lips against hers. She softened beneath him and leaned into the kiss. Everything felt right in the world again. The puzzle pieces slid into place until she pulled away.

"I need to go." She left him standing there and went into his bedroom. Stunned for a moment, he could hear her picking up her things and putting them in the bag.

He followed her and grabbed her free hand, pulling her to a stop. "Morgan, please, talk to me. What's going on?"

She sank down on the edge of his bed, set the bag on the floor, and looked up at him. Her eyes were filled with pain. It rocked him to his core.

"We need to stop. We've been lucky so far that no one has found out, but I can't lose my job over this." She gestured between them.

He sat next to her and she stood. He grabbed her hand, stopping her from walking away. "Why now?"

She looked at the ceiling. "Today? Tomorrow? Friday? What does it matter? It has to end. It's been fun, but that's all it's been."

Her fist in his gut would have been easier to take. "Fun?"

A tear rolled down her cheek when she looked at him, but she smiled. "Yeah, fun. The whole cloak and dagger routine is wearing thin though. If Phoebe could figure it out—"

"Phoebe knows," he whispered. He nodded as if everything finally made sense. Why Morgan turned suddenly cold to him. Phoebe found out and that terrified Morgan. "You said she's your friend. She won't do anything to hurt you, like tell the boss."

"But if she found out, someone else is bound to. We're risking too much. I like you, Drew—"

"I like you, too." He stood and closed the distance between them physically, wishing it was just as easy to bridge the other gaps she kept throwing between them. "It's only two more days."

She pressed her hands against his chest, not to push him back though. Her smile bordered on the edge of regret. "It has to end, and now is as good as two days from now. We need sleep and focus for the interviews and the decision. We can't continue this once one of us is the boss. I've enjoyed working with you, and it will be easier to adjust afterward if we end it now."

He didn't want this, but what could he do? He couldn't guarantee they wouldn't be found out. He couldn't guarantee there wouldn't be repercussions at work if someone did turn them in. Just two weeks ago, corporate had sent that memo and it had been clear that corporate didn't want employees being more than friends. He sighed, feeling all the fight leave his body. "If this is what you want. . . ."

She nodded and dropped her hands. "At least we know we work well together now."

Better than that. He nodded and watched her pick up her bag and glance around his room as if leaving a hotel room and not wanting to leave anything behind. No trace of her for him to hold on to.

She held out her hand to shake. "I'll see you tomorrow."

Stifling the urge to laugh at her attempt at distance after the intimacy they'd shared, he took her hand as professionally as he could. She wasn't out of his life yet. Maybe he couldn't change her mind tonight, but maybe he could change corporate's. It was possible the memo wouldn't be enforced. They could have been covering their own asses. "Tomorrow."

~

MORGAN MADE it all the way to her apartment and closed the door before her courage deserted her. She was exhausted mentally, physically, emotionally.

She sagged against the door and dropped her bag. The nervous energy that had carried her drained from her body. Her head pressed against the solid wood. It was for the best. She had to tell herself that over and over. But then why did it feel like she'd cut off something vital? A piece of her that made her feel good and safe and. . . . She shook the word "loved" out of her head.

The hurt in his eyes had almost broken her.

It should have been easier to call it quits. If this had been about sex, she should have been able to stop no matter what he said or did. Instead, she kept wanting him to convince her she was being foolish and they should continue regardless of the consequences. This thing between them amounted to more than an accidental booty call.

A simple knock at her door made her heart leap. She wanted it to be Drew.

She turned and opened it. Her heart dropped back down as Phoebe held up a bottle of wine. "Ready to indulge?"

Morgan stepped back to let Phoebe in, went to the couch and sank onto it. Glasses rattled in her kitchen, followed by the release of the cork, and finally the liquid splashed into the glasses.

"How'd he take it?" Phoebe held out a glass.

Morgan drank a healthy mouthful. "He didn't beg if that's what you were hoping for."

Phoebe eyed her suspiciously. "Is that what you were hoping for?"

"No." Morgan took another drink. "Maybe? Something. A fight. It doesn't matter now. It's over." She took a deep breath and rubbed at the ache in her chest. The knot in her stomach wouldn't give way.

Phoebe took a sip. "It's okay if you wanted more."

Had Morgan wanted more? Maybe one last time that lasted forever? Dinner on his couch with a movie playing? Working together side by side?

"It's not always straightforward. Sleeping with someone. Sometimes we could even start to like someone." Phoebe set her glass down. "But this is important. . . ."

Morgan lifted her gaze to Phoebe's. Hoping that what she said next would make Morgan's decision feel right. Instead of this lingering wrongness in the emptiness of her chest.

"It's against the rules at work. Not to mention your own code. He's off limits. You'll find someone else. Until then you always have me."

Morgan smiled sadly. Phoebe wasn't wrong. Morgan had never been a rule breaker before. Even her blue streak was hidden during the day. "I'm glad I have you to talk me down off the ledge."

"What are friends for?" Phoebe picked up her glass and clinked it against Morgan's. She took a drink. "Okay, now spill. After all, I've seen the man's forearms and have my suspicions, but is he cut? Is he overcompensating for a lack below the belt? Does he have any tricks that make your toes curl?"

"Yes, and no, and way too soon to spill the details. The body is barely cold." Morgan shook her head. When the numbness wore off, she'd be able to deal with whatever residual feelings remained. It would suck to see Drew tomorrow. and in the future, but eventually things would return to normal. Or at least something resembling normal.

"At least you weren't in love with the guy." Phoebe took another drink. "Okay, what's on crap TV tonight?"

As Phoebe flipped on the TV and pulled up a reality show, Morgan's thoughts centered on a single word. Love? She hadn't been in love with him. That was impossible. How could you go from hating someone to loving them in less than two weeks?

She definitely had liked the sex and sleeping with him. Waking up with him warming her body and his silky hair entwined in her fingers. The way he made her laugh even when she tried to be serious. The way he'd taken a story from her childhood and made it a thing for them. Always sharing his brownie with her. The way she felt when he came into a room. How she missed him when he wasn't there. His smile.

The pain in his eyes when she'd ended it. She rubbed at the ache again. It was only infatuation inspired by lust. It couldn't have possibly been love.

CHAPTER 22

"Do you feel more comfortable with the product line?" Thomas asked as he made a note on the legal pad on his desk.

Drew smiled, thinking of Morgan helping him through the product lines those first days. He ignored the punch in his chest, choosing to focus on the interview. "I got a crash course on it over the previous weeks. But yes, I definitely feel like luxury goods is a direction I can handle."

"It's not very different from beverages, I imagine." Thomas leaned back in his chair, completely relaxed. "You've been in beverages for years and done an outstanding job. Your previous employer spoke highly of you and hated to lose you. But he also understood you needed the room for growth they couldn't offer you. Do you think luxury goods could be the growth opportunity you needed?"

Drew mimicked his stance. "Definitely. As compared to doing an ad for soda, luxury goods requires more sex appeal but overall not different."

"Good, good. How has it been working with the team? Morgan?"

"The team is efficient and smooth running." Drew took a

breath and ignored the ache at the thought of Morgan. She hadn't even given them a chance to fizzle out. "Morgan is an amazing asset. I can see why Allison nominated her to take her place. She's intelligent and takes charge of meetings with ease. She understands the product lines and gets along well with the clients."

"Careful. It sounds like you think Morgan should be the next Creative Director." Thomas leaned forward, his gaze intent on Drew.

"She's up for the job for a reason, and she'd be exactly what you need in the position." Drew knew he could be stabbing himself in the foot, but he couldn't seem to help himself. He didn't want this job if the only reason he gained it boiled down to some arbitrary rule of experience, or worse, because he was male. Morgan had every right to the position. She'd earned it. And if he lost it to her, he'd completely understand why.

"I'm glad you think she's such an asset. I do think experience is important in this field, but I also know sometimes the right person won't have all the qualifications necessary for the written job but are perfectly capable of handling the work required. We have a lot to consider in our HR meeting later today. I should have an answer for you both in the morning."

"Thank you for this opportunity, Thomas." Drew stood and held out his hand.

Thomas joined him and shook his hand. "I'm glad we were able to steal you away from your previous firm."

"One more thing, Thomas, if you don't mind." Drew remained standing. He had Thomas's attention, and now might be the perfect opportunity to ask about the corporate rules. "Not in regard to the promotion."

"What's on your mind?" Thomas sat down and resumed his relaxed pose.

"A few weeks ago, corporate sent out that memo about employees dating. . . ."

Thomas smiled slyly. "Got your eye on someone, do you?"

"No," Drew lied. He didn't need to drag Morgan into this. Besides even if corporate changed their minds about the policy, a boss still couldn't date a direct report. But if Morgan got the job, maybe he could switch to another department. Even if he enjoyed working with her, it would be worth it to have her back in his arms. "I was just wondering how set in stone it is. It's hard to meet new people when you're working all the time. I'd understand if someone found love in the office. If I'm someone's manager, how enforceable is that rule, or do we enforce it?"

Thomas templed his fingers against his lips in a pose of thoughtfulness. "Honestly, we hope the memo will keep people from dating. If someone complains about something happening at work, we'll have to apply the current rules, which have punishments ranging from suspension without pay, all the way to termination."

Drew nodded thoughtfully. "Do you think corporate will eventually back down on this?"

Thomas slowly shook his head no. "They're worried about sexual harassment charges and their liability if they allow some employees to date and others not to. They've been working on getting this through for a while now, so I don't see it ending anytime soon."

Drew smiled and thanked Thomas as he left. His interview went well, but it sounded like the no dating rule appeared solid. Meaning, if he pursued Morgan and they got caught, they'd be punished. Potentially fired. He turned down the hall and bumped into someone. He reached out automatically and steadied Morgan. His fingers tightened into the soft flesh of her arms slightly. Everything in him wanted to do more. To take her in his arms and kiss her until she came to her senses, but that would destroy everything they both had worked for. She was right; the risk was too high.

"Morgan." He nodded and dropped his hands from her arms.

"Excuse me." She straightened her shirt and met his eyes. She was all work right now. Her eyes resembled frozen pools of ice and not a hair dared to be out of place. His urge to mess her up kept trying to surface.

Instead, he nodded an acknowledgement and watched her disappear into Thomas's office. He inhaled and looked at the ceiling. He couldn't do anything about corporate. Which meant he couldn't do anything more with Morgan. It would be hell for a while working with her, but eventually they should be okay again. At least they weren't enemies any longer.

~

MORGAN MANAGED to get her emotions under control while Thomas made a few notes. She thought she would be prepared to see Drew. After all, they would both be interviewed, and the office wasn't big enough to avoid someone in your department you would have to work with every single day for the foreseeable future.

And that must be why corporate didn't want people dating in the office.

"Drew assures me you helped him get caught up. How do you think things went?"

Morgan folded her hands in her lap and met Thomas's eyes. "I can see why he's up for the promotion. He quickly learned the line and added value to each of the campaigns we've worked on together. He's got a knack for this, but you already knew that."

"He had nothing but praise about you and your work ethic." Thomas leaned forward.

She didn't know what he expected her to say to that. "We get along fine and are able to bounce ideas off each other well."

"What are your thoughts on the campaigns you've put together?" Thomas picked up his pen.

"The campaigns were interesting, and he brought some new ideas to the board. We worked together to make them as good as possible." Morgan mashed down the smile that tried to take over her face when she thought about their vodka-soaked brainstorming. Thinking about Drew wouldn't help anything right now. She couldn't miss her opportunity to claim the job as her own. "He was able to come up with sketches to help sell the client when we didn't have art available."

"The Foxx Vodka ad?" Thomas asked.

"Yes. We knew we wanted a concept from art for the cologne since we'd previously lost their business due to the perfume ad. With such a limited amount of time to pull together three campaigns, we made the decision and it ended up paying off for us."

"But without his sketches you might not have been able to present the vodka portion?"

Morgan's pulse kicked up a notch, and her leg desperately wanted to bounce. "The drawings were definitely helpful, but I'm sure art would have been able to create something Monday morning to help if we'd needed them to. Fortunately, we felt his drawings were good enough to get the concept across and knew that art would have time to refine them for the final client presentation if we got the account."

Thomas nodded and marked something down on his pad. She resisted the urge to strain to see what he wrote. She had no idea what Thomas's thought process was for this interview. Maybe he only asked her questions to see if Drew was right for the job? She hadn't stopped to consider how she'd feel if he got the position. They would work together, yes, but who took the lead had been up in the air. Over the past days, they'd worked as partners, equals, more than supervisor and assistant.

"I wouldn't have said this two weeks ago, but I think Drew and I make a good team." Morgan took a deep breath. "At different times throughout our projects, we each took charge, but we always had a common goal and a common objective. To make the client want to sign with us no matter what."

Thomas leaned back and gave her a once-over. "You aren't planning on pushing out any children anytime soon. Are you?"

Heat flushed through Morgan. Everything inside her went on alert. She was fairly certain Drew hadn't gotten a similar line of questioning. Technically HR didn't allow Thomas to ask those kinds of questions, but apparently it hadn't stopped him. "If you are asking if I have plans to start a family. . . ." She waited for his nod before continuing, "Not for the foreseeable future."

He made a note.

"If you are asking if I'm devoted to this company, I am. I've been with Hart Association since college. I've devoted nights and weekends and given up on finding a healthy relationship that can endure the hours I give to my job. This promotion is what I've been working for, and I believe I'm the right person for the Creative Director."

Thomas set his pen down. "We've always considered you an invaluable addition to our team, Morgan. Regardless of which one of you we put in the position of Creative Director, we know you are a team, and to succeed we need both of you happy and working to your full potential."

Morgan didn't know what to say to that, but she nodded.

Thomas smiled. "We should have an answer for you both by the morning. HR has to go over a few things first, and I'll discuss both of you with the CEO."

"Thank you for the opportunity." Morgan rose to stand and thankfully, her knees had stopped shaking.

"Always a pleasure." He shook her hand.

She let herself out of his office and as soon as the door closed behind her, she took a deep breath. She had done what she could to make the position hers without throwing Drew under the bus. Maybe if things had been different, she might have left out the compliments, but Drew really had been an asset to her work. They played well off each other. Both at work and in bed.

Now she just had to get through the rest of the day without running into him again.

~

AFTER FIVE, the office still pulsed with energy. Another division had a project to finish. A number of people worked in the conference room and spread around the office. Phoebe and Robin finished some details on the Avalon presentation.

Morgan got up from her desk and stretched. She needed some coffee and a snack. Her gaze fell on Drew's door across the way. His light was still on, but his office appeared empty. Probably in the break room. The snack machine downstairs would be better than being alone with him in the break room. Again.

Too many memories. Too much longing.

Tonight would have been their last night together before they ended it. But she'd ended it early, and she had to believe it was for the best. Now she wasn't figuring out how to rush out of here to spend the night with him. She could finally focus on work—after all, it was all she had left.

She grabbed some change and headed for the stairs. It would be less noticeable than waiting for the elevator in case he came out and saw her. Not that he'd come over to talk, but she couldn't risk it. Her insides felt too raw to deal with him. One last night. One final send-off before never again. And she'd cut them short, denying them.

She entered the stairwell and let the door bang shut behind her. It was always quiet in here, as if the other floors and all the workers in the building ceased to exist. For a moment, she stood and let the coolness of the concrete seep into her.

As she made it down one flight of stairs, she heard a door open on the floor below and slam shut. Footsteps on the landing echoed as someone proceeded up. When dark curly hair came into view, she almost turned and ran back the way she came. Instead she froze at the landing as Drew came up toward her.

"How'd the interview go?" He stopped in front of her, giving her space, trying to be cordial. Exactly what she'd wanted.

She cleared the lump that formed in her throat. "It went well. And yours?"

"Same." He smiled. "Going to the vending machines?"

She nodded. "Obviously," was what she wanted to say, but she didn't. The old her would have rolled her eyes as well. Now she couldn't even look him in his eyes. Instead she focused somewhere near his shoulder.

"I got you something." He reached into his pocket and held out a brownie.

She stared at it. Her heartbeat echoed in her ears as her insides melted.

"We don't have to split it. . . ."

She lifted her gaze to his eyes. Those eyes were always her Achilles' heel. Before she could change her mind, she stepped into him, closing the distance between them and threaded her fingers through his stupid hair. He could have stopped her when she brought his head down, but he let her, and she raised up on her toes to meet his lips with hers. One last kiss.

He'd followed her wishes and left her alone. Why was it when he gave her what she wanted, she ended up hating it?

His hands went to her hips and pulled her close as they fit together. When they kissed, the whole world could fall apart around her and she wouldn't notice. She missed this, and she would miss this in the future. But right now, she just wanted to chase the high she got when she lost herself in his arms. Like he made her somehow whole.

She couldn't have him, and it killed her inside. But when he kissed her, she found herself again. She was alive.

A noise sounded behind her, and Drew lifted his head from hers to look over her shoulder. When he returned his gaze to her, his eyes had turned into molten pools of blue and all she wanted was to lose herself in him, and for him to keep kissing her forever. She let out a shaky breath, suddenly aware of her feelings.

She loved him. Holy crap, she loved him and her insides froze as her heart thumped against her rib cage. She couldn't have him and her career. She had to choose. And that was why she stepped back.

"I'm sorry," she said as she took her hands off him. A chill settled through her at the lack of his warmth. She wrapped her arms around herself. "I shouldn't have done that."

He cleared his throat. "Well, I did offer you the whole brownie, so I guess you could say I asked for it."

She glanced up at his smile and her heart broke a little more. "Thank you," she said softly.

He held out the brownie and she took it. Turning her back on him, she walked up the stairs and opened the door to the office. He stood at the bottom of the landing watching her. She nodded in acknowledgement and went into the office.

She really hated when he gave her what she wanted.

It was a dreary rainy day when Morgan hustled into work the next morning. She wasn't late, but she wasn't early like normal. Everything was soaked even though her umbrella had tried its hardest. She made it onto their air-conditioned floor and shivered, glad she had a sweater for these kinds of days.

She'd just finished putting her stuff down and pulling on the sweater when Robin stopped at her door.

"HR asked me to let you know they want to see you." Robin didn't look Morgan in the eyes and wrung her hands together. She turned and left immediately after delivering the message. Weird.

When Morgan walked into the HR conference room, Drew sat in the other chair across from HR. She hadn't figured they'd be told who got the promotion together, but it made sense. Bonnie from HR sat across the conference table from them. She had always struck Morgan as a stodgy librarian type. Bonnie's sweater had more bulk than Morgan's, and she pressed her glasses firmly up her nose.

"Please sit down," Bonnie said, indicating the chair next to

Drew. Morgan sat and Bonnie just frowned at them both. Obviously, they were waiting on something. Morgan tried not to notice the heat pouring off Drew. She wished she still hated that about him. Instead it reminded her of softly spoken promises in the dark.

"Sorry to keep you waiting." Thomas came into the room and shut the door. "Had a last minute phone call."

This was it. One of them would be promoted. Morgan's stomach rolled and she wished she had time for one more coffee before this.

"I'm really sorry to have to call you both in for this."

Sorry?

Thomas turned to Drew. "An employee has come forward with claims the two of you were seen kissing last night. And they believe you've been in a relationship for a while now. Apparently, they overheard someone talking about it."

Morgan's breath caught in her throat and her hands started to shake on her lap. No. No. No. Her stomach felt like it was in a free fall. This couldn't be happening. What could they possibly say to this?

"Corporate has very tight rules on fraternization, which I'm sure you both are aware of." Thomas opened up a folder Bonnie had slid in front of him. "We have to ask some questions."

Drew tensed next to her. At least they hadn't asked them separately. This way their stories could be straight. Who had snitched on them? No one had been in the stairwell last night. She would have known, wouldn't she?

The building could have fallen around her while his lips were on hers and she wouldn't have known. Fuck.

"Are you two dating?"

"No," Morgan said, quickly. "Not at all."

"Have you ever dated?"

The word stuck in her throat. They hadn't actually dated.

Though they'd eaten together and slept together. But if semantics would save them, so be it.

"No," Drew said, his voice tight. She fought the urge to look at him, to try to see what he was thinking.

"Morgan, has Drew ever made advances toward you that you considered inappropriate or unwanted?"

She could feel Drew looking at her and a bead of water ran down her spine. She wasn't sure if it was nervous sweat or rainwater. "No."

Thomas turned to Drew. "Has Morgan ever made advances toward you that you considered inappropriate or unwanted?"

Morgan couldn't stop herself from glancing at Drew. She had been the one to initiate everything. He might throw her under the bus to save himself. A muscle ticked in his jaw, but he didn't let any other sign of stress creep through.

"No," he said.

"Good, good." Thomas made a few marks on the paper in front of him. "This isn't that hard now, is it?"

Morgan swallowed and half expected Drew to make some offhanded remark, but he stayed surprisingly quiet. No relationship. No unwanted advances. They should be good to go. Maybe they'd actually salvaged this.

"Sir, you have to ask the other questions." Bonnie pointed with her pen at the paper in front of Thomas.

He blew out a breath and glared at Bonnie. "Is it true that you kissed in the stairway yesterday evening?"

She should say no. This would all be over, and they could go back to being exactly what they were before. She wasn't the best liar, but who would press the issue?

Whoever turned them in in the first place probably.

"I'm not asking for an essay on the subject, just a simple yes or no."

Morgan glanced at Drew and caught his eyes. Fuck.

They'd really dug themselves a hole here. Maybe Thomas would be lenient. Maybe this was a slap on the wrist offense. Canoodling in the staircase. Maybe suspension at the worst. Surely they weren't the only ones who had ever crossed that line.

"Yes," Morgan finally said.

"But it wasn't unwanted," Drew specified.

She closed her eyes, not sure if his statement would hurt them or help them. They were sunk.

Thomas set down his pencil. "Has this happened before?"

"Yes," Drew said.

"But you aren't in a relationship?"

They looked at each other and then away quickly. As if that glance alone would condemn them. What they had was temporary. It should have never been more than just sex.

"Is this why you asked about the corporate policy yesterday, Drew?" Thomas seemed actually upset. Drew had asked about that? Why? And what did Thomas expect them to say? They were just screwing around? It hadn't meant anything, even though it had started to feel more real than anything she'd had in the past? Even if she'd fallen in love with him.

"You do know that corporate would never approve a director dating the assistant director even if the no dating policy didn't exist. In fact, even before this rule, they didn't allow people in the same department to date."

For a brief second, she almost blurted out that they'd just been sleeping together and had ended it before the promotion was announced so no harm, no foul? But she stopped herself, knowing it wouldn't help matters. They were in the same department now.

"Have you been sexually active with each other?"

The heat crept over Morgan, reaching her face. This was horrifying. This wasn't how today was supposed to go. One of them was supposed to be promoted. And the world would keep turning.

"I'll take from your silence the answer is yes?" Thomas looked at both of them and then sighed. "The company is clear about fraternization, especially within departments, and we have to deal with it fairly every time. Meaning I have no choice."

Bonnie pushed two folders toward them. Drew reached out and pulled them over, giving one to Morgan.

"I'd had much higher hopes for the two of you." Thomas shook his head and stood. "You have thirty minutes to clean out your desks."

DREW COULDN'T MOVE. Seriously sacked for a kiss in the stairwell? All that time he'd spent sucking up to the boss obviously hadn't amounted to much in the end. Sure, the non-answer to the sex question had probably been the final nail in the coffin, but he'd figured they'd get suspended at worst.

He couldn't look at Morgan. Her dreams had just been crushed. She'd been right; they had risked too much for what had amounted to sex. Though he'd been feeling more, he couldn't say the same for her.

"You'll find your severance package outlined in the folder as well as your 401k rollover and COBRA information." Bonnie got up from the table. "You are welcome to file an appeal to corporate. The paperwork to do so is in the packet as well."

Bonnie left the conference room and they both sat there.

"Did that just happen?" Drew asked and pushed a hand through his hair.

"Apparently." Morgan's hands shook as she picked up the folder. She scooted her chair back and stood.

"I mean, we came in today for a promotion. Both of us had done such a good job." Drew looked up at Morgan's face.

It was blank, but he knew her well enough now he could see the fraying at the edges. She was barely keeping it together. After all, this job meant everything to her.

"Do you want me to help—"

"No." She held up her hand. "I think we've finally figured out what happens when the two of us get together. Mutual destruction."

She started out the door, and he quickly rose to his feet, grabbed his folder, and followed her down the hallway. The office was abuzz with activity. No one gave them a second glance except Robin, who met his eyes before she quickly looked away.

They each went to their offices. It didn't take Drew long to get his things. He'd only been there for a little over a month. Not like Morgan who'd been there for years.

Who had turned them in? It couldn't have been Phoebe. There would have been no question regarding sexual activity if that had been the case. Robin seemed to be the only one interested in what he and Morgan were doing today. She'd been the one to tell him HR wanted to see him. He lifted his box of things and said goodbye to a few coworkers from beverages, hoping to give Morgan enough time so they could ride the elevator down together.

Morgan still hadn't finished, but he couldn't make up any more excuses to hang around. As soon as he got into the elevator, he moved his box to one side and got out his phone. He'd used a recruiter to get this job, so he dialed the guy's number, hoping to have at least a lead or two. He also made a note to call his lawyer friend to see how legal this whole termination was.

He left a message for the recruiter and got out of the elevator but didn't go far. The lobby bustled around him. No one paid him any attention as he leaned against the wall. He needed to make sure Morgan was okay. It sucked for him, but he was used to bouncing around jobs. She'd been at the same place since college.

It felt weird to be out of work and have nothing to do all day. It wasn't like he'd get an interview scheduled right away. He'd always gone from one job to the next. His savings would get him through, and hopefully he could find a position even though he'd just been fired. Which would be a sticky issue.

Every time the elevator came down, he looked for Morgan. After a while, she finally got off and swept past him. He grabbed his box and followed her.

"I've got a Lyft if you want a ride home. I also have the name of a recruiter—"

She stopped him with a look. If daggers could come out of someone's eyes, he'd be a dead man.

"Thank you, but I can see to myself," she said and continued toward the door.

"Can we talk?" he asked catching up to her.

"No." She stopped at the doors. The rainy weather loomed outside.

"Can I at least give you a ride to your place?" Drew didn't know what to do in this situation. "It's the least I can do."

She closed her eyes. "The least?"

He rebalanced his box. His stomach tied in knots.

"The least you could have done was lie. Tell them we had never nor would we ever have sex in a million years, because how ridiculous would it be if we started something sexual in the first place."

"But you didn't say anything—"

"I have never been more mortified in my life." She set her

box down and pushed her finger into his chest. "I knew you were trouble when I first met you. Your stupid hair and pretty eyes. The biggest suck-up in the world. But I didn't think you'd get me fired."

Okay, now that was getting him riled up too. "I didn't text you at one a.m."

"You should have known that text wasn't meant for you." She threw her hands in the air. "I hated you. I couldn't stand to be around you. How did you *ever* think that text had been for *you*?"

"By the looks you gave me."

"Oh, you mean the times I rolled my eyes?" She picked up her box and went out into the rain. Her eyes scanned the street for a cab.

He followed her out. "Don't act so innocent now."

"I have never looked at you with anything but disdain."

"Then your disdain looks a lot like interest."

Rain soaked them both quickly.

"You know what?" she said as she spotted a cab.

"What?"

"I wish the other Drew had shown up. Sure the sex might have been mediocre, but at least I'd still have a job."

She crossed over to the curb and let herself into the cab without looking back at him.

That one had stung. The fact that the only reason they'd ever gotten closer was due to a messed up text and his misinterpretation of the situation had always been a sore point with him. How could he apologize? Why should he apologize? He'd lost his job too.

MORGAN SAT on her couch with her laptop. Dressed in her PJs and comforted by some chocolate ice cream, she was ready to look for a new job. She scanned the job postings on a few sites, uploaded her updated resume to a few more, and answered a few emails.

When she finished, she glanced at the clock. Eleven a.m. She hadn't had a vacation for a long time, and it had been ages since she had unscheduled time off. She honestly didn't know what to do with herself. The only other person who didn't have a job now was Drew, and she wouldn't call him for a playdate ever again.

How's work? She sent to Phoebe and flicked on the TV.

Quiet. Phoebe responded. *Want me to bring you lunch on my break?*

Yes, please.

On it. Be there in thirty.

Morgan managed to sidetrack herself with flipping through the channels and landed on a *Friends* episode.

A knock came at the end of the episode. Morgan turned the TV off and opened the door.

"Fatty foods to the rescue." Phoebe put down a few bags from the bar on Morgan's table. "I got some wings and fries and a salad just in case you want to pretend to be healthy."

"Thank you." Morgan joined Phoebe, and they sat across from each other. "You don't know how bad I need this."

"So. . . ." Phoebe popped a fry in her mouth. "What happened?"

Morgan flinched. "What did Thomas say?"

"You two had violated the fraternization policy and had to be let go."

"That about sums it up." Morgan drowned a fry in ranch dressing before eating it.

"But how did they find out? I thought you ended things." Phoebe pulled the drinks out of the carrier and handed one to Morgan.

Morgan flushed. "I kissed Drew in the stairwell last night."

"And they had video?"

"No, thank God." Morgan said around a wing. "Someone saw us."

"Who?"

Morgan shrugged. "They didn't say."

"Okay, well that's bullshit." Phoebe pointed a fry at her. "You have a right to face your accuser. They should have told you who it was."

"It didn't matter who it was. We didn't lie."

"Why not?"

Morgan shrugged. Why hadn't she said no they hadn't kissed and no they hadn't been sexually active? And no she hadn't been falling for him. Not really, anyway. It couldn't be love. It had all been an illusion fueled by hormones. Obviously.

"If you can't lie, you should never run for Congress." Phoebe shook her head. After a minute she held up a chicken wing and said, "You know what?"

Morgan lifted her gaze from her own chicken. "What?"

"Robin has been acting fishy. And she has a huge crush on Drew. I bet you a hundred dollars she's the snitch."

"Does it matter? We're still fired."

Phoebe gave her a conspiratorial wink. "Snitches get stitches."

Morgan chuckled and rolled her eyes. "Don't you get fired for this too. I might need a place to stay if I can't find a new job quickly."

"Did they give you a severance package?"

"Yeah, a couple of months, which should be long enough. I'm sure Drew got the same even though he worked less time at the company." Morgan scoffed. The way he had sucked up to Thomas it was a wonder they fired him at all.

"Well, you know my door is always open." Phoebe winked. "Unless there is a sock on the handle. In that case give me an hour or two."

Morgan shook her head. "What am I supposed to do for the next several hours?"

"Watch TV, knit a blanket, call up Drew for sex."

"Not going to happen." That road was officially closed.

"Knitting? Yeah, probably not unless you secretly already know how." Phoebe giggled.

Morgan shook her head. "I'm not going to call Drew. He's trouble."

"But it was such fun trouble. And it's no longer against the rules." Phoebe propped her elbows on the table and put her head in her hands as if it were story time. "You never did tell me about all the trouble."

Morgan shook her head and pressed at the ache in her chest. "It was fun while it lasted, but getting fired kind of sucked the fun right out of it."

Phoebe nodded. "I get that. But you guys seemed to be more than just fuck-buddies. Don't hit me, but I think he might have actually had feelings for you."

Morgan tried to laugh, but it came out broken. "I think I ended that too by telling him I wished the other Drew had shown up."

"Ouch. Yeah, that's not exactly nice." Phoebe glanced at her phone. "I need to head back to the office. Want me to punch Robin for you? I bet I'd only get written up. Especially if I don't sleep with her afterwards."

"We both don't need to be out of a job."

After Phoebe left, Morgan looked at her phone. Drew had mentioned a recruiter… She shook her head and went back to her computer to find her own recruiter. She didn't need to owe Drew anything.

CHAPTER 24

MORGAN DOUBLE-CHECKED her skirt and blouse in the bathroom mirror. She had three interviews lined up this week, and this was the first one. She needed to make a strong first impression, because eventually they'd have to ask for references and why they fired her. She wasn't looking forward to that conversation.

She reapplied her lipstick and patted her hair. After taking a deep breath and mentally telling herself she could do this, she headed out of the bathroom and into the lobby. Stepping up to the receptionist, Morgan waited for her to stop working for a moment.

"I'm Morgan Taylor. I have a three o'clock appointment with Ms. Sandy Knight."

"I'll let her know you're here," the receptionist said and indicated some seats. "You can wait over there."

Morgan sat down and crossed her legs. She kept her posture tight and didn't play on her phone. You only got one chance for a first impression.

The sound of a conversation floated down the hallway getting closer. A man and a woman. As they got close enough for Morgan to distinguish voices, she recognized Drew's voice. Her heartbeat skipped, and she took in a deep breath, ready to be blindsided by him.

"It's been a pleasure talking with you, Mr. King." Morgan assumed that was Ms. Knight talking. The open position was for an Assistant Creative Director in the luxury goods division for an inhouse marketing team. At least she had more experience in the line. It would suck to lose the job to the guy she basically trained.

"Thank you again for this opportunity. I look forward to hearing from you." They came around the corner, and Drew shook the woman's hand. When he turned, his eyes scanned the reception area quickly, and then did a double take and came back to her. She gave him a tight smile, acknowledging this was awkward. He looked good though. Of course, he always looked good.

"Oh, Ms. Taylor, I'm glad you are early," Ms. Knight said. She was in her late forties with dark brown hair pulled up in a bun and dancing hazel eyes. "We'll be in touch, Mr. King."

Morgan stood and passed Drew on her way to meet Ms. Knight. His heat radiated over her, and his sandalwood scent stirred a longing deep inside her. But she didn't even spare him a side glance as she greeted Ms. Knight and shook her hand. The hairs stood up on the back of her neck as if somehow, she knew he'd checked her out.

"If you'll follow me."

Morgan followed Ms. Knight but glanced back in the direction of the lobby to see if she could catch one final glimpse of Drew. He stood near the elevators and happened to glance up to catch her looking at him. She turned away quickly but not before catching the heat in his eyes. She took another cleansing breath to be ready for her interview.

She wouldn't let Drew King screw up another job.

~

IT MADE sense when Drew thought about it the next day, as he waited in the lobby for his next interview. He'd arrived early and happened to see the interviewer giving Morgan a tour of the company's office space. Her pencil skirt and blouse were as attractive as usual. He couldn't just call her up after their spectacular exit from Hart Association. She'd made it clear she wanted nothing more to do with him, but then he'd bumped into her yesterday and thought for a moment maybe he should call her.

But he also knew he should give her the space she needed. No matter how much it tore him up inside.

However, both Morgan and he had been assistants to the Creative Director. There were only so many of those positions available without having to change cities. Ergo, at every interview, he'd be up against Morgan for the position just like Hart Association all over again.

He hadn't taken her words to heart when they'd left each other at the building. She'd been upset and frustrated. While he was partly at fault for their firing, he wouldn't take the whole burden. It took two to do what they did. And they did it so well together.

It had been awkward yesterday when Ms. Knight asked him why he'd left his current company. *I got caught with a coworker fraternizing and was lucky they didn't have security cameras in the break room because they would have caught me fraternizing her brains out the week before.* Probably wouldn't go over well.

Instead, he chose to say the company had rules against fraternization, and a coworker had turned him in for dating another coworker. Not his smoothest moment, but he showed the proper amount of chagrin when he explained about the memo of no dating and how he had no intentions of making the same mistake ever again.

Morgan wasn't a mistake, but for the purpose of getting a job and paying his bills, he could stretch that truth a little. After all, he was sure Morgan had told them she'd made a mistake. Of course, the people interviewing them would be able to tell they'd worked at the same company and had the same termination date and the same story, so. . . . If the interviewers were halfway intelligent, they'd make the connection they had fraternized together. And if he had any say in it, hopefully would fraternize in the future.

Morgan and a Mr. Smith, he believed, came around the corner.

"I really appreciate you seeing me." Morgan smiled that frozen smile of hers and her gaze flicked over to him for a moment, before adding, "I look forward to hearing from you."

"We should have a decision shortly. It was a pleasure to meet you." Mr. Smith shook her hand and glanced at Drew before moving to speak quietly with the receptionist. Then he disappeared into the back again. Apparently, he needed a breather between interviews.

Morgan walked toward the elevator, but she had to pass within grabbing distance of him to do that. As she started past him, he said, "Lovely weather we're having, isn't it?"

She sighed as she stopped, but she didn't roll her eyes like she would have three weeks ago. "Sure. It's great."

"Let me guess. Tomorrow you have an interview with PR Franks?" He didn't look up from his phone.

She startled and then smiled. "Going for the gold, huh?"

The position was for a Creative Director, not the assistant. Technically they'd both been up for the position prior to leaving, so why not get the promotion in a strategic career move.

"I'd expect you to do the same." Drew gave her a crooked smile. "I guess I'll see you tomorrow then."

She nodded and headed out to the elevator. After pressing the button, she glanced back at him before looking away.

God, he missed her.

It didn't matter they'd fucked up each other's careers. If they both got one of these positions, they wouldn't be working together. That meant they could try to figure out what was between them without any rules keeping them apart. Of course, then their schedules may never match up again.

He wanted to text or call her, but she may not want to hear from him. He just wished he could know if what she felt for him was more than attraction.

If he admitted he had fallen in love with her and she didn't feel anything comparable, he'd be shredded. It wasn't like they had discussed feelings at any point. Because that would have been admitting it was more than a fling. More than sex. And wouldn't end when the promotion happened.

He took a deep breath as she slipped into the elevator and back out of his life.

"Mr. King? Mr. Smith is ready for you now."

Morgan almost stumbled off her heels as she entered the offices of PR Franks and saw Drew sitting in the decidedly small reception area. She went up to the receptionist and told her her name. The receptionist asked her to take a seat.

There were three seats in the reception area and Drew had taken the middle one. Of course. She released a breath and headed over.

"Is this seat taken?" *By your enormous ego?*

"No, go ahead." Drew straightened in his seat and adjusted his tie.

She sat and edged away from him and his intoxicating heat.

"I figured you were already in there," Drew said.

"My appointment is at three."

"Mine too."

That made her turn to look at him. "What?"

"Double booked?" Drew shrugged. "Maybe they just like to crank through these. Maybe they have two people interviewing separately."

"Maybe they've heard the stories." Morgan rolled her eyes and opened her phone to her email. She read it over and nothing appeared out of the ordinary. She made sure her phone was set to silent and slid it back in her purse. "Or connected the dots."

"Two employees from Hart Association applying for the same job with the same termination date. Yeah, that would be a little suspicious." Drew crossed his ankles and stared at the picture on the wall across from them. It was one of those contemporary designs that complemented a space without adding too much clutter.

She let the silence hang in the air for a few minutes, but it felt ridiculous. "What have you been saying about being fired?"

"That I had an awesomely torrid affair that completely wrecked me, but I still got my job done and would have gotten the promotion too, if it hadn't been for those damn kids." Drew delivered the statement in a flat matter of fact way, but his smile at the end ruined the effect.

She relaxed a little. "Almost correct, except the promotion would have been mine."

"We may have to call up Thomas and ask him so we can

finally have the answer to who's the boss." Drew gave her a wink.

"Can't you just ask him when you golf next, or is the bromance over?" Morgan raised an eyebrow at him.

He put his hand to his heart. "Ouch, that one stung."

She shook her head but couldn't stop the little smile that tugged at the corners of her mouth. She'd missed this most of all. The little verbal sparring they did.

He glanced toward the receptionist, but there hadn't been any movement from that front yet.

Her voice was soft when she finally built up the nerve to ask, "Did I really 'wreck' you?"

His eyes crinkled in the corners as he took a deep breath. "Worse than when Elizabeth rejected Darcy, even though he totally deserved it."

A warmth spread through her, starting at her heart. "Maybe she wouldn't have been so heartless if she'd had the full story."

"Mr. King, Ms. Taylor."

They both looked up at the receptionist.

"If you'll follow me, they'll see you now."

Within a minute, they were settled on the same side of a conference table with two people across from them: a man in his late fifties with salt and pepper hair and a woman in her mid-thirties who seemed to smile all the time. At least she had since Morgan met her, which was only a few seconds ago.

Morgan would be a lot more comfortable if she didn't have Drew's sandalwood scent filling her nose and his presence directly beside her for an interview she thought she'd be having alone. He always tended to throw her off her game.

"I'm sorry if this is uncomfortable for you two, but seeing as you are both coming from Hart Association and as Assistant Creative Directors, we figured we could kill two birds with one stone." This was from the smiling woman. "I'm May Ashby and this is Anthony Cook."

Everyone stood to shake hands over the table and then settled back in their seats.

"No problem at all," Drew said with his suck-up smile. "We actually worked together for the last few weeks, competing for the same position of Creative Director."

"That's why we were interested in you two," Anthony said. "We were also up for the Bradbury Industries account. They had nothing but good things to say about you two when we asked them about it. In fact, your dismissal frankly surprised them after such a strong showing. They loved what you did for Foxx Vodka."

"It was a shock to us too," Morgan said, trying not to be too forthcoming in details but trying to connect on a human level with the interviewers too.

"From what Bradbury could tell, you worked well together and even though you'd only been together for a short time, they could tell you made a dynamic team." May leaned back in her chair. "We don't work the same way Hart Association does. Our structure is slightly different. We like to build a team of people to collaborate on projects without labeling someone the boss. Our teams work on whatever projects we feel that particular team would do a good job on."

"That makes sense." Drew leaned forward. "I found similarities in both beverages and luxury goods, but I also feel you could stagnate in one department if you don't have a chance to look at it from a different angle."

"The variety was one of the things I appreciated in luxury goods," Morgan said. "It wasn't always about alcohol or perfume, where there are only so many ideas before you are basically copying yourself from four years ago. The ability to put a new spin on products really fascinates me."

"That's exactly why we were interested in you both."

Anthony smiled at each of them, before turning more serious. "However, we've talked to Thomas already and know there were some issues with fraternization. Our corporate policy is very similar to Hart Association's."

Morgan didn't dare look at Drew. She needed to project professionalism, and if she looked at him, she was afraid she'd give away that at some point she'd fallen head over heels in love with the guy. Maybe it was their vodka-soaked evening or the day they'd spent watching movies or maybe it was that first kiss. But somewhere along the way, she'd lost her heart to him and his stupid hair.

However, she needed a job. She could cure whatever lovesickness she had if it meant she would get a job and another chance for her promotion.

"We would be open to considering you as a pair for the Creative Director position. We understand sometimes two minds work best when pitted against each other, and I believe that's what we are seeing here," May said before looking to Anthony.

Anthony set down his pen. "Frankly, we can't have employees in the same department dating each other, but if you are willing to assure us you can work together and that's all, we'd like to consider you for the position."

Morgan's knee started to bounce under the table. Could she just work with Drew? Would she ever get over him if she had to see him every day and not be able to have crazy conversations about inappropriate work topics? And what happened when a sexy campaign made her weak? If they worked together, it would only be a matter of time before she ended up stupidly kissing him in the stairwell where someone could catch them.

"You're absolutely right, Mr. Cook," Drew said, bringing her back to the interview. "We do make an amazing team and it's definitely an interesting proposal."

Morgan glanced over at him, not exactly sure where he headed with this line of thought.

Facing the interviewers again, he said, "The problem is, if I'm close to Morgan my brain turns to mush and I can't help but want to be with her. Sure, we get the work done, but I can't imagine not being able to be with her outside of work as well. It wouldn't last long until I'd want to kiss her again and not because work makes her convenient, but because I love her."

Her breath caught and her hands shook.

He turned to her. His blue eyes locking on hers. "'My affections and wishes have not changed, but one word from you will silence me forever. If, however, your feelings have changed, I will have to tell you: you have bewitched me, body and soul, and I love, I love, I love you. I never wish to be parted from you from this day on.'"

Morgan gasped and covered her mouth. He'd perfectly quoted the words from the final proposal scene of Pride & Prejudice. Her throat choked up.

"We could work for you, but then I'd have to give her up. I'm not willing to do that." He stood and reached his hand down to her. "How about it, Morgan? What if we could have it all?"

May's smile turned almost into awe, but Anthony just looked disappointed.

"I'm sorry we wasted your time." Drew said.

Morgan looked up at him, still in shock. He'd said he loved her. . . in an interview. . . for the position of a lifetime. And turned down that job for her. His gaze never wavered from hers. All she'd been looking for her whole life reflected back in those amazing eyes of his.

"Thank you for the interview and for considering us, but my colleague is right. We may be a package deal, but that means the whole package, not just the work portion." She slid her hand into Drew's and everything fell into place. Those knots that had been her constant companions since getting fired loosened. He pulled her up. God, she wanted him to kiss her.

"It was a pleasure meeting with you both," May said, practically squealing in delight.

"Thank you both." Morgan smiled. "I'm sorry we can't take this position."

CHAPTER 25

"WELL, THAT WAS WEIRD," Morgan said as the elevator closed them in.

"I'm sorry. I know that was your dream job." Drew leaned against the back wall of the elevator. "Wanna grab a drink and maybe an appetizer to discuss our. . . situation?"

"That sounds great." Morgan pulled her phone out and quickly texted Phoebe to let her know where she was going. She could feel Drew reading over her shoulder.

"Worried I might abduct you?"

Hopefully. Her heart pounded as she put her phone away. He'd just told strangers he loved her, but what did that mean for them? What did having it all mean?

The elevator stopped and he led her through the lobby to a waiting Lyft. She climbed into the back and he joined her.

The bar was only a five-minute ride away. Thankfully. She reached over and took his hand. He gave her a soft smile and squeezed her hand. She took in a breath and everything inside her settled.

They still had a lot to figure out. He didn't want to work together obviously. Especially if they couldn't be together.

But where did that leave them? What situation did they still need to discuss? How would they work and ever see each other?

Torrid affair that completely wrecked me, echoed in her mind. She took a deep breath and stared out the window. She desperately wanted to tease him about quoting Jane Austen to her, but her insides were a flood of butterflies all trying to escape.

She loved him, but how would they ever make this work?

After they arrived, he held the door to the bar open and within a few minutes they were settled into opposite sides of a booth, each with a beer and orders for a couple of appetizers on their way to the kitchen.

She kept waiting for him to say something. Anything. Did he love her or was that just a stunt to get out of that job interview?

He took a drink of beer and looked around the bar as if trying to gather the words he wanted to say from anywhere else. *Wrecked.* She watched him curiously. How wrecked? More than Darcy? Besides the sex and her unintentional feelings, they obviously had become friends, but friendship wasn't the issue.

Drew sighed and finally looked at her. "Cards on the table?"

"O-kay." Morgan wasn't sure what he was about to say. She didn't want to get her hopes up in case he just wanted what they had before. Incredible, mind-blowing sex.

But he'd said he loved her.

Drew took another drink and leaned forward. "I haven't slept well in a week. My apartment is a hellscape because *you* are everywhere I look, but nowhere at the same time. I can't even eat a burger without getting turned on because of you."

She waited. Everything in her held still, waiting. She needed to hear the words.

"I think it was a great career opportunity, but personally, I can barely keep from touching you now. I want to hold your hand and play with your fingers. I want to make you laugh and smile. I want you to tease me about my hair but be completely possessive about it all at once. I want to be able to get drunk on vodka and sleep with you in my arms.

"I love you more than Darcy loved Lizzie. I don't want to work with you and not be with you at home. I want to work with you and have you in my apartment, my bed, and my life because without you, I'm frankly going crazy."

"Oh," she said. Her heart raced as her head tried to catch up. She knew she would sound stupid, but she couldn't help asking for clarity. "You love me?"

He nodded, his normally cheerful expression worried.

"You want to work with me?"

"You have to admit we were a crazy good team together. There's no one else I'd prefer to have at my side. You're intelligent. You have the ability to describe the sexiest situations I've ever heard that would make me buy anything you were willing to sell me. You're calm and cool under pressure. And so put together that even though I want to mess you up, I love seeing you present to the world this perfect image, and know only I can make you produce the most undignified noises."

Heat rushed to her cheeks. "I don't—"

"You do, and I love that about you. I love everything about you." He threaded his hand through his hair. "I don't know what I can do to convince you this isn't just lust or sex or who comes out on top. I want to be your partner in all things."

She put her hand over her racing heart. His sapphire eyes sparkled in the dim light. He waited for her to respond. She could almost feel his tension as he waited.

"Nachos and wings?" The server stopped at the table and set the plates down. "Do you need anything else?"

He loved her. He wanted to be with her. He loved her.

"No, thank you," Drew said, still holding Morgan's gaze. "Enjoy."

Morgan cleared her throat of the frog lodged there. "So, do we wait to hear from the other firms and hope one of us gets a job? Keep interviewing?" Her hands shook as Morgan took a plate and dished out some of the nachos and some of the wings onto it, just to keep herself from getting lost in his eyes. This was crazy.

"Morgan?"

She inhaled and looked up at him. He was all hope, and she loved him truly, completely. Her heart swelled so much she felt like she could fly away as long as he went with her. She couldn't keep the huge grin off her face.

"Will you please just tell me?"

"Tell you what?" She took a bite of nachos.

His eyes sparkled as he grabbed a wing off her plate and not out of the basket.

"That I fucked up when I said all those things before. That I didn't mean any of them." She paused and swallowed. "That you are the only Drew I have ever wanted or ever will want."

He smiled at her and it damn near made her heart burst.

"That I think your ego couldn't handle what I think about you? That it would explode beyond any reasonable size, making you impossible to live with?" Morgan smiled and took his hand. "That I love you and never wish to be parted from you again or whatever that line is that Darcy says."

Drew's fingers tangled in hers. "Don't say it unless you mean it, because I'm going to need to hear it frequently."

"Have to feed the beast." She squeezed his hand. "I love you, probably since that first night. I don't know how it happened and don't tell Phoebe, but you're my best friend."

"Now, about work?" His grin was practically ear to ear.

She shook her head. "I don't know what company is going to want a partnership that involves tons of extracurricular activities. Even PR Franks wanted us but only as a work partnership."

"I have some savings and the ear of some investors—"

"I'm sure you do." She rolled her eyes. Him and his networking.

"I think we could put together a boutique agency. You and me, a few employees for copywriting and art and such, against the world. What do you say?"

This whole thing felt new and exciting. Her insides were so light, like he'd lifted a huge boulder off her. He loved her. If he asked, she could fly. "When can we start?"

EPILOGUE

FOUR MONTHS LATER

AFTER A LONG DAY at the office, the last thing Drew wanted was to share Morgan with their ragtag group of employees. The bar was packed this Friday night. Drew sat in the chair next to Morgan as the rest of their staff spread out around the table. Morgan smiled at him and leaned back into his arms before turning back to a conversation with Phoebe.

"All right," Drew said. "I hope everyone is having a good time. Morgan and I wanted to thank all of you for your dedication this past week. So margaritas and beers are on us. Thanks for helping us land our first client!"

Everyone clapped and clinked glasses together before settling back into their conversations.

"You know, I was planning on doing that." Morgan turned to him and raised her eyebrow.

"As the first name in King and Taylor—"

"It's Taylor and King," she reminded. "I won that battle easily."

Heat flushed through him at the inventive way they had used to determine which name came out on top. She'd definitely won that battle. But so had he.

"I believe you had an unfair advantage." Drew slid his arm around her. "I think a rematch might be in order."

"Not a chance. The URL has already been bought." She tweaked one of his curls.

"Fine. But don't expect me to cave to all of your demands." He smiled and pressed his lips against hers for a brief second.

"You didn't cave. I earned—"

This time he captured her mouth to remind her why he'd let her win. He couldn't imagine kissing anyone but her for the rest of his days.

"Office PDA," Phoebe shouted, and the rest of the staff chanted with her. "Office PDA. Office PDA."

Drew pulled back from Morgan and smiled. It was the only way Phoebe had agreed to come work for them. If and when there were public displays of affection, she would get something worthwhile out of it. In this case, alcohol.

"You got next," Phoebe said.

"We're already paying for the drinks," Morgan reminded her.

"Yeah, but now you have to go get them too." Phoebe stuck out her tongue at Morgan who just laughed.

Drew and Morgan headed to the bar. Drew ordered a pitcher of beer and margaritas and turned back to Morgan, draping his arms around her waist and pulling her in close.

"We really should rethink that policy," Drew said. "We're going to be broke at the rate we're going."

"Phoebe's right, though. We needed something to keep office PDA down to a minimum." Her hands pressed in the center of his back. "Apparently, your bank account will make you behave."

He sighed. "I suppose, but we're going to have to win a whole lot more clients to pay for all the alcohol we're buying our employees."

Morgan pressed her mouth to his. "At least we have the weekend free."

"Oh, do you want to go golfing with the boss?" The pitchers were waiting for them and he handed her one before following her back.

When they sat down, she turned to him and held up her finger. "One, you are not the boss." She held up another finger. "Two, I can think of more enjoyable things to do than golf."

"You really make this no office PDA hard to follow. Especially when we aren't in the office." Drew glanced around the table but at least one person would see them if he kissed her. He sighed. "I don't know if I can afford to kiss you. They might want shots next."

She laughed. "You really are crazy."

He leaned in and kissed her, ignoring the others. When he pulled away, he leaned his forehead against hers and said, "Only for you."

THE END

ACKNOWLEDGMENTS

I started Not Quite Enemies in 2017 to break myself out of burnout. Without Kate Pearce's permission to stop beating the dead horses in my unfinished projects file, this book and this series might have never have seen the light of day. Obviously it still took me time to finish it and then to complete the other books, but here we are. Thank you, Kate!

Thank you to Gwen Hayes for doing the initial edits on this book. Even though it's called a critique, you helped me refine this book. MK Book Editing for providing copy edits and keeping me on track with my characters. Amanda Bonilla for proofreading and catching the things my eyes just can't find at this stage. Amy Halter for your excellent beta reading skills.

My writing life wouldn't happen without Jeannie Lin, Shawntelle Madison, and Sela Carsen. We've been together since the start of this crazy journey. The encouragement and help we provide each other is necessary to keep us sane in this career.

To the friends I've made during the pandemic and who kept me accountable for every word written. Who knew video sprints were what I was always looking for? To Carrie, Sarah, Holly, Selena, Danielle, Ivy, and a whole host of others: Thank you for being my daily push I need to stop procrastinating and do!

ABOUT THE AUTHOR

Amy Lark is a contemporary romance author. A Midwest girl stuck in the swamps of the South, she lives with her husband, her dog, and two cats. When not writing steamy romance, she's doling out advice to her children and bowing to her pets many demands. Find out more about upcoming books at amylark.com.

ALSO BY AMY LARK

Just Ad Love Series

Coming soon!!!

Not Quite Roommates

Not Quite the Boss

Not Quite Faking It

Also by Amanda Berry

L.A. Cinderella

PUBLISHED BY HARLEQUIN

Fox Creek Series

Yours at Last

One Night with the Best Man

PUBLISHED BY HARLEQUIN

More Than Friends